Three Degrees From Justice

By John Bobo

Copyright

This book is a work of fiction. Names, characters, places, and incidents are the product of the author's imagination or are used fictitiously. Any resemblance to actual events, locales or persons, living or dead, business establishments, corporations, events, or locals is entirely coincidental.

Copyright © 2020 by John Bobo
Originally e-published © 2013
All rights reserved.

ISBN: 978-1-935689-88-1(ePub)

Cover Photo: © 2013 John Bobo
Cover Design: Hubert Longfield

All rights reserved. This book was self-published by the author John Bobo. No part of this book may be reproduced in any form by any means without the express permission of the author. This includes excerpts, photocopying, recording, or any future means of reproducing text.

If you would like to do any of the above, please seek permission by first contacting the author at beststorywins@gmail.com.

For Pegs

"So I find it to be a law that when I want to do what is good, evil lies close at hand."
Romans 7:21

Prologue

April 18, 1985

If God ever needed to send a personal letter of apology to everyone in the world for creating someone, that someone would be Otis Whitaker. The letter, perhaps an engraved scroll on cream-colored parchment, maybe something on the wall, would read:

"I never should have given free will to that twisted bastard. Of all people, I should have known how much havoc could be inflicted by the jawbone of an ass.

Regrets, G. Almighty."

I got my apology of sorts. Not through a letter or a burning hydrangea, but through coincidences that only God could arrange.

True story. I met Otis Whitaker once in 1985, and like any political blowhard, I heard him before I saw him.

I was standing in line with twenty-four people in a conference room at the University of Tennessee's Student Center in Knoxville. At the time, I was only 21, and only one of the few students allowed to meet with our luncheon guest. The rest were university bigwigs and political hoo-has.

"Ladies and gentlemen, the President of the United States."

The door swung open and in walked Ronald Reagan.

"I can't believe it," said a voice behind me. "He's wearing a *brown* suit."

The suit was more of a subdued chestnut color, but brown enough to stand out like a chocolate oil slick in a sea of black, navy, and charcoal-gray.

Reagan's aide walked him to an imaginary spot in front of a photographer, and people in line ahead of me began walking forward for the handshake of a lifetime.

What amazed me was what happened next. Each person would take Reagan's hand, turn toward the camera, and strike a pose. Nobody said anything to him more than hello; then, they waited for the flash and moved on.

This was probably my one time to meet the President of the United States, and I wasn't about to turn and mug for some snap shot. I wanted to really meet the man. I wanted to look him in the eye and take the measure of the most powerful man in the world.

When my turn finally came, I took his hand, looked him directly in the eyes. But whatever plans I had for a real dialogue went out the window as soon as the dry croaks masquerading as words escaped from my mouth:

"*Mister... Prez...mah...nam...is...*"

Flash!

By the time I got to *Jack Henley*, someone had put their arm around my shoulder and was escorting me to the dining room.

I'd completely blown it. Reagan would be sitting two tables away during lunch.

But I figured I might as well make the best of the meal. I turned to my left to a gentleman sitting at the head of the table. He had ruddy cheeks framing a bourbon nose. He looked to be about sixty, and he was using his fat belly as a shelf on which to rest his clasped hands.

"How are you doing?" I said. "I'm Jack Henley, president of the Student Government Association."

The man didn't acknowledge me at first, but finally cut his eyes in my direction. "I'm Lt. Governor Otis Whitaker, and I've been in politics for 30 years, you young pup."

His tone was not friendly or even remotely droll, and I immediately recognized his voice as the one criticizing the President's choice in suit color. His gaze quickly returned to his fingernails, which he inspected until Congressman Jimmy Quillan joined our table.

I have never taken such an instant dislike to anyone as I did to Otis Whitaker. I didn't say another word to him, but I'll never forget a conversation he had with a state senator from West Tennessee over dessert.

"Otis, how long's this prison meeting going to last on Thursday?"

"It's beyond me. The AG told me this morning that if the over-crowding gets any worse there's a real chance that the *federal* courts will step in," Whitaker said. His nostrils flared on the word *federal*. "But with our budget, I don't know where we are going to get the money for more space. Hell, if we try to actually solve the problem, we'll be there for months, but if we just stick about 500 extra beds in the hallways, we can make it to the golf course by 3:30."

He was not joking. That was his plan.

In hindsight, I probably should have crawled up on the table and put my fork through his throat. But I didn't know then that Whitaker would be the architect for the Criminal Reform Sentencing Act. I didn't know then that the biggest fight of my life would be against his intellectual sloth.

That day I dismissed him as an idiot –as only an arrogant college boy can. What I should have done was recognize him as dangerous and run for his spot. Years later, I still had recurring dreams about that lunch. Sometimes I was able to speak to Reagan. Other times, not. But I was always able to recognize Whitaker as an evil SOB who needed killing.

In my dreams, I'm sitting at the table staring at 26 forks to the left of my plate. I have to pick the correct fork for putting through the throat of a Lt. Governor, so the Secret Service won't shoot me. I always pick the wrong fork. Hot metal slugs from Secret Service MP-5's thump into my body.

Perhaps I worry too much about doing the right thing.

I only met him once. But once was enough.

PART I
Black Monday

Chapter 1

September 22, 1997

Black Monday began with the usual courtroom tedium that comes with sentencing.

Judge Raymond Sacs spent the morning going through his docket with a precision that can only be only accomplished using glacial speeds, and now we had become bogged down in the sentencing hearing of one of Chattanooga's more inept burglars.

"I can't go to jail," Denetta Lynn Cousins said. "There's no one to take care of my babies."

Sitting in the witness box, Denetta looked as if she'd just gotten off the truck from *The Grapes of Wrath*. She wore a red flowered print blouse under faded overalls. She was only 32 years old but looked a withered, alcoholic 55.

She sank her protruding front teeth into her lower lip and squinted tears from the wrinkled corners of her eyes. From where I sat at the prosecutor's table, the crying appeared convincing; even Denetta could drum up some sincere emotion for her children.

"Bailiff," Judge Sacs said, "get the defendant some Kleenex."

A brooding man in his late sixties, Judge Sacs was able to muster civility for anyone who sat in his witness box.

"Thank you, Judge."

Marta Boling, Denetta's public defender, turned to her client. "Ms. Cousins, tell the judge how many children you have."

"I got three young'uns," Denetta said ticking them off on her fingers. "Tommy, he's eight, Kelly, she's five, and Peyton, he's near about two."

"And there's no one you can count on to look after them?"

"No ma'am. Their daddy caught a federal charge down in Atlanta. I just don't know what I'll do if I go to jail. I can't stand to think of the State splitting up my babies."

Denetta used an expression common among defendants –*caught a charge.* As if an arrest was something viral that could randomly happen to anyone.

"Ms. Cousins," Marta said, "do you understand it's up to the judge to decide if you go to jail or get probation?"

"Yes, Ma'am."

"And if he gives you probation, you'll have to follow certain rules and restrictions. Do you think you can do that?"

"Oh yes, I'll do anything he wants. Pick up trash on the highway. Community service. Go to those A.A. or N.A. meetings. Anything. I just want to take care of my babies. They need me, and they don't got no one else. No one."

Judge Sacs eyed Denetta with a slight scowl. After seven years in that courtroom, I knew when he was feeling sympathetic. Unfortunately, it was up to me to ruin the moment.

"General Henley," said Sacs. "You may cross examine."

Sacs called me "General" because I was an Assistant District Attorney *General*. Only in court would such an archaic title still be adhered to, but all the lawyers in Chattanooga's District Attorney's Office were called "General" by the judges and other court personnel.

When I took the podium, Denetta glanced up. Her tears instantly vanished; I was the enemy.

"Ms. Cousins, you're here because eight weeks ago a jury found you guilty of burglary, correct?"

"Yes, sir, that's right."

"You were caught inside the home of Gordon Winston in East Brainered at 1:00 in the morning, right?"

"That's right."

"Who was watching your kids then?"

"Excuse me?"

"Who was caring for your three children while you were breaking into Mr. Winston's home?"

"Objection," Marta said, standing up at the defense table. "This is a sentencing hearing not a--"

"Overruled. Ms. Cousins, answer the question."

"My husband."

"And in 1996 when you were arrested for burglary, who was watching your kids then?"

"I don't remember," she said, crossing her arms.

"It couldn't have been your husband," I said. "He was in the workhouse. And what about the time you were caught with crack cocaine in 1995, who was with your kids then?"

"Why, I have no idea."

"What about when you were arrested for shoplifting?"

Denetta's glared at me as if her psychic power could implode my head. Denetta didn't even have the ability to do long division, so I ignored the threat. "Did you take your kids along when you were shoplifting? Was Mommy teaching them how to be thieves?"

Marta hit her feet. "Objection!"

"Sustained." Sacs said.

"What about it, Ms. Cousins? Who watched your children when you were shoplifting?"

"I can't recall," she said. "I used different people, and there was a lot of different times."

"Eight times to be exact. Now let me ask you about your job. It's at the Blue Deli Sandwich Shop?"

"That's right."

"How long have you been working there?"

"Six weeks."

"According to your probation records, this is your first job in over two years. Was that something you did just for the hearing today?"

"Absolutely not," she said. "I'd been talking to the manager down there for months."

"Ms. Cousins, I see you're wearing a beeper. Is that in case you have to go make an emergency sandwich or something?"

"Objection!" Marta said. "Your honor, that is so inappropriate."

"It was, your honor. I apologize. No further questions."

I walked back to the prosecution table and sank into the leather counsel's chair.

The victim, Gordon Winston, sat in the front row behind the rail. A barrel-shaped man with sandy hair, Gordon leaned over and patted my shoulder. "Good job," he whispered. "You really showed her for what she is." Over a year had passed since Denetta had climbed through the utility room window of Gordon's home. After a day of drinking Listerine and popping Xanex, she was looking for something to trade for the next high. She tried to steal a $20,000 baseball card collection that had taken Gordon fifteen years to build. Luckily, she was caught inside, and Gordon's insurance company covered all the break-in damage, including the profane words Denetta had etched on his bedroom walls with a butcher knife (Police said her spelling was as offensive as her word choice). I doubted she remembered anything at all from the incident.

An engineer for the Tennessee Valley Authority, Gordon had a hard time believing that someone like Denetta was allowed to roam free on the streets, and he was incredulous that she'd found the way to his bedroom. But today, Gordon truly believed the judge was going to make it right.

"Does council wish to be heard?" Judge Sacs said.

I looked over to Marta with eyebrows raised. I wasn't going to argue unless she did. My habit of restraint on such matters had clearly endeared me to the judge. If Marta was smart, she'd do the same thing. Then again, she might want to put on a show for her client.

"Yes, your honor." She walked to the podium. "I'd like to be heard."

All I can say is that her argument was passionate, earnest, and at least ten minutes too long.

"So in closing, your honor, I would ask the court to remember that the entire community wins if Ms. Cousins receives probation. That keeps her working at the Blue Deli and keeps her kids at home. Taxpayers won't have to foot the bill for prison and foster care."

Judge Sacs barely looked up from his paper work. "Care to respond, General Henley?"

"Briefly, your honor. I'd just point out that Ms. Cousins has never taken any personal responsibility for the burglary. She's never shown any remorse, and there's been no desire on her part to seek help for chemical dependency. Ms. Cousins has worked hard through the years to build an impressive resume as a thief. I'd ask the court to reward her for her efforts."

"Is the victim out-of-pocket on anything?" Sacs asked.

"No, your honor. His deductible was already met."

Sacs nodded. "After listening to the proof at trial and the testimony in today's hearing, I find the defendant guilty of a class C felony of burglary of a habitation. I find that despite one felony conviction and lengthy misdemeanor history, she is a Range I Standard Offender...."

Sacs didn't have the discretion people thought he did. He wasn't going to dream up some Solomon-like remedy; he was inputting the facts into a grid that was sort of like a multiplication table. You took the criminal offense on one side and the criminal record on top, and where the columns intersected, a range of years was provided in a tiny box. All the judge had to do was make a decision in that range.

Sort of.

For Denetta, the judge could choose between three and six years, but the legislature said he had to start at a presumptive minimum of three years. If the facts met certain statutory enhancing factors, a judge could bump the sentence higher.

And now, Sacs was reciting his grid logic so the Court of Appeals could see he hadn't applied any justice outside the lines.

"...Therefore, I sentence Ms. Cousins to the presumptive minimum of three years in the Department of Corrections. Bailiff take the defendant into custody."

I sat back stunned. Active time. The old man had pulled the trigger.

"Your honor," Marta said, "May my client have some time to put her affairs in order?"

"*Affairs?*" the judge said. "No, she's known for eight weeks that this hearing was set today. Bailiff, take her into custody."

Denetta started crying hysterically. Real racking sobs. The officer took her by the arm and walked her to a wood paneled doorway that led to a holding cell built behind the courtroom.

Once court was adjourned, Gordon grabbed my arm. "Fantastic job! That's three years she'll be off the streets."

"Now hold on, Mr. Winston," I said. "That doesn't really mean three years."

"But the judge gave her three years?"

"No, the judge gave her three fairy tale years."

***

"But, I don't understand," said Gordon as we walked down the hallway of the DA's office. "You think she's only going to serve five months?"

"If that," I said. "Come into my office. I'll explain."

Gordon's face was red. The veins in his neck looked like a relief map of Georgia's state highways. Throbbing little blue and red lines crisscrossed down his open collar. His Adam's apple was about where Atlanta should be.

I led the way into my small governmental office, complete with the regulation simulated wood desk, filing cabinet and bookshelf. Along the floor, piles of dark brown file folders crammed with papers leaned against the walls. Most lawyers are known to have an ego wall with diplomas and photographs. Me? I had an id, ego and super ego wall.

On my id wall hung my diploma from the University of Tennessee in Knoxville. After all, my sophomore year was the best two years of my life. Actually, the entire five years had been indulgent, but I somehow managed to pick up an English degree.

When I graduated, I realized an English degree qualified me to be a waiter most anywhere, so on my ego wall hung a diploma from the University Of Memphis School Of Law. It represented three years of teeth-grinding determination. Over a third of my class dropped out, but along the way, I discovered I had a talent for trial work.

Now, I don't mean litigation. Attorneys who call themselves litigators are generally paper tigers who have rarely seen a live jury. I like to think of trial lawyers as quick-on-your-feet people who can walk into fire and enjoy the heat. A true warrior class. To me, it's the difference between cargo pilots and fighter pilots.

And like a fighter pilot, I had a super ego and a wall to go with it. I hung every useless certificate that had a frame. I had a certificate for completing the prosecutor's applied trial technique course at the National Advocacy College in Columbia, S.C. I had a certificate of appreciation from the Hamilton County Commission where I prosecuted two county employees for embezzling, and I had a picture of me shaking hands with Ronald Reagan.

I didn't look like that 21-year-old kid anymore. I was now a heavier 33 year-old, reasonably tall with too much gray peppering the sides of my black hair. Of course I welcomed the gray, so juries wouldn't think I looked too young.

Gordon spied the picture of me and Reagan. Still upset, he said the first thing that popped in his head. "You look scared to death."

"I was," I said, taking a seat. To my back were two windows looking at downtown Chattanooga and the ribbon of green mountains that surrounded the city.

"Mr. Winston, the sentencing act is *designed* to get people out of jail. The prisons are overcrowded, and the legislature didn't like the federal courts controlling the state penal system. So, they came up with this. Now, Ms. Cousins got three years. She's eligible for parole after serving 30 percent of her sentence, so that's about one year. You with me so far?"

"Yeah," he said shifting back and forth in the chair.

"Now, there are federal caps on our prison population, and when it gets too crowded, they start kicking people out of prison. It's called the safety valve, which means Denetta automatically gets another forty percent off that thirty percent. So that means she'll be out in just under five months."

"But that's ridiculous."

"I agree," I said. "I hate it. We refer to the safety valve as the danger valve. The Department of Corrections says it only gives safety valve time to non-violent offenders--your burglars, crack dealers, car thieves--but in reality, they have released armed robbers. A policeman was killed in Nashville last year by a guy who had just been released."

"That's insane."

"No, sir, that's the law. The irony is people do more time in the county workhouse on a misdemeanor than on a class B felony."

"So in other words, this has been a complete waste of our time. She'll be back on the street in a few months, and for all we know back at my house pissed off that I testified. And then, nothing will happen again. What a farce."

"Farce? Do you know how hard it is to get a burglar *active time*? Our case couldn't have gone any better. It was as good as it gets.

"But—"

"Mr. Winston, I'm afraid you're finding out what every criminal already knows and what the average citizen doesn't discover until they become a victim. The criminal rarely goes to jail, and if he does, it won't be for long."

"I don't understand why you're not infuriated by this."

"Hey, on the up-side, her next felony will be her third, so she'll be considered a Range II multiple offender."

"Does that mean she'll stay in jail?"

"No, it means she'll serve about ten months."

As soon as I spoke the words, I realized how lame they sounded. Then, my beeper went off. Even before my fingers fumbled to silence it, I knew who was paging.

Gordon was pacing and shaking his head. "So what are we going to do?"

"Write your legislators," I said. "They're the only ones who can fix it. And I hate to run, but I'm late for something important."

Gordon stopped in mid-pace. "I'm not important? The idea that in five months Denetta Lynn Cousins could find her way back to my house is not important?"

"Mr. Winston, did you lose any blood?"

"What?"

"If you'll look around the floor of my office, almost every file you see lining the walls represents a dead person. At any given time, I have about 400 cases going, and what makes a case a priority is if you've lost blood. You were lucky this office even had the time to try your case. Please keep that in perspective, and remember the best thing you can do is write your legislator. Now, if you'll excuse me, I really am running late. You can find your own way out."

As I was leaving my office, I heard Gordon behind me. "Well, I am the victim you know. She wasn't in your home. She was in mine. I'm the victim."

Crazy freakin' victim, I thought. Crazy like every other freakin' victim.

Chapter 2

"Well, finally!"

Maisy Kirkland was standing in the flagstone courtyard of St. Paul's Episcopal, the oldest church in Chattanooga. The noonday sun shined on her long blond hair, making it shimmer like a supermodel's.

"Sorry, I got hung up in court." I said. "How late am I?"

"You're not," Maisy said with a wry smile. "I may have fibbed a bit about the time of our appointment."

"How much of a fib?"

"Half hour."

"I can't believe I fell for that again."

She gave me a quick kiss and led me through the colossal gothic doors of the church. Moments later, we were sitting on hard wooden chairs before the desk of Father Nicholas Humphreys.

Father Nick stared at us through thick black-framed glasses that stood out sharply against his shaggy white eyebrows and woolly white hair. His mouth was in a grim frown. Gone was a warm jocularity that we had grown accustomed to in our previous three sessions of pre-marital counseling.

"I'm afraid we have a problem," he said after a tense moment of silence. "I got the results back on your personality tests. As you can see from the results I plotted this morning, the bride's chart forms an almost perfect parabola. But the groom's..."

He held up a graph showing a drunken line weaving haphazardly down the page. "The groom's, you see, is another story entirely."

"You sound concerned, father?" Maisy said, lacing her fingers through mine. "Isn't this test just a formality?"

"Not exactly. The truth is that I'm not supposed to marry the two of you until your test scores are closer."

"But that's absurd!" I said. "It's only a—"

Maisy squeezed my hand so hard that her nails almost broke the skin of my hand. She was under enough stress with the wedding, and the idea of some standardized test making problems for us now seemed too crazy for words.

"The diocese checks all our counseling paperwork, you see," Father Nick was saying. "It's all part of the bishop's new initiative, to cut down on the divorce rate with better counseling on the front end."

Maisy scooted to the edge of her chair. "So are you saying this test indicates we shouldn't get married? That we aren't right for each other?"

"What it indicates is that Jack has some issues that may or may not cause difficulty later for both of you. The test is designed to raise a red flag and hopefully engender some frank discussions about potential problems."

"Problems?" I said, with more surprise than anger. "Like what?"

"Frankly, Jack, the test shows you've got some control issues. Maisy, that's not hard to understand. When Jack's parents died his senior year of high school, he had to take on an incredible amount of responsibility."

"What's wrong with that?"

"Nothing whatsoever." Father Nick said. "What's worrying me is that as a result of taking on so much so young, perhaps he is a bit obsessive when it comes to matters of control."

"So I'm a little type-A," I said, waving a hand. "Find me a lawyer who isn't."

Maisy started laughing. "A *little* type-A?"

"I take it you agree then?"

"Well, after seeing him in court..."

A year ago, Maisy Kirkland was the gorgeous jury foreman who uttered that sexy little word to the judge – "*Gill-tee*." Two notes forming a perfect harmonic that rippled through the courtroom and wormed their way into drug enforcer Cecil Harris's ears to let him know that even 12 people off the street didn't believe he set Eric Lambert on fire in self-defense. Of course, I was learning how that amazing stroke of luck in jury selection was going to be used against me.

"So how did his behavior in court make you think he's type-A?"

"He's sort of like an espresso machine," she said. "You know, all this repressed steam that's only released in controlled, focused bursts."

"Controlled bursts?" Father Nick nodded, a smile tugging at the corners of his mouth." Interesting choice of words, wouldn't you say?"

Maisy grinned at me. "It's in a good way, father, I assure you. And while I'm sure we both appreciate your point, keep in mind that your test overlooks something important."

Like the fact we love each other! And I was about to say that too, but something told me to keep my mouth shut.

"That's lawyer Jack you're reading about in the test answers there," Maisy continued. "Boyfriend Jack is open-minded, spontaneous, and in the year I've known him, anything but controlling when it comes to our relationship."

Father Nick nodded as he listened. "That's certainly encouraging, but I think there could be more to the issue. What about it, Jack? Where does all this repressed steam come from?"

I looked at him blankly for a moment. If Maisy understood me, wasn't that enough? Why the hell should I have to convince the church of our love?

"Perhaps some of your anger is rooted in feeling abandoned by your parents?"

"Abandoned?" I sat upright and looked directly at him. "I'm sorry, Father, but that's ridiculous. My parents didn't abandon me. Their car hit a patch of ice and slammed into a telephone pole. And, of *course*, I try to be controlling in court. I'm paid to win."

"What about anger, then? Is that what's being released in these controlled bursts Maisy mentioned?"

I took a deep breath and thought for a moment. Sure, inside court I probably did vent some self-righteous anger. But for the last seven years, I had been up to my chin in shovel and knife fights, drug deals gone bad, thugs killing other thugs, convenience store stick-up idiots and stoned drivers slaughtering entire families with a left turn.

But that stayed in court, right where it belonged. Most of the time, anyway.

"Father," I said. "What do I have to do to marry this woman on Saturday?"

He smiled and looked at us with a slight glint of mischief in his eye. "Take the test again, but before you do I want the two of you to talk about where your answers differed. And remember, Jack, there is a lot you can learn from Maisy."

Two minutes later, I was seated in a Sunday School classroom looking at the test. Maisy was pacing while flipping through her test booklet.

"How can you fail our compatibility test," she said, "as if I wasn't a nervous wreck already."

"What are you telling me?" I said. "That this stupid graph on a piece of paper means something? I love you, Maisy, and nothing will ever change that or convince me otherwise."

And nothing would. I had known that from the moment I kissed her for the first time.

Maisy continued to pace, her heels keeping time like a metronome. "Do you realize my family will be here tomorrow afternoon? What am I supposed to tell them?"

"Look at number three," I said. "How am I supposed to answer that?"

She stopped pacing and read over my shoulder. "'Do you consider yourself to be neat and orderly?' That's easy, circle *no*."

"Now, I know I'm not neat, but I *am* orderly. The two words are—"

"Let's not forget my results show I'm perfect."

I circled *no*. "Well, I'm glad to see we're working through these issues."

"Listen, Buster, I'm coordinating two hundred guests, the caterers, the reception, seven bridesmaids, thirty two relatives and a horse drawn carriage. Not to mention, I'm attending two engagement parties, a rehearsal dinner, a bridesmaid luncheon and maybe a wedding. Now, I've got to hold your hand through this test, so the bishop okays our marriage because you're the only person on the planet who's orderly but not neat!"

"Give me the copy of your test?"

"Why?" she, handing it over.

I didn't say anything as I began using her answers to mark my test.

"Jack, you can't... That's cheating."

"I have never cheated on a test in my life, Maisy, but I refuse to have my life dictated by circles you color with a number two lead pencil. I gave that up after high school. And I'm not going to let these ridiculous questions designed by some egg-heads – who for all I know aren't even Episcopalian– shake anyone's confidence in our marriage. I know in my heart that you're my best friend, my soul mate, my ravenous sex partner and my early morning snuggling buddy. This test does not mean anything."

*

When we turned the papers in to Father Nick, he gave them a quick perusal and nodded approvingly. "Looks good. I'll see you at the rehearsal Friday."

Maisy had calmed down by the time we got back to the parking lot. "So you'll pick me up at the hospital for the party tonight?"

"How about this," I said speaking in the smokiest, most suggestive voice I could muster. "It just occurred to me that this may be the only hour we get to ourselves until after the wedding. How about a two-hour lunch?"

Maisy flipped her hair over her shoulder and nodded with a full-lipped sensuous smile. "You drive."

Our town house was in Heritage Landing, a gated community just across the river from downtown. As soon as we pulled into the garage, clothes were flying off, and we were giggling as I chased her into the living room. We never made it past the couch. And it's true what they say, nothing–and I mean nothing–is as good as make-up exam sex.

I just never imagined it would be the last time we made love.

Chapter 3

I wasn't back in my office two minutes when our receptionist Sharon buzzed me on the intercom. "The General wants to see you in his office right away."

In court, assistant DA's may be called *General*, but around the office, that term referred to one man and one man only. And I never kept him waiting.

Harlan Griffin was the elected District Attorney and chief law enforcement officer for Hamilton County and, for my money, the least political DA in the state. When I say *political*, I mean he wasn't using the position as a platform to run for Congress or the Governor's Mansion. He was a career prosecutor because that was what he loved doing.

Less than 30 seconds later, I whirled into his office – a plush dark green cave with textured wall-paper, expensive prints of ancient Greece and a mahogany desk with a finish as clear as a mountain lake. "Sorry to bother you, Jack, but I'm afraid I've got some bad news."

I quickly inventoried the cases that kept me awake in the middle of the night and proffered the one that kept me up the most. "The Rawlins case?"

"That's right." Harlan sat down in a stuffed chair by the couch flipping through sheaf of white faxed legal pages. He looked young for 53, but the half-glasses resting on his nose bespoke of an impending AARP membership.

"It's not good, Jack." He tossed the papers on the coffee table. "Barbara Briggs wrote the opinion."

"Damn." I sat down on the couch with a sigh.

"Damn is right. She says that it was improper for you to argue that repeated blows of the hammer to Fran Weitzman's skull were proof of premeditation."

The law has always recognized that premeditation can occur in an instant. Many people assume premeditation is akin to the last chapter of a murder mystery where an elaborate plan of action is revealed. But, point a gun at someone for ten seconds and imagine how many times the thought of pulling the trigger goes through your head. *Hundreds!* So take the drug dealer who sees his customer who owes him money. He may spot the target, grab his gun and fire within 20 seconds, but his premeditation formed in the time it took to click the safety off his 9 millimeter. Why would anyone want to live in a world where that dealer was not guilty of first degree murder?

And along these lines, the law had also allowed prosecutors to argue that repeated blows of a weapon were proof of premeditation. Waling away repeatedly at someone's head with a hammer must mean he had had given some reflection to wanting that person dead. Even Rawlins' defense attorneys did not blink at an argument prosecutors had been making for more than 100 years. "I don't recall the defense raising that issue on appeal?"

"They didn't," Harlan said. "She reached into the record and found it all on her own. One of the worst examples of judicial activism I've ever seen."

"Amazing. So she thinks if you hit someone in the head 26 times, it's not a premeditated crime."

"I don't know if we'll ever be able to prove first degree murder again without a written diary outlining the killing," Harlan said.

"And that means less chances for us to push for the death penalty," I said.

That was the logical conclusion. As the newest member of the Tennessee Supreme Court, Barbara Briggs was a sworn enemy of capital punishment. In fact, her love of criminals seemed to know no bounds.

Last month, she'd reduced the 40-year sentence given to a man for violently raping a 72 year-old woman to 15 years with no explanation other than 'fifteen years is enough for this brutal rapist.'

And she wasn't even being sarcastic!

What offended me, besides the obvious, was that as an appellate judge she had no firsthand experience with the victim or the defendant, or anyone else who had been affected by the crime. She had no idea about the rapist's demeanor in court...of how he smirked and winked at his victim when she testified. All Barbara Briggs did was read a transcript and dream up her decisions. And they were real nightmares.

Last year, she had set aside a murder conviction because of a three-inch pocket knife. When the medical examiner was beginning his autopsy, he made a list of the personal property that was on the victim, including the knife. None of the witnesses had seen the knife, nor had the defendant testified to seeing the victim with a knife. Nonetheless, she said that evidence could have been used to build a self-defense case, so the case was reversed because prosecutors failed to show the personal property list to defense attorneys. Never mind that the prosecutors didn't even know the list existed. But that was Barbara Briggs for you. I sometimes wondered if she was the kind of woman who secretly penned hot steamy letters to death row inmates.

I hadn't read her opinion from today but one thing was sure; Lorenzo Rawlins would be allowed to return from prison to Hamilton County to stand trial one more time for the rape and murder of Fran Weitzman.

The attack had been exceptionally vicious, thanks in part to a hammer Rawlins found on a washing machine while chasing Fran through her house. She had been trying to get outside where someone might hear her screams, but a few feet from the back door, Rawlins got a handful of hair. He yanked her down and beat her face and head 26 times. Then, he raped her corpse for over an hour and stuffed her body in the crawl space of the house.

The memory of this poor woman's death already had my stomach churning, but making matters worse was that, thanks to Justice Briggs, Rawlins now had a state constitutional right to bond.

"Was a bond set?" I said.

"No, but I expect a bond hearing next week."

"This is unreal. To think that piece of human garbage can get out of jail. Well, I shouldn't have any problem convincing the trial judge to set an astronomical bond."

"Aren't you forgetting something?" Harlan said. "Like your honeymoon?"

I slapped my forehead. "Well, there's that."

"Don't worry about a thing. I'll personally handle it."

"You?" I said. "Are you sure you remember how to find the courtroom?"

"Funny," he said, "How soon can you be ready to try this again?"

"Two months...maybe three. You're sure you're up for the bond hearing?"

"Positive. But right now, you need to track down Isaac Weitzman and give him the bad news before he hears it from the media."

"It'd sound better coming from the top dog--"

"Nice try," Harlan said. "I'm not talking to that lunatic any more than I have to. I want my best victim-handler to work his magic. As for Briggs, I'll call the DA's Conference in Nashville. We have to try and get around her legislatively on this. She's made a mess out of every first degree murder case in the state."

I nodded. I didn't relish the idea of dealing with Weitzman, who was high maintenance at best and capable of doing anything, given the opportunity. But I really couldn't blame the guy for how he'd behaved through the trial. Had it been my wife, I don't think I'd be acting any differently.

"Here's a copy of the opinion," Harlan said. "Read it and then haul ass over to Weitzman's."

We both knew Weitzman could afford to have Rawlins killed if he wanted to, and with this 11-page push from Barbara Briggs, he might just be predisposed to do it.

I nodded. "I'll take care of it, General."

"That's why I like you, Jack. You always do."

*

On the fourth floor of Erlanger Hospital, a surgical nurse tied a green robe around me and led me to the scrub room. Standing by the sink was Isaac Weitzman, wearing purple surgical scrubs and scouring his fingers with a brush.

Bald, tall, and in pretty good shape for a guy in his late forties, Weitzman had the unmistakable bearing of a surgeon. But Weitzman wasn't your everyday doctor either; at his core was a tough, rowdy kid who grew up on the streets of South Boston, and a seven-digit income had clearly not dulled his street-fighter mentality.

"Well, well, well, this must really be bad if you came here to tell me." Fifteen years in Chattanooga hadn't dulled his thick Boston accent either.

I only had about five minutes before Weitzman went into surgery, and I had no idea how to begin. The nurse had told me he was going to rebuild the face of a cleft-faced Guatemalan boy.

Children with abnormalities from all over the world flew to Chattanooga where Weitzman would build them a new face for free. His third-world work had built him quite a good reputation in Chattanooga, but for me Weitzman remained a rather large pain in the rear. He was always the angry customer who needed special handling.

"Dr. Weitzman, I'm sorry to have to tell you that the Tennessee Supreme Court reversed Rawlins' conviction and ordered a new trial."

Weitzman's body tensed, but he said nothing. He kept scrubbing his fingers with the brush, harder and harder, so hard that I thought the bristles would draw blood.

"I'm so sorry," I said. "It was a really bizarre ruling. No one expected it."

With his lips pressed together in a thin line, he clenched his hands into fists as though he was going to put them through the wall. I had no doubt that if he hadn't been sterilizing his hands he would have, but he did the next best thing. With a guttural yell, he kicked the side of the sink with a ferocity that thundered throughout the OR. His surgical nurse ran to the door, but I sent her away with a shake of my head.

"YOU!" he said pointing a soapy finger at me. "You tell me how this could have happened."

"The Court felt the judge had incorrectly applied the law in allowing prosecutors to argue–"

"Enough with the lawyer talk! I want you to tell me why."

I thought for a moment and decided he deserved nothing less from me. "The truth is that the Court hates the death penalty. We're guessing that--"

"That's ridiculous. This wasn't even a capital case."

"Doesn't matter. Their real agenda has nothing to do with Rawlins himself. They're looking for every excuse to weaken our ability to prosecute first degree murder cases."

"Was it this Briggs woman we talked about?"

"Yes, and I need to warn you... There's a bond hearing next week, but no one seriously believes he'll make bond."

"Are you telling me this nut-job could be released?"

"No one believes it will happen." I spoke in a slow cadence as if my voice could soothe him.

"And no one believed the case would be overturned. Now tell me, Henley. Is there a chance he could make bond? Yes or no?"

"There's always that possibility."

"So the answer to my question is YES."

"That's right."

"Are you handling the hearing?"

"No, Harlan Griffin will be handling it personally."

"Unacceptable," he said. "I want you."

"I'll be on my honeymoon."

"Cancel it," he said. "You owe me that much after screwing up my case."

"First of all, I didn't screw up anything. We got a bad ruling from an insane Supreme Court Justice. It happens. But, let's not forget, I'm the only one who was willing to try this case when everyone else wanted to plead it."

"I know," he said, "you're the only son of a bitch up there that knows how to fight. I don't want to go into court with some pantywaist District Attorney that hasn't been in a courtroom brawl for over a decade. Because while you're screwing your brains out in the Bahamas or Cancun, Lorenzo Rawlins could very well get bond and disappear. Then you guys in the DA's office will cover your ass with some bullshit lawyer talk, and I'll be left holding my Johnson while my wife's killer roams free to kill again."

He peered at me though narrow eyes, his gaze angry and pleading all at the same time. "*That's* why you should take your honeymoon after the hearing."

"I tell you what," I said. "I'll handle the case however you want me to, but only if you let me stand next to you in the OR and tell you exactly how to perform the operation on that boy."

"You're such a smartass, Henley. This isn't a turf thing, and you know it. This is about Fran. Can't you at least put off the hearing until after the honeymoon?"

"No, Rawlins has a right to have the hearing sooner than later, and he will never agree to a reset."

The surgical nurse tapped on the window of the door and pointed to the clock on the wall.

"We can talk more about this tomorrow," I said.

"Oh, we will."

"Dr. Weitzman, I may be out of line here, but perhaps you should think about joining a victim support group. They could really help you work through these things. I've sent a number of people to them through the years with great results."

Weitzman leaned his back against the door that led into the O.R. with his hands raised in front of him. "Henley, go fuck yourself."

Chapter 4

Maisy had been delayed at work, so we were already about 30 minutes past fashionable for the party at Harlan's house on top of Signal Mountain. Sauntering in late to a friend's party may be okay, but it's bad form when it's a party in your honor at your boss's home. So I drove as fast as I dared while I filled her in on how things had gone today.

"So how did Weitzman handle it?" she said.

"He kicked things, told me it was my fault and demanded I postpone our honeymoon until after the bond hearing."

"What an ego! Thank God I didn't become a surgeon; I'd probably be just as intolerable. Did you tell him to stuff it?"

"He was on his way into surgery, so I told him we'd talk about it in the morning."

"Well, I hope it's a quick conversation. Because if you think for one minute that I'm going to play second fiddle to Isaac Weitzman, you're nuts. I know how much this case means to you, but postponing our honeymoon? I can't believe he even suggested it."

"I know. I know." I waved my hand in surrender. "You're right."

"Oh, the ice, Harlan wanted us to bring some ice!" She pointed to a Golden Gallon Exxon convenience market at the corner of Mountain Creek Road and Signal Mountain Boulevard.

I parked in front of a battered ice storage freezer about 30 feet to the left of the front door and threw a couple of crumpled bills at Maisy. "You go pay, and I'll put the ice in the car. And hurry. We're late."

Maisy grabbed the money and scampered towards the door.

I popped out of the car and opened the ice cooler. The whir of an ancient motor shook the box, and I had just gotten a grip on two five-pound bags, when I heard the muffled bang of what sounded like a shotgun.

I jerked my head out of the cooler and heard another blast from inside the store. *What the hell?*

I dropped the ice and went for the glove compartment of the car. I fumbled with the latch and grabbed my .357 Magnum, left there from a late night visit to a homicide in a gang-infested neighborhood the week before.

Odds were that we had stumbled into a robbery, and I knew there was no one more stupid and more dangerous than armed robbers. They took maximum risks for the least amount of gain. Surely, Maisy had the good sense to hand over anything they asked for and not try anything that would provoke a wigged-out gunman.

I crouched beneath the store's waist high windows and began a duck-walk toward the door.

I hadn't taken three steps when the door slammed open so hard that the glass shattered. Out came a man wearing a black ski mask, a Members Only Jacket and white painters' pants. In his right hand, he held a pump shotgun; in left hand was a white plastic Golden Gallon bag filled with cash.

To my great relief, he never looked left or right and never saw me squatted down beside the building. He hightailed it to a boxy black Maxima idling on the other side of the pumps.

I didn't try to stop him. If he wanted to leave, that was fine with me. As the man started to drive away, he tore off his ski mask and threw it out the window.

I only got a look for an instant. Not even a whole second, but I didn't need a whole second to recognize Jimmy Ray McElvy. I had tried him about two years ago for an armed robbery of a Bi-lo store on Highway 58.

McElvy's made parole, I thought. McElvy? But he got 10 years!

McElvy turned left onto Mountain Creek, and I yanked the remains of the door open and ran inside, my hands suddenly jittery. A cold sweat had formed on my back and my mind was suffocating in its worst fears.

I almost tripped over Maisy, who was lying a few feet in front of the door. She was moaning and pressing her hands to her stomach.

MAISY!

My leather soles slid on the slick linoleum now wet with Maisy's blood. My feet shot out our from under me as if it was my first day on ice skates. I crashed into a potato chip rack, sending its contents toppling down all over me.

"Oh, Jack," she said taking big gulps of air. "It hurts so bad."

I backhanded the rack and sloshed through the bags of chips to my knees. Her stomach was bleeding in a circular pattern about the size of a dessert plate, and I could see awful things bulging out – folded tubes of sanguine-white tissue. Blood seeped around my fingers as I pressed her intestines back into the cavity. I jerked off my tie and shirt, pressing the shirt to her stomach to stop the bleeding.

"I must have surprised him when I came in."

"Shhh, don't talk. *Someone call an ambulance!*"

"Is the clerk okay? I saw her go for a gun."

I glanced up towards the counter. No one was standing there, and the wall behind the counter was streaked with red and green. Through the years, I had seen enough brain spatter to know it when I saw it.

"Don't worry about the clerk," I said. "Am I putting too much pressure on your stomach? Am I hurting you?"

"It hurts. But keeping blood is more important."

I had no idea of how hard to press. Too hard and damage her organs or cause unnecessary pain. Not hard enough and lose too much blood.

I had just started hyperventilating when I glanced up and saw the blue uniform of a Chattanooga police officer coming in the door.

"Thank God, call for help," I said.

"Sure thing, Mr. Henley."

I looked up again and saw that it was George Cash. I had tried a number of his cases through the years. I couldn't have asked for a more professional officer to be on the scene.

"George, this is my fiancée, we need an ambulance right now."

George began talking into his radio rig strapped to the epaulet of his shirt.

"And George, the shooter's name is Jimmy Ray McElvy. He's driving a late eighties black Nissan Maxima with a drive out tag, and he's armed with a pump shotgun. Call Burglary/Robbery. They know everything about him."

George nodded went out the door mumbling into his radio. He returned wearing aqua blue latex gloves and carrying a first aid kit.

"The ambulance will be here in one minute," he said getting on his knees beside me. He pressed a large gauze pad on her stomach.

Maisy gave a sharp yelp.

"Sorry," George said, "but we need to stop this bleeding."

"We certainly do," Maisy said, her voice noticeably weaker. "Jack and I are getting married Saturday."

George didn't say anything, but from his expression, I could tell he didn't believe her.

*

In the ambulance, two EMT's worked to stop the bleeding. I was holding Maisy's hand and giving her shoulder squeezes of encouragement. She was white as chalk and having a hard time catching her breath.

"Doctor, you're going to be okay," said one of the EMT's.

"Hear that?" I said. "You're going to be fine."

Maisy moved the plastic oxygen mask off her mouth. "Oh God Jack! I don't want to die."

"You're not going to."

"I don't want to die!"

"Shhh, we'll be at the hospital soon."

I glanced out the window. We were at Fourth and Walnut Street, and two police cars had cleared the intersection. We had not gone another half block when I spied three police cars blocking Third and Lindsay streets.

My eyes welled with tears. The only time police would clear every single intersection to the hospital was for a fallen officer. This was a huge compliment from George Cash, and I'd never been more appreciative of a human gesture in all my life.

Lying on her back, Maisy's tears rolled across her temples towards her ears. I gently brushed them away with my fingertips and rubbed her head.

"Jack, I wanted nothing more in life than to marry you. Being your wife would have been so wonderful."

"And we are going to get married," I said. "If I know one thing about my life, it's that I was meant to marry you."

"What if I don't make it to Saturday, Jack? What if I can't..."

"Shhh," I said, putting her oxygen mask over her nose and mouth. "It's going to happen, I promise."

I patted her hand and crawled forward to the driver. "Hey, can you please radio ahead for a priest."

"They'll do that for you at the hospital," the driver said. "We're only a few blocks away."

"I'm not asking you. I'm telling you to get us a priest. I need him there the second this ambulance hits the ER."

The driver looked at me for a second through his mirrored aviator sunglasses. His red-haired moustache did little to hide his freckles; he couldn't have been more than 25.

I don't know if it was my tone of voice or the expression in my eyes, but he nodded. "Okay, Okay.

You must be pretty important. I've never had the police give me an escort like this."

"Oh, I'm a nobody. She's the important one."

*

I held Maisy's hand as they wheeled her into Erlanger Hospital. I was wearing a blood stained white T-shirt and blue poplin pants. The socks in my loafers were wet from her blood and squished when I walked.

An unusual number of nurses and doctors were waiting for us. Apparently, they knew how to take care of their own too. They swarmed around me and Maisy shouting orders and working on her.

A man in a black suit put his hand on my elbow. "Son, I'm the hospital chaplain. Why don't you come sit with me and let's get out of everyone's way?"

"What are you? Methodist? Presbyterian?"

"Southern Baptist."

"That'll do. I need you to marry us, right this minute."

"I'm sure that can wait until after the surgery."

"No, sir, I need you to marry us now." I looked down at Maisy. "Is that all right with you, Honey? Will you marry me five days early?"

Her eyes sparkled as she nodded yes.

My request must have surprised everyone because they paused for a second before resuming their work.

A tall man wearing surgical scrubs stepped up. "I'm Dr. Bill Allen, chief attending. You're going to have to leave us alone and let us do our job."

"I'm not leaving until I'm married to this woman."

"Sir, this is neither the time nor the place. She has multiple organ damage, and we have to get her into surgery as soon as possible."

"We're not signing a single consent form until you marry us."

"Call security. I want this man removed."

"Please, Bill," Maisy said, as she held her oxygen mask to the side. "Give us a moment."

"Are you sure?"

"Yes."

Dr. Allen turned to me. "You got 60 seconds, and we'll be working around you."

"That makes you my best man, Doc." I waved the Chaplain to the table with a nod of my head. "Padre, give us the best you got."

I have to say the Chaplain rose to the task. He put his hand on top of Maisy's and mine and said: "Dear God, we stand before you with two people very much in love who come to be joined in holy matrimony. Do you, uh...?"

"Jack"

"...Jack, take this woman to be your lawfully wedded wife. To love and to hold in sickness and in health until death do you part?"

"I do."

"Do you, uh...?"

"I need a chest tube," the doctor said.

"Maisy," I said.

"...Maisy take this man to be your lawfully wedded husband. To have and to hold in sickness and in health, until death do you part?"

Her ash-blue eyes found mine, and she nodded. "Until death do us part, I do."

"Nurse, let me have an 18 French silk."

"I now pronounce you man and wife. You may now kiss the bride and get out of the way of these good people."

A nurse yanked Maisy's diamond solitaire off her finger and put it in my hand. "For safe keeping," she said.

"Call time of marriage," Dr. Allen said.

"20:11," said a nurse writing on the chart.

"I love you, Maisy," I said kissing her gently on the mouth. "Now, let them make you better, so we can get started on our honeymoon."

"I love you, Jack." She managed a weak smile. "And thank you."

Then she turned her head to the side and began throwing up on the side of the table and floor.

"Don't let her aspirate!" Dr. Allen said.

"Come on, son." The chaplain tugged me gently by the arm.

"Doctor, take good care of Mrs. Henley."

Nurses were wiping her chin, but Maisy's eyes flashed a smile when I said it.

I turned to follow the chaplain, and as soon as Maisy could no longer see my face, I began weeping. My eyes were like open faucets flooding my vision.

The chaplain put his arm around my shoulder and led me towards the waiting room. "Who can I call for you?"

Chapter 5

The linoleum floor in the surgical waiting room was artic cold. A nurse had given me some scrubs to wear but nothing for my feet. Harlan found me stamping my feet, trying to keep warm, as I waited for word on how Maisy was doing.

"Jack, I'm so sorry," he said. "I stopped by the scene on the way. It was horrible. How's Maisy?"

"She's in surgery now. She was hit in the stomach at close range. Her insides are torn up pretty bad."

"Homicide will be by when they finish processing the scene. I've got Skerret and Jenkins there now."

Dave Skerret was the executive assistant DA in the office, Harlan's number two man. A former Army JAG officer, Skerret was aggressive, smart and creative. And Saul Jenkins was one of our best investigators. He had a gift for watching a prosecutor's back.

"Who's working the case?"

"I'm not sure, but from the looks of it the entire homicide squad. Charlie Shane was there, calling the shots himself."

"Any sign of McElvy?"

"Not yet."

"General, how did this guy get out? I just put him in."

"I don't know, Jack, but believe me I'm looking into it." He paused for a moment and looked at me appraisingly. "Anything I can do for you, Jack?"

"I could use some shoes. Or even real pants for that matter."

"Done. I'll have an investigator drop by your place."

"Here's the big favor, General. Could you call Maisy's family? Remember, you met them last summer at the lake. I'm afraid I couldn't get through it all. Here's their numbers. Her parents live with her sister in Berkley. They're all scheduled to fly in tomorrow."

I handed him a slip of paper.

"Sure thing."

The chaplain came into the room waving a piece of paper over his head. "It took some wrangling, but I got you a marriage license. I had the ER nurses sign as witnesses, so it's all official."

"What's official?" Harlan said.

"Oh yeah," I said. "Before they took Maisy to surgery, we got married."

Harlan was speechless for a moment. "So she was that bad."

*

An hour later, the waiting room was filled with people. In the corner, Harlan was on his cell phone tracking down Maisy's family and keeping tabs on the investigation. A few prosecutors and their spouses had trickled in from the engagement party. Father Nick was in another corner discussing the marriage with the chaplain, whose name I still hadn't learned. Several of Maisy's coworkers were there as well.

All in all, it was the most maudlin wedding reception in the history of wedding receptions. And for some reason, everybody kept wanting to bring me coffee. As if caffeine would make me feel better.

I jumped when the waiting room phone rang. One of the nurses who worked with Maisy picked it up. She hung up the phone and shook her head. "That was Channel 9."

"Don't worry about the media, Jack," said Harlan. "I'll handle them."

Who cares!

Charlie Shane from homicide arrived next. "I brought you some coffee."

He was alone, and I appreciated him not bringing an entourage of detectives.

Harlan, Shane and I took a stroll in the hall, so we could talk privately. I told them everything that I had seen.

"When you wrap up things here," Shane said, "I need you to come by the department, so we can tape your statement."

"I understand. Anything you need."

"One last thing," he said. "Skerret recommended we do a photo lineup."

"He's right. I haven't seen McElvy in two years."

Shane reached into his folder and pulled out a manila board with six photographs of middle-aged white males with scruffy black hair. Then, he formally asked the magic legal question: "Do you see the man you saw tonight running out of the Golden Gallon with the shot gun and money?"

"Yes, I do," I said. "That's him."

I pointed to a picture in the upper right corner. McElvy's eyes leapt off the page at me --brown swirls of stupidity, cowardice and B-movie machismo. They were a little too far apart and set so deeply that his eyebrows were dark scraggly over-hangs. His nose hooked over a sneer originally given to a booking officer who must have wondered if McElvy's parents were first cousins.

"Put your initials and the date underneath his mug shot."

"Charlie, when the hell did this guy get out? He had a ten-year sentence."

"All I know is that he served sixteen months and somehow got released. In the four months he's been out, we believe he's committed four other armed robberies. I got every man in the squad out looking for him."

"Have you seen the store video?"

Charlie nodded sympathetically. "She really surprised him, Jack. I think he would have shot her again, but he saw the clerk going for a gun. After he killed her, he got scared. Grabbed the money and ran."

"Who was she?"

"Katrina Jones, mother of four, worked days at the Seaboard chicken plant. What's weird is McElvy's had two types of shells in the gun. The first round, which hit Maisy, was birdshot. The clerk was hit with buckshot, which took most of her head off. You're lucky it wasn't the other way around."

A door opened and Saul Jenkins came in carrying a gym bag with a change of clothes and some other things I had asked for from home. He nodded briefly to me and then inspected something on the toe of his shoe when he handed me the bag.

I went into a bathroom at the end of the hall and slipped into some Levi's and a Polo shirt. Socks warmed my feet as I tied on a pair of Nike running shoes. I leaned against the stall gulping for air and rubbing tears out of my eyes. Fear, hope and panic fighting for prominence but only numbness winning out. No man likes crying, but I'll be damned if I didn't think that right at that moment that rolling around and sobbing on the floor might ease the pain in my chest.

Come on, Jack. Hold it together, Jack. Come on, Maisy needs you.

A splash of water in the face, a deep breath and I was out the door. When I came out, Dr. Allen, Father

Nick, and Harlan were huddled together talking quietly.

Dr. Allen stepped forward and nodded solemnly. "The surgery on your wife revealed multiple organ damage. She lost her pancreas and liver along with all kidney function. And there was some significant lung damage as well."

Oh God, no! Not her liver! You can't live without a liver!

"We did everything we could, but the damage from the shotgun was too great. Let me just say how personally sorry I am for your loss. She was an outstanding physician and a wonderful person."

Words choked in my throat, so I swallowed hard and whispered, "Where is she? I'd like to see her."

"She's still in the OR. I can show you the way."

I looked at the solemn faces of the men. And then, I found Father Nick's eyes, filled with concern and compassion, yet there was also a toughness to them. I had met those same eyes 15 years ago when a doctor told me my parents had died.

I had drawn strength from them then. My parents' bodies were too mangled for viewing, but Father Nick went with me to collect their personal effects. On my wrist hung my father's gold Omega Constellation he had bought on a trip to New York.

For Father Nick and me, there was a familiarity to the moment that neither of us enjoyed.

"Father, could you come with me?"

His eyes filled with tears, and he whispered, "You bet."

*

Maisy was draped with a clean hospital sheet folded down at her shoulders with her hands resting on her chest --an unmistakable casket pose.

Father Nick rubbed the sign of the cross on her forehead with his thumb and began reading from the Book of Common Prayer: "Into your hands, O merciful Savior, we commend your servant Maisy Kirkland Henley. Acknowledge, we humbly beseech you, a sheep of your own fold, a lamb of your own flock, a sinner of your own redeeming. Receive her into the arms of your mercy, into the blessed rest of everlasting peace, and into the glorious company of the saints in light. Amen."

"Amen."

"May her soul and the souls of all the departed, through the mercy of God, rest in peace. Amen."

"Amen."

I slipped Maisy's engagement ring onto her ring finger on her left hand. Her hand was cool but not yet stiff. I then opened the gym bag and took out her wedding band, sliding it snug against the engagement ring. It had been my mother's. I reached into the bag again and put on my own finger a bright new gold band that Maisy had bought for me last week at Fischer Evans.

Father Nick rubbed my head with his hand and left me alone with my wife.

Chapter 6

I sat in the passenger seat of Saul Jenkin's Crown Victoria staring ahead at Amnicola Highway but not really seeing anything. The ride passed in oppressive silence, interrupted only by occasional bursts of chatter from his police radio. I was in such a daze that that I nearly jumped out of my skin when Jenkins' cell phone rang.

"Jenkins." He frowned as he listened. "Where?...I'll try, but I need to get Henley to homicide first...."

He flipped the phone shut and slipped it into his coat pocket. "Looks like they've found McElvy. He's holed up at his mother's house in East Lake. They may have to call the SWAT team."

"Good," I said. The Chattanooga police SWAT team had such a high kill rate, the threat of their presence alone was often enough to persuade people to give up. Either result was fine with me. "Did you get an address?"

"Let's just get you over to homicide, okay?"

"Why? Every homicide detective on the payroll is probably in East Lake."

"Maybe so," he said, "but I'm still not sure it's a good idea to take you there."

"Come on, Saul. I've earned the right to see this guy taken down."

There was no way he could argue with that. Saul nodded as he slowed the car for a U-turn, "I guess it wouldn't hurt to go check it out."

*

The street leading to McElvy's mother's house was blocked at each end by several police cars. Jenkins found a parking spot about 50 feet from one barricade, close to a cluster of men including Harlan and Dave Skerret. Several cruiser side-mounted spotlights were trained on a small house made out of concrete block. Spray painted on the side of a telephone pole out front was the telltale tag of an all-white gang called the South East Thugs.

"Some neighborhood," I said.

Jenkins opened his door and stepped out. "You better stay in the car, okay? I'll find out what I can and be back in a minute."

"Take your time."

I rolled down my window and listened as Shane talked from a bullhorn from behind a Crown Victoria pulled in front of the house. "Come on, Jimmy Ray. The longer you stay in there, the worse it'll be for you."

A window broke in front of the house, and the tip of a shotgun emerged from the remains of the window. The taste of bile shot up the back of my throat; that had to be the same gun that killed Maisy.

"I got some demands!" McElvy screamed.

"I guess a new window will be your first one," Shane said.

I had to hand it to Shane for trying to keep it light. Yet, as I spat the bile out of my mouth through the open car window, my fists clenched and unclenched rapidly. If they didn't get this son-of-a-bitch soon, I was going to take his fucking house apart and drag him out myself.

"I want some pizza!"

Fuck this!

While Harlan and company were all watching Shane, I got out of the car and beelined it to the back yard of a nearby house.

After making sure my badge was visible, I crept through the next two backyards, past a tire swing and a grill made out of the side of a steel drum and concrete blocks. I found a patrolman squatting in the overgrowth in the shadows behind a tree. He had his gun trained 30 yards away on McElvy's backdoor, or what was left of it. An old wooden screen door hung by one rusted hinge at the bottom. The main back door was open on the inside.

My guess was that the door was open on purpose, so McElvy could demonstrate why they called this a shotgun house. If he was in the living room, he had a clear line of sight from to the back door.

"Officer," I said. "I'm with the DA's office. Lt. Shane sent me. Any activity back here?"

I didn't recognize him. He looked about 21 years-old. To be working this shift in this neighborhood, he was probably fresh out of the academy. *Perfect!*

"No, sir. No sign that anyone else is in the house."

"Anyone else covering the back?"

"Abernathy and Moody have the other corner. We're just covering the exits until the SWAT team gets here."

From the front of the house, I heard McElvy yelling, "And I don't want no mushrooms or olives on it. I hate 'em."

"Officer, this is a bunch of crap! Listen, Lt. Shane believes he's listening to police traffic on a scanner, so I need you to sneak around and tell Abernathy and Moody that we're going in at exactly 11:35. That's in five minutes. I'll cover this corner for you."

"Where's your gun?"

"Ankle holster," I lied.

The officer wiggled through the bushes and kudzu until making it to the other side where he could talk with Abernathy and Moody. That's when I got up and walked as quickly as I could towards McElvy's back door. If I ran, someone would probably shoot me--either from the woods behind or the house ahead of me.

As I opened the screen door, McElvy yelled, "And make sure it's deep dish. I'll blow your head-off if it's that thin crust shit!

"Now, Jimmy Ray," Shane said. "You're going to have to give me a good reason to not shoot you. Did you know I get two weeks off if I shoot you? It's an automatic suspension *with pay!* So, I'm thinking it's win/win for me."

Once inside, I was in a dark kitchen. The smell of marijuana was overpowering, but I didn't slow my pace at all. Not even when I grabbed an iron off the ironing board. I kept walking--and fast.

Within five seconds, I was in the living room. Police lights slashed through the blinds across the darkness. McElvy was still wearing his *Member's Only* Jacket and painters' pants. His shotgun was poked out of the window, and he was hunched over the stock staring at the police. Next to him, smoke rose from a bong that must have been two feet tall.

By the time he heard me it was too late. I reverse-gripped the iron so the bottom faced up and its sharp point faced forward and swung with all my might. I heard something crack and watched as his skin on his face split open and start spewing blood.

With my left hand, I slapped the butt of the gun sending it out the window. My left foot delivered a sharp blow to his groin while I hit him again and again with the iron.

And I hate to admit it, but I have never felt more in tune with my being. My DNA, encoded for survival thousands of years ago, told every ounce of me that this was what had to be done. Killers like McElvy had to be taken out; then, we would all be safe again.

Finally, I felt a hand grab my forearm while another wrapped across my chest and hoisted me away from McElvy.

"What are you doing!" It was the young officer from the backyard. "Ease off!"

"What's the big idea!" McElvy shouted. He was shaking, and red spittle hung from his bottom lip. The left side of his face looked like hamburger meat with spaghetti sauce. "I was gonna turn myself in right after I had the pizza."

"You want free food while my wife lies in the morgue?"

"Oh, shit!" McElvy, unable to respond, fell back in pain with his hands over his eye.

Harlan and Jenkins came in the front door. "What the hell's going on? My God, Jack! Have you lost your mind?"

"What were you going to do with him, General? Put him in jail! Well I already did that, and it doesn't work, all right! Unless we put this fucking animal down-- "

"Enough!" Harlan said, cutting me off with the wave of a hand and taking control of the scene. "Officer, let's get this piece of shit to the hospital."

The rookie released his grip and moved to help carry McElvy outside as EMT'S rolled a stretcher up to the house. Other officers began moving about the house pulling open cabinets and drawers hoping to turn up anything linking McElvy to the Golden

Gallon. One officer bagged and tagged two crack pipes he found on a coffee table.

"If you want to commit murder, that's your business, but do it on your own time. Not in a way that will get me sued. You've really screwed the pooch this time, Jack. I don't care if your girlfriend–"

"Wife! My wife!"

"–wife was killed today. We don't have absolute immunity anymore. Do you realize the personal liability you've exposed me to? Give me your badge."

"What?"

"Your badge. Give it to me. You're suspended while we investigate what happened here tonight. With your badge in my pocket, I might be able to convince Shane not to arrest you until tomorrow morning.

"Jenkins, take him home and guard him. If he tries to leave, arrest him. If he tries to kill himself, arrest him. I'll have someone there in the morning to relieve you."

*

Jenkins took me home, removed all the sharp objects from my bathroom and searched the bedroom for guns. I gave him some blankets and a pillow for the couch in the living room.

He wasn't speaking to me, and I couldn't blame him. He could expect one hell of an ass chewing from Harlan in the morning, if not worse.

For the second time that day, I took off blood-stained clothes, showered and lay on the bed. The digital clock on Maisy's side of the bed read 1:25 a.m.

Black Monday had ended over an hour ago with a critically injured man and two dead bodies. I'd been married for two hours and 17 minutes, the biggest murder case I'd ever tried had been reversed on appeal, and I'd been suspended and placed under guard. Legally, I could be arrested for attempted murder, but even if that went away, I knew McElvy would sue me into financial oblivion. A life time of tuna and garnished wages.

I could smell Maisy on the sheets. I rolled onto her pillow and took a deep drag. I buried my face deeper to drown myself in her scent.

PART II
Sliced Lives

Chapter 7

I heard the phone ringing as I watched the morning sun stream in through the bedroom blinds. I was lying in bed looking at the ceiling and wondering if I had actually slept at all.

After a light tap at the door, Saul Jenkins stuck his head in. "Good, you're still alive. I realized when I woke up this morning that I forgot to take all your shoelaces and belts."

"I don't think you forgot. You were pretty sore at me last night."

"Well, that was last night. If I was in your shoes, I'd have done the same thing. Come on. Get up. I'm making breakfast."

I didn't want to get out of bed. I couldn't think of a single reason why I should. "No thanks. I'm not in the mood."

"Of course you're not. But you need to eat and get cleaned up. We're going by homicide and then to the airport to meet your in-laws. You'll need to pull together as best you can for them."

Maisy was the youngest of five girls. Her sisters were all wildly successful: a dentist, a lawyer, a Ph.D. teaching chemistry at Berkeley, and a financial expert in acquisitions and mergers at a Fortune 500 company. But worse than that for Maisy, they were all married and had at least one child.

Maisy would turn away her mother's probing little questions with typical younger sibling aplomb: *"But Mom, they're so much older than I am."*

Yet, Maisy had felt the pressure. Her dad was a retired Air Force pilot not too concerned about having more grandkids, but her mother was a different story. Maisy would say, *"Mom, I don't need to marry a doctor when I AM a doctor."*

I felt bad that I hadn't talked to them yet, but how could I explain that, because I was worried about being late, I'd forced Maisy to run directly into an armed robbery?

I shuffled into the kitchen wearing boxers and a UT football T-shirt and sat down on a stool at the kitchen counter.

"Here's some coffee." Jenkins pointed to a table piled high with wedding gifts in the adjoining living room. "I didn't know which of your five new coffee makers to make it from, so I used the one in the kitchen.

The gift table was an overwhelming testament to the generosity of our friends and family. For the last two months, our house had been a regular stop for the UPS truck. The table was crammed with silverware, toasters, a bread oven, ice tea maker, coffee machines, our everyday Lenox Blue-pin stripes, and more than a complete set of formal ware.

"I couldn't help taking a look," Jenkins said, pointing at a sterling silver tea service. "I can tell which gifts came from Maisy's doctor friends."

"That reminds me, thanks for the sombrero chip & dip tray."

"Don't mention it." Jenkins was scraping a spoon through a pool of watery looking eggs in a skillet. "I guess you get to keep all of this since you got married."

"What the hell would I do with it?"

"Yeah..."

"Anyway, who was it that called?"

"The General. McElvy's had some brain-swelling and went into a coma."

My hand shook as I set my coffee mug on the counter. If he died, I could be facing a manslaughter or murder charge, but death was the perfect remedy. No appellate court reversals. No parole. No freedom to kill again. "I should have taken him all the way out when I had the chance."

"Tempting prospect, but I'm afraid you missed your chance. Get anywhere close to McElvy now, and the General says I have to shoot you."

He tried to make a joke out of it, but if Harlan told him to shoot me, he would.

"Ahh...so, should I plan on being arrested today?"

"Only if you don't do what I tell you--Hey, check that out!"

Jenkins grabbed the remote, pointed it at the television on the kitchen counter and pushed up the volume. On the screen, a throng of television cameras and microphones were surrounding Stan Nelson, public information officer for the Chattanooga Police Department.

Stan wasn't a professional public relations man, but a traffic investigation retread marking time in the main office until his pension hit. His on-camera appearances always sounded like bad police reports, but his strength was that he looked incapable of lying. And to the department, looks were everything.

"....as I said, this matter is still under investigation. All I can tell you are the facts we have at this time. What we do know is that subsequent to Mr. McElvy shooting and killing two women, he exited the store with $242 in cash. Mr. McElvy, who has a lengthy criminal history for violent crimes, fled to his mother's house in East Lake. When Lt. Charlie Shane arrived, Mr. McElvy produced a shotgun and threatened his life. That's when Assistant District Attorney Jack Henley, with no regard for his own personal safety, entered the back door of the residence and wrestled the gun from Mr. McElvy. The fight over the gun didn't last long, but it appears that Mr. McElvy got the worst of it...."

"Why was Jack Henley there?" one of the reporters shouted.

"Mr. Henley successfully prosecuted Mr. McElvy two years ago. He knows more about him than anyone. That's why police requested his assistance at the scene. The department is indebted to Mr. Henley for saving the life of Lt. Shane as well as protecting other officers at the scene from this killer. And our deepest sympathy and regrets go out to Mr. Henley right now. But as I said, we're still investigating...."

I snatched the remote from Saul and turned off the television. If I had screwed up, that meant the police had screwed up by letting me walk into the house. By all rights, I should have been charged with attempted first-degree murder because the truth was that I'd have kept swinging that iron until McElvy was dead.

I was no stranger to the department covering their ass, but on this, the department's spin was supersonic.

Jenkins could see I was confused and turned off the stove. "Jack, this is good news, and they're right. I hadn't thought about it, but if you hadn't gone in there and broken things up, some good people may have gotten hurt."

"That's a rationalization."

"More like a perfectly legitimate interpretation of the facts. And that will stay the best interpretation as long as you keep your mouth shut. Would you rather be arrested? Do you know how long a prosecutor lasts in prison?"

"Well, I did leave CPD with a mess. They probably didn't have much choice."

"That's right. And more importantly, you don't want that to be an issue in the trial against McElvy."

"It doesn't matter, Saul. Nothing does anymore."

The doorbell rang.

"Could you get that while I put on some jeans?" I said.

"Sure."

When I came out of the bedroom, Jenkins pointed to the screened-in porch. "You got a visitor."

There was no mistaking the bald head looking toward the Tennessee River. Above those broad shoulders sat a plump melon so barren that not even kudzu could grow. *Weitzman*.

"Thanks, Saul. Give me five minutes and then pull me out with a phone call, would you?"

"You got it."

Across the river, an eight-man rowing team was shoving off from the Lookout Rowing Club, and Weitzman was studying how the men feathered their oars.

"Did you come to gloat, Doctor?"

Weitzman spun around, and in some universal sign of sympathy, he put both hands over his heart as if he was suffering from heartburn. "Jack, I came to tell you how deeply sorry I am. Maisy was a terrific doctor with a great reputation. Everyone at the hospital really respected her."

"Okay. Are you sure you're not here to see how the shoe looks on the other foot? What a happy day this must be for you!"

"Come on, Jack. You know I wouldn't wish this on anyone."

"Whatever." Today of all days I wasn't in the mood to handle Weitzman. "What can I do for you?"

Weitzman looked at me and chuckled fondly. "I don't care who you see today or who comes by to lend support. No one, and I mean no one, will know how you feel as much as I do."

I didn't say anything. He had this smug expression on his face that I wanted to remove with a tire iron. Having a wife murdered suddenly made me good enough for Isaac Weitzman. In my past encounters, Weitzman was always insufferable because he judged his own suffering in life as morally superior to mine. But, not today, and I resented the hell out of it.

"Jack, I only came by to give my condolences and make an offer. I've been part of a victim support group for about a year, and a number of fellows in there have gone through exactly what you're going through. Give me a call anytime, and I'll give you a ride."

"You've been in a group?" I was about as surprised as if he was confessing to the Hoffa slaying.

"Yeah, we meet once a week, but I get together with a few of the guys two or three times a week. That's why I got so mad when you suggested it."

"*You* are in a group? *Three times a week!*"

"It's like that old Vince Lombardi story. You see there was this pro football player who got traded to the Green Bay Packers, and he couldn't wait to meet

Vince Lombardi. He'd heard that Lombardi went to Mass every day. *Every day!* And he couldn't wait to meet such a devout Catholic. So after the player had been in Green Bay for awhile, one of his friends asked him about meeting Lombardi. And do you know what he said? He said, 'That son of a bitch *needs* to go to mass everyday!' Well that's me Jack. I *need* to go to this group as much as possible. And so will you."

"Look, I appreciate the offer, but--"

"Just come with me tomorrow night," he said. "You don't have to say anything. Just come and listen."

"Hey, Jack!" said Saul from the next room. "Phone call. It's the General."

"Really, Doctor, I might appreciate this more at another time, but not right now. Besides, all I did was prosecute your case. I don't owe you anything."

"I know that, Jack. I'm here because I felt like I owed you something."

Jenkins stepped out on the porch with his cell phone. "Harlan says it's urgent."

I took the phone from Jenkins and covered the mouthpiece with my hand. "Thanks for stopping by."

Weitzman shrugged and started walking back toward the front door. "I wouldn't have come unless I thought you were in bad shape. During rounds this morning I stopped in the ICU and got a look at McElvy." Weitzman let loose with a low reverent whistle. "I told you that you were the only son of a bitch up there that knew how to fight."

Chapter 8

"So *there* you are." Harlan stepped out the sanctuary of St. Paul's into a small garden. On what should have been my wedding day, I sat on a stone bench underneath the red leaves of a Japanese maple, hiding from funeral well-wishers. "Everyone's looking for you, you know."

"Sorry, General. I guess I needed a few minutes."

I could hear the murmur of people originally invited to our wedding filing into the church for the funeral. I felt awful sequestering myself, especially considering how supportive Maisy's family had been through the past few days. Her sisters had taken care of everything – canceling the rehearsal dinner, the bridesmaid luncheon and the reception. Her parents had made all the funeral arrangements. These wonderful people were as devastated as I was, but they somehow managed keep it together in a way I just couldn't. It was all I could do to get up in the morning, and sometimes I didn't even care about doing that.

As much as I appreciated them, their presence had been oddly unsettling in some respects. Every time I looked at them I saw Maisy--in the angular line of a sister's jaw or the ash-blue tint of her father's eyes, in the way they said certain words or phrases.

Sometimes I would even jerk my head around as if I'd heard Maisy, but she was never there.

"I'm sure everyone will understand." Harlan was saying. "I know what you must be going through."

I knew Harlan meant well, but how could he know?

And Weitzman's comments began nagging me again. *Is that maniac the only one who knows how I feel?*

"This is for you, General," I said pulling an envelope out of my inside coat pocket. "It's my resignation."

"What?"

"My resignation. I was out of line at McElvy's, and I created a real mess for the office."

With strong sharp moves of his fingers, Harlan tore the envelope up into tiny pieces and put them in the outside pocket of his suit. "I'm not accepting it."

"Listen, you don't want me. I'm no good to you anymore. I think what we do is a joke. How many cases did we handle in criminal court last year? Fifteen thousand? And what did we accomplish? *Nothing!*"

"Jack, we did the best we could with what we had."

"Maybe so, but in the end all we really do is memorialize people's guilt. You know, I really believed we were the thin gray flannel line between civilization and chaos. Now, I know the truth. We are nothing but paper-pushers in an elaborate, taxpayer-funded catch-and-release program."

Harlan sat down on the bench next to me. "I really do understand your frustration, but what you're saying just isn't true. What happened with Maisy was awful, heartbreaking… a hard, hard lesson in what's currently wrong with our justice system. But this is not the norm—"

"Tell that to Isaac Weitzman."

Harlan took a white linen handkerchief out of his pocket and wiped the back of his neck. "The pendulum swings both ways, Jack, and while you're right, there's a lot shitty politics getting in the way of dealing with garbage like McElvy, the pendulum *will* swing back in our favor. It always does."

"When?"

"When things get bad enough."

Geez, what more did it take?

"I guess I'm just too close to it, General. I don't know if I have the stomach for this anymore."

"Now's not the time to worry about that," Harlan said, standing up. "By the way, you're no longer suspended. You're now officially on a two-month paid leave of absence. I want you to take some time and clear your head."

"I don't know, General."

"Of course you don't, but when you get back, I'm putting you in Sessions Court until we see how you're doing. No need to gear up for the pressure of a trial court."

Sessions Court was a misdemeanor court where the office burnout cases usually ended up. You just showed up, did your thing and went home at the end of the day. Nothing you screwed up mattered that much one way or another.

The idea did appeal to me. Dealing with Maisy's death was proving hard enough, and the prospect of looking for a new job was overwhelming.

"Thanks, Harlan." I said. "That makes sense."

"But I do have one condition."

"What's that?"

"At McElvy's, you were out of control. You really scared me, so before you come back, I want you to go to a victims' support group. It could really do you some good."

I don't know how many times I had said what Harlan had just said to victims, and for the first time I understood just why it could make people so angry. All the support in world wouldn't bring Maisy back, and that was really all that mattered.

"General, I've been around long enough to know if I need that or not, and I'm telling you I don't."

"Unacceptable."

"Listen, I'm fine. Do you expect me to attend a group where I personally referred half the room? Don't you know how crazy they are? Hanging out with people like Weitzman is supposed to help me?"

"Actually, Weitzman called and suggested it."

I sprung to my feet. "Now, I *know* I'm not going."

"Yes, you are, Jack. If you want to keep working for me."

Before I could respond, Harlan reached in his pocket and pulled out a gold shield. "I believe this is yours."

In the palm of his hand was my badge. In the center of the gold was the enamel blue seal of the State of Tennessee and etched above the seal were the words *Assistant District Attorney General*.

Seven years ago, I had raised my right hand and sworn to support the Constitution of the United States and the Constitution of the State of Tennessee, and Harlan had presented me with a leather case with my credentials and badge. It was one of the best days of my life. Finally, I belonged to something bigger than myself.

Now, as I was about to go pray over my wife's dead body, none of that seemed too important, but I wasn't sure what else I had.

I took my badge out of Harlan's hands and put it in my pocket. "Thanks."

Harlan nodded graciously and patted me on the back. "Now let's get you back inside."

Chapter 9

Well after midnight, I leaned over the rail of the Walnut Street Bridge and looked at the rippling reflection of a full moon in the murky water. I wondered if the quickest path out of sadness was somewhere in the darkness of the river below.

I climbed over the railing. The heels of my Nike's caught the ends of the wooden planks from the bridge's walkway. My arms stretched behind me holding onto the metal bars. I leaned forward as far as I could and stared at the water. All I had to do was drop, inhale and let the river fill my lungs.

After all, I already knew exactly how it would feel. When I was 21, swimming with some friends in the Hiawasse River, I got caught up in its fast-moving rapids. The current was really strong that day and in a split second of carelessness, I realized I had swum too far out. Next thing I knew, my body was being slammed into the boulders of Devil's Shoals.

Spent from fighting the current, I took several deep breaths of whitewater. I suddenly had no idea which was up or down, and all I could see was brown water churning around me. One of my buddies –the one smart enough to wear a life-jacket– plunged his arm through the foam and managed to get hold of me.

Now, maybe Maisy would be on the other side ready to pull me up.

All I had to do was let go.

But I was too much of a coward, and part of me also believed that I deserved to suffer from allowing her to be killed. And all that seemed nothing but another betrayal of our relationship.

As I climbed back over the rail, I told myself I could always try again tomorrow.

"Hey, you okay?"

I jerked my head up and saw a park ranger heading up from the downtown side. Twenty years ago, the Walnut Street Bridge was used by cars, but now it had been converted into a blue-steel foot-bridge linking parks and trails. It spanned from the River Bluff's Arts District to the kitschy restaurants and hip boutiques on the Fraizer Avenue side.

I knew how it looked – a man in running clothes with a leg stuck up on the railing of the bridge at 1:30 in the morning. I stretched my right leg and bobbed my head toward my knee. "I'm fine. Just working out some kinks."

"You've picked a weird time to run, mister."

"I know, but I don't sleep much anymore."

The officer was getting closer, and he squinted at me when I moved directly under a street light. "Oh hey, Mr. Henley. I didn't recognize you."

I had seen the ranger in court, but I couldn't remember his name.

"How you doing?" I said.

"Good. Been a pretty quiet night, so I guess I can't complain."

"Glad to hear it. Well, have a good one," I said and began jogging back toward home. I would have talked longer, but I didn't think I could.

As the bridge sloped down toward Fraizer Avenue, I ran faster. I swung around the Blue Angel Café to Coolidge Park. By the time I hit the back road that lead to Heritage Landing, I was in a dead sprint.

The faster I ran the better I felt.

Tonight was the first time since Maisy had died that I was left alone. Somehow, not being around well-meaning people was a huge relief.

At home, I pulled off my sweatshirt, flipped on the television and headed for the kitchen. Tupperware fell out of the refrigerator as I opened the door. I caught a container of fried chicken before it hit the floor.

I'm still not sure if it was cleverly orchestrated, or if I had fallen victim to the Southern tradition of over-loading the bereaved with food, but every evening since Maisy had died, someone showed up at the door with a huge meal.

I found it touching really, but I didn't have the heart to tell my friends that I had no appetite. They would stand awkwardly at the door and say they were sorry. I would thank them and let them know I was fine and then promptly throw everything in the refrigerator.

I grabbed a bottle of PowerAde and lay on the living room floor. As soon as I caught my breath, I was going to do some ab crunches.

On television was a C-Span conference on criminal justice. One of the O.J. lawyers was babbling about how we had too many people in prison. *Too many prosecutors abuse their power. Too many innocent people are forced to serve time. And why are victims getting such a big say in sentencing? They have a civil remedy. Prosecutors are only using victims for political gain when they should only be concerned with the idea of justice.*

I got an instant headache just listening to him. What did an O.J. lawyer know about being a servant to justice? I wondered if he thought about justice when he paid for things with his O.J. money.

Yes, my good man, he would say to the sales clerk, *I'd like to buy that $4,000 TAG Heuer watch.*

Excellent choice! Will that be cash or charge?

Oh, it will be cash. You know I still have buckets of money thanks to the death of Nicole Brown Simpson. Don't mind the blood stains on the one hundreds. Most of it's dry.

In the bathroom, I fumbled with the childproof cap on the Advil. Push. Turn. Line up the arrows. Nothing. My hands couldn't work the process. I stormed into the kitchen and yanked a hammer out of the drawer. With three blows, I had the plastic top cracked open.

I had just swallowed a couple of pills when I heard the defense attorney yapping again. His words were like a spinal tap performed with a jack hammer.

I stand by what I said earlier. All police officers are trained to lie. They call it test-i-lying. That's why so many innocent people are convicted wrongfully. You know, it is the prosecutors who teach them to lie....In America, it's better that 10 guilty men go free than one innocent man goes to prison. That's why we just can't hand over our courtrooms to victims. The system was never designed for victims to be parties to the suit because our founding father knew they're all crackers.

"You son of a bitch!"

I bounded down the stairs to the garage and returned in less than thirty seconds with goggles and a Pouland chainsaw.

The 10-horsepower engine started with one yank of the cord, and I glared at the defense lawyer as he kept flapping his mouth like a rabid, empty-headed terrier.

With one downward stroke of the blade, I cut through the wooden top of the entertainment system and into my 35" Sony television. Plastic, wood and metal slivers began flying. The screen burst and crumbled onto the oriental carpet in tiny shards of glass. Sparks began to arc from the television set and wall outlet. I heard a deafening pop over the sound of the engine and a blue flash zapped towards me from the motor.

That must have been when I blacked out.

I woke up a half-hour later. My left hand caught in the handle of the chainsaw that was sticking out of my living room floor. A few inches to the right, the blade would have dug into my head instead of the floor.

I sat up on my elbows and looked at the damage. My entertainment center sagged in the middle. A twisted burnt casing of what was once my television.

My legs were shaky as I stood. I gave the chainsaw a tug, but it wouldn't budge. Then, I grabbed it with both hands and used my legs and pulled up, but it still wouldn't move.

My chainsaw just wobbled back and forth. Instead of the sword in the stone, I had a chainsaw stuck in the hardwood floor. And I'd also ruined an oriental carpet my parents had brought back from Morocco.

"This is nuts."

I grabbed the phone and attacked the keypad. Within ten seconds, I heard a groggy voice answer on the other end.

"Weitzman!" I said. "I'll go to your damn group."

"Henley? It's three in the morning."

"Does the group use puppets?"

"What?"

"Puppets! For therapy! Does the group use puppets?"

"What? Are you kidding?"

"If I see one puppet, I'm out of there. And the same goes if I have to talk, or if I'm put in the position of having to defend how the DA's office handled somebody's case, or if I have to listen to you too much, or even if I just don't like it."

"Jack--"

"...And another thing, if I have to hold hands during the Serenity Prayer, I'm out of there...."

"-Jack."

"*What?*"

"I'll pick you up at six thirty."

Chapter 10

Weitzman and I were late and slid quietly onto two folding metal chairs in the gym at East Brainerd Church of Christ. We were at the back of some twenty odd rows filled with people just like us.

I think that's what surprised me as I looked around the room. Everyone there had lost a spouse, child or friend in horrific fashion. Some sat with pictures of loved-ones in their hands. One woman in a denim jumper had a framed picture of her husband hanging around her neck with a piece of cord. An elderly man whose face sagged from deep wrinkles wore a tee shirt with a picture of his daughter screen-printed on the front.

There was so much sorrow in the room you could put your arms around it – a palpable energy of grief that radiated from each person like body odor.

At the podium, a woman in her fifties was speaking. I recognized her from the news as Mary Lou Hinch, the group's president. I had never met her, but over the years, I had spoken to her on the phone a few times.

"If you're new or a visitor, I'd like to welcome you to the Greater Chattanooga Victims of Crime Support Group." she said. "As you know, our group has three main goals: To support family and friends of murder victims, to memorialize those we've lost, and to advocate for victims' rights legislation.

"Before I introduce this week's speaker, I want to remind everyone that if you haven't sent a letter to the state delegation to please go ahead and do so now. Fall is the time they draft new legislation to take to Nashville in January. If you need a sample letter spelling out exactly what we're supporting, see me after the meeting."

She picked up an index card off the podium. "Tonight, our speaker is county school superintendent Dr. Tom Lynch, who has been a member of this group for almost nine months now. Tom's wife was murdered a year ago today. As you know, this is one of the toughest days any of us go through. Tom."

With a nod to Mary Lou, a tall light-skinned black man took the podium. He wore a light gray double-breasted suit with white pinpoint lines. He was in his late forties about six feet with a solid build.

As he waited to talk, his eyes burned with an intensity that astonished me. This was the most self-contained man I had ever seen, and I was baffled that anyone could get up and talk about his wife's killing for no other reason than to help others deal with the same loss.

"At the time, we lived in Memphis. Chrissy worked as an accountant for Promis Corporation. One night while I was at a school board meeting, she stopped off at Sessel's Grocery Store. There are no Sessel's here in Chattanooga, but they have the best salad bars in the world. And Chrissy could never get enough of them, so she had stopped that night for a salad.

"As she was getting in her car with her dinner, a fifteen year-old put a gun to her head, and with the help of two other teenagers, forced her into our car. First, they went to an ATM and cleaned out what they could of our accounts."

Lynch's voice started cracking, but he maintained his composure pretty well. "Then they drove Chrissy to Overton Park where she was repeatedly raped by all three teenagers in every way imaginable."

A heavy tear rolled down his left cheek and clung to the bottom of his chin. "Then, they shot her twice in the head before putting her in the trunk of the car."

Lynch squeezed the sides of the podium to steady his hands.

"The police finally caught the boys, if I can even use the word *boys*. These were little sociopaths-- not anything that resembles humanity. In fact, the three of them were already in legal custody of the Department of Children's Services for an armed robbery six months earlier. The Juvenile Court had recommended they be locked in a secure facility.

"But the Department of Children's Services didn't have the beds, so the kids were sent home. Sent to the same homes that had allowed them to commit armed robberies and assaults and eventually rape and murder. When a reporter told me that Tennessee had not added any more beds for juveniles in over a decade, I felt a sense of betrayal unlike anything I have ever experienced."

I leaned over to Weitzman. "Why's he telling us all this?"

"You have to talk about it," he said. "If you don't, you'll go crazy. And if you shut up and listen, you might find people have actually gone through worse things than you."

I crossed my arms and leaned back in the chair. Maybe being understood was overrated. I could never see myself doing this.

Lynch prattled on with his pitiful story. A woman got up to say she knew exactly how he felt. Her son had been abducted at an interstate rest stop. An older man rose to his feet; the same thing had happened to his daughter at the mall.

Why had I agreed to join such a pathetic group? So I could wallow in the world's grief? Didn't I have enough of my own?

And maybe that was it? My own hurt was so raw and fresh that I couldn't see the good in "sharing." In fact, I could barely stand to listen to it. Only my respect for the losses of people around me kept me in my chair.

At the end, everyone stood up for the serenity prayer. I couldn't help but wonder what god Weitzman prayed to, or if he actually prayed to himself. Being a doctor, I'm sure he thought prayer was valuable as some sort of self-hypnosis.

Of course, while I was railing on Weitzman for his ego, I had nothing to pray about. Since Maisy had died, I had nothing to say to God. At the hospital, I had made all sorts of promises to God: if you save her, I'll dedicate my life to you. If you let her live, I'll become a priest. If you let her return to my arms, I'll give my entire life over to your works. And I had meant it, too.

But God had let her die, and I hated Him for that.

As we started to leave, a frail black woman in her late sixties came over and touched me on the arm. "Mr. Henley?"

"Yes, ma'am." She had an oval face with deep lines and a sharp nose. I had already spotted a number of familiar faces in the group, but hers I couldn't place.

"Mr. Henley. I'm Chenester Jones. Katrina Jones' mother."

"Okay," I said, still not making any connection.

"My daughter was the clerk in the Golden Gallon with your wife."

My mind flashed to the image of brains oozing down the wall while Maisy gasped in pain. Her daughter's brains. I looked right at Chenester Jones, and in her sad yet compassionate gaze, I felt a connection with another human being such as I've never known.

"Mrs. Jones, I'm so sorry," I said as my eyes watered. "I was there, but I couldn't do anything."

She hugged me and said, "Oh Mr. Henley, you're lucky the Lord let you live."

I hugged her back hard. "How are the children?"

"They live with me now and cry themselves to sleep most every night. I was so sorry to hear about your wife. Know I'm praying for you."

When I started to leave, I had sworn that I'd never return, but now from someone I least expected it – a connection. Chenester Jones knew how I felt. If only I had her quiet strength. How else could she keep going forward and raise her daughter's four children?

"Mrs. Jones, if I can help you in any way with anything, please call me."

She squeezed my hand and nodded. "I appreciate it. I may just do that."

I watched her walk away toward the door. You could tell she had arthritis in her left hip. Each step looked painful, but for some reason I found myself looking forward to seeing her next week. Maybe there was something to this after all.

Weitzman broke away from a cluster of people and nodded his head toward the door in his typically impatient fashion. "Come on," he said with a knowing grin. "Time to check out the *real* support group."

Chapter 11

"It's a place called Jimmy's Diner," Weitzman said as he pulled his Lexus onto Bonnie Oaks Drive. "Me and a couple other guys from the group meet here twice a week, and sometimes for breakfast on Saturday as well."

"That's an awful lot of togetherness," I said.

"What else are we going to do, stay at home and feel sorry for ourselves? You've got to hang out with people who know what's really happening to you and can see through all the 'I'm fine' bullshit you give everyone else."

Jimmy's was in the corner of a Best Western motel. Run down and outdated, it reminded me of one of those all-night diners my college buddies and I used to hit about three in the morning--the kind of place where the food only tasted good if you were drunk.

We parked across from the main entrance. Inside the restaurant, Tom Lynch was sitting at the table with his coat off and tie down. Next to him was Bert Cawood.

I recognized Cawood from the papers. He was a local developer with a good reputation for building drug rehab centers and habitat for humanity houses for free. He also owned some of the most profitable malls in town. With an MBA from the University of Georgia, he was a skillful money player in Chattanooga's post-aquarium development boom.

I hadn't handled his case, but I remember when Cawood came through the office after his wife was killed. Her throat had been cut 14 times by a roofer who worked occasionally for her husband. Cawood had had a beef with Kyle Burnette for not showing up at work, and after months of back and forth animosity, Burnette decided to settle the score using Cawood's wife.

He left her body in the foyer of Cawood's Mountain Shadows home. In blood, he drew a cartoon bubble coming from his dead wife's mouth – "Honey, you should have paid the roofers."

Burnette was found not guilty by reason of insanity and was now in a mental institution in middle Tennessee.

I also remembered Cawood because he was the only witness I knew who had gotten away with constantly referring to the defendant in front of the jury as a "peckerwood."

Cawood took up his entire side of the table at Jimmy's. He looked like an NFL linebacker, and his hands seemed like catcher's mitts palming a menu.

Weitzman introduced me around. The handshakes were all firm, and nobody treated me like a victim.

As we were sitting down, Weitzman said, "Hey, Lynch, Henley here couldn't understand why you were telling your story tonight. I got the impression he thought he was attending a big pity party."

Lynch laughed. "That's what I thought at my first meeting too."

"He may be characterizing that a little harshly," I said.

"Don't worry about it," Tom said.

Cawood closed his menu and nodded in agreement. "Yeah, it's not like anyone wants to go to a group like this. But the truth is we all need to go, so we don't eat the barrel of a gun."

Cawood has thought about suicide too?

Weitzman saw my look of surprise and shame, and he leaned in closer. "I thought about it for months. I even developed this special cocktail of gin and barbiturates. Even mixed it up once, but then I thought, shit, why give Rawlins two victims, right?"

"I was going to use dynamite from one of my construction sites," Cawood said. "That way, maybe I could take out a couple of defense attorneys with me."

"That's another reason we all go," Lynch said. "Not only are we all victims of the scum allowed to live in our communities, but we are also all victims of the criminal justice system, Mr. Assistant DA."

"Look, I just work in the system. I don't defend it."

"What a cop out!" Weitzman said. "The system's only as good as the people in it."

"Maybe, but in the end it's only as good as the law."

Finally, a waitress came over and took our order. Cawood actually ordered four fried eggs. He must have seen my surprised expression.

"I tend to mask my aggression with food. You got a problem with that?"

"Not at all. Have some crackers," I said passing the basket.

Lynch and Weitzman started laughing.

"You need to watch him, Cawood," Weitzman said. "I've seen him in court. His tongue's a razor that cuts to the bone."

"Actually, it's more like a butter knife," I said, "but thanks."

"Ok, Mr. Assistant DA, let me ask you this," Lynch said. "Before my wife was killed, I'd spent years teaching school children about the Constitution, but I really didn't know anything about the criminal justice system. Then my wife is murdered, and I find out there's nothing to really expect from the system. Not a damned thing."

"That may be true for us," I said. "But there are plenty of cases where violent criminals get exactly what they deserved."

"So you're disagreeing?"

"Not exactly, I said. "I mean, does a victim's common sense, real-world expectations of justice correspond to what they'll find in the courts? Absolutely not. But on rare occasions, the system works like it should, and on all the other times, victims can take comfort knowing that at least one person in the courtroom is dedicated to learning the truth and seeing the guilty held accountable. And that's the prosecutor."

"Fat lot of good a prosecutor can do," Cawood said. "Especially when you consider how little time criminals actually serve."

"Don't forget that it's not because people want violent criminals on the street. But in the end, it's all about the Benjamin's, and Tennessee simply does not have enough of them to pay for the number of prisons it needs."

"Bullshit," Cawood said. "There's plenty of money. It's just being spent in the wrong places. So what the hell can a prosecutor do when there's no place to put these assholes for longer than a year or two?"

"We can still mess with people," I said, "but sometimes that's all we do. Jerk them around on their way through the system."

"Like the way you messed with McElvy?" Lynch said, eyes wide with interest and approval.

I jerked my head up and looked around the table.

"Don't look so startled. Weitzman told us everything."

Weitzman grinned and slapped my back. "I was bragging on you, Henley."

"Must have felt pretty damn good," Cawood said. "I'd pay $100,000 for the same privilege."

"Not worth your money," I said with a shrug. "I got no more pleasure beating McElvy than a man gets killing a cockroach underneath the heel of his shoe. The truth is McElvy's a pathetic animal, and our communities will always have people like him. Statistics show that 87 percent of all crime is committed by seven percent of the population. Of that, two percent are violent criminals.

"How safe would our society be if we simply had the courage to lock up the 2 percent of our population that needs locking up? If we had that kind of courage, I can guarantee you our wives would be alive.

"So you see, Bert, I beat up the wrong guy. The asses that need kicking are the guys in Nashville who let him out."

"I'd still pay!" Cawood slapped the table rattling everyone's glasses and silverware. "I'd pay every stinking penny I had to get that kind of chance." Cawood's face had turned a scalded red, and in his voice, I heard the desperation that I truly felt.

I put my elbows on the table and leaned toward him whispering, "But at the same time, I'd be lying if I told you I didn't want a second crack at the guy."

Cawood grinned and popped a whole cracker in his mouth.

"Well, I'm sick of hearing that a society is judged on how it treats its criminals," Lynch said. "Why not judge a society on how it treats its victims? That's a place I'd want to live!"

"So what are we going to do about it?" Weitzman said. "Hire a lobbyist and storm Nashville for changes?"

"Now that sounds like a great idea," Cawood said. "I could pony up for a lobbyist."

"Me, too," Lynch said.

"Now hold on." I said. "I've been to Nashville year after year, stood on my soapbox and flooded their chambers with my outrage. I've spoken to the Governor, legislative sub-committees, regular committees and special interest groups. The point is, I've tried and tried and ended up with absolutely nothing to show for it."

I thought about Maisy and the cruel irony in McElvy being one of my own cases. My breath caught in my throat, but I swallowed hard and kept on.

"And all I've ever wanted these people to understand is one idea. That America ought to be a place where violence never goes unsanctioned. But that's not the way it works. We live in a country that has an incredible tolerance for violence, a tolerance that's permeated all of our institutions. The only thing that is likely to make enough of an impression on our bone-headed Governor is if we..." My voice tapered off as my thoughts outpaced my words.

"What?" Cawood said.

"Well, I'm not exactly sure. But something to give him a perspective on what it's like to be a victim."

Weitzman snapped his finger and pointed at me. "Beat his ass to a pulp, that's what. I bet we'd see some improvements then."

"Why stop with him?" Cawood said. "Let's open up a six-pack of whupass on a few legislators too, show them what it feels like."

"That would fix Barbara Briggs, wouldn't it?" I said. "Let her get robbed at gun point, and suddenly, we'd be seeing a different type of Supreme Court."

"Fact is, no one truly understands until they become a victim," Weitzman said.

"Can you imagine what our state legislators would do if a third of them were victims of crime?" Lynch said.

"We should do it," Weitzman said.

I started laughing. "I'd never actually do anything like that in a million years. But I've got to say, it is fun to think about."

"Then what *would* you do?"

"Excuse me?"

"You don't really expect things to change in Nashville just because they're wrong, do you?" Lynch said. "The segregation laws didn't magically change overnight just because they were wrong. It required good people taking chances and risks, and at some lunch counters, people even broke the law. So what do you suggest we do?"

It was a good question. And if I'd been thinking straight, I'd have told Tom Lynch that two wrongs never make a right and that nothing we did would ever bring us our wives back.

Hell, what I should have done was walk out into the cool night air and clear my head. Instead, my grieving heart found a home with all the anger and pain these men offered. It was as if we were the only four people in the world to take the trip to Damascus. Why could no one else see how bad things were? We all knew why, and we all knew what it would take to help them see.

"I don't know Tom," I said. "I don't know."

*

Weitzman's Lexus crested Missionary Ridge, and I could make out the lights below of downtown Chattanooga glowing in the darkness. We had driven in silence since Jimmy's.

"Fran always use to love the city lights," Weitzman said. "One of our favorite things to do was drive up Signal Mountain at night and just sit for awhile."

"Speaking of Fran, I understand you got some good news today. I heard Rawlins didn't make bond."

"Yeah, Harlan Griffin did okay."

"He's still a great trial lawyer," I said. "I know I've been kinda nuts, so I just wanted to say thanks for taking me tonight."

"Don't mention it, and if you weren't going a little nuts, I'd worry about you. Guys like you and me, Jack, don't handle these things like normal people."

"What do you mean?"

"We're doers. We make life happen to us, not the other way around."

"Whatever," I said, turning back toward the lights.

That shut him up for a moment, but as he pulled off the interstate onto Martin Luther King Blvd., he said, "Jack, I saw a bunch of white horses tonight in the diner parking lot. Apparently a bunch of do-gooders meet there three times a week and bitch about how bad things are. But none of them has the cahones to do anything more than write their legislators.

"Well, I'm tired of riding a white horse while every month our support group grows larger and larger. I tell you what I'm going to do, Jack. I'm trading my white horse in for a low-slung, armor-plated mule. That's what I'm going to do. Get me an armor-plated mule and *ride*."

"I'm not sure I'm following you."

"That idea you came up with at the diner. I think you're on to something."

"What? To order scrambled eggs?" I knew what he was talking about, but I wanted him to say it.

"No, about going after the Governor. Fucking A-One Brilliant."

I didn't say a word. Not another word.

Chapter 12

My first day back at work started with commuter congestion every bit as irritating as I remembered it. Behind a line of cars on Walnut Street, I sat waiting to turn into the parking garage next to the jail.

Traffic was angling around a bus for the Tennessee Department of Corrections, a large stainless-steel affair with tinted windows and bars.

The bus door opened to swallow 20 handcuffed men in orange jumpsuits and leg shackles trudging out from the jail. A thin chain linked their wrists to the hands of a deputy leading the string of men to the bus.

Every man in the row needed a hair cut and a shave. Tattoos decorated their arms and hands. Long ago, I had noticed a ratio between tattoos and teeth; the more tattoos a guy had, the fewer number of teeth. This group was no exception.

As the long orange line shuffled toward the bus, the rhythm of the chains and their feet beat out a methodical rhythm. *Stomp, clap, three, four. Stomp, clap, three, four.* The identical back-beat to Pink Floyd's "We don't need no education." *Stomp, clap, three, four. Stomp, clap, three, four.*

All their lives, they had carried the anthem forward of no education and no self-control: dropping out of junior high school and smoking pot, boosting cars and knocking around their women, mixing booze and pills and sticking some dude with a knife 'cause he spilled ketchup on their brother.

Stomp, clap, three, four. Stomp, clap, three, four.

This bus would take them to a classification center in middle-Tennessee before scattering them to any number of prisons across the state. But most of these guys would be back on the streets within a year. I just hoped that when McElvy got on that bus, he'd be going away forever.

*

At the office, I laid the sombrero chip and dip tray on Saul Jenkins' desk, when I heard his voice behind me.

"Well look who's back," he said setting his coffee down and pumping my hand.

"Good to see you, Saul."

"So what's this?" He nodded at the chip ensemble, still in its box.

"I really appreciate the gesture, but I just can't keep any of the wedding gifts. I'm sure your wife will understand."

"You may not believe it," Saul said leaning forward as if he was about to give me insider-trading information, "but I'm the one who picked this out."

From the looks of his salmon-colored polyester coat and sans-a-belt slacks with cuffs riding about an inch above his shoes, I did believe it.

"I appreciate your thoughtfulness, but if I return one, I have to return them all."

"You look like you've lost some weight."

"Yeah, that's what happens when you run 10 miles a day and don't eat, but believe me, I wouldn't recommend my diet plan to anyone."

"Hey, did you hear? McElvy came out of his coma this morning."

Jenkins might as well have plunged his pudgy square hand into my navel and yanked out a handful of intestines. I felt the acid hit my stomach and my colon tighten. "When?"

"Sometime about five or six o'clock. Have you seen The General yet?"

"Not yet. Thanks, Saul."

Back in my office, I jerked open the bottom left-hand drawer. I knew it had to be in there. I groped among files, a laser pointer, some big markers and a Nagra tape recorder. I finally uprooted a bottle of Pepto Bismol, shook it as if there was no tomorrow, and took a long pull. I remembered a professor in law school who said you weren't a real lawyer unless you had a bottle of Pepto in one draw and a bottle of Jack Daniels in another. Frankly, I'd always found the Pepto more comforting than the whiskey.

I heard a knock at my open door and saw Harlan leaning against the jam. "Not back an hour and already hitting the pink stuff."

"Sorry," I said. "I just heard about McElvy. I wasn't expecting it, that's all."

"You really thought he wouldn't make it?"

"No, I was hoping he'd stay in some agonizing vegetative state for years."

Harlan studied my face. He was trying to tell if I was being sarcastic, but from the bottle my hands, he knew I wasn't.

"A fellow can hope, right?" I said.

"Well, *sure*," he said in the slow cadence most people reserve for mental patients. For an instant, concern clouded his face, but then it was gone. "By the way, Mike Steelman from over in Rhea County has been appointed pro temp on McElvy's case, but nothing's going to happen until McElvy's well enough to be booked. We expect a full report on his condition this afternoon."

"Steelman's good. I've got no problem with him."

Mike Steelman was the District Attorney for the 12th Judicial District which included Rhea, Sequatchie, Grundy and Marion counties. Whenever a member of the DA's office had a conflict of interest, such as the victim was the wife of an assistant district attorney, a prosecutor pro temp was appointed from the DA's Conference in Nashville.

"So, how are you *doing*?" said Harlan as if the harder he punched the word *doing* the greater he empathized with me. "I hear you've been attending the group."

I had continued to go to both support groups-- the one at the church and the one at Jimmy's Diner. And as much as I hated to admit it, there was always something about the meetings that made life less suffocating.

"Yeah, the group's worked out okay, General. Thanks for the tip."

"*Good*! Good for you! We want to do everything we can to help you get through this. I know it's been a God-awful ordeal. So I want you to ease back into the routine. These first few days back I don't want you doing much of anything. I've told the guys in Sessions you'll be there by the end of the week."

"General, I'm fine. Really..."

"You and I both know that what you've been through may have forever ruined you as a prosecutor. How anyone in your shoes can muster any objectivity at all, I don't know. We'll just have to wait and see."

"General, the sooner I can put someone in jail the better I will feel."

"Jack, you've always had a keen eye for evaluating the proof. Don't let a personal experience cloud that. Remember when Skerret had a ladder stolen from his garage. For over a year, he gave active time to anyone who stole a ladder. I don't want to see that kind of thing out of you on a bigger scale."

"You won't, General. Not from me."

"Good. Well, go get 'em. We're glad to have you back."

I gave him a thumbs-up and a forced smile. As soon as he was gone I grabbed the Pepto and took another swallow. Harlan just didn't get it. I knew that now. And I wasn't going to waste time arguing with him that losing your wife is not some "personal experience" to overcome like having a ladder stolen. Every cell of my body burned with Maisy's absence, and people like Harlan whose lives were untouched by death didn't have a clue what that was like.

I threw the Pepto back in the drawer and plopped into my black leather chair. Looking directly at me from a mahogany frame on my desk were Maisy's ash-blue eyes. The picture was from last spring on a hiking trip to Cades Cove in the Smokey Mountains.

We'd spent the night in a little dome tent nestled among the mountain laurel by a creek. In the moonlight, we'd lain naked and sweaty on a sleeping bag listening to the katydids, crickets and a creek swollen by spring rains.

My lips brushed Maisy's ear: "I want you to be my wife."

"What did you say?" Maisy sat up on her elbows.

"Maisy, be my wife and make love with me forever. I love you as I've loved no one –simply and totally and with my whole heart. I don't want this to ever end. Say you'll marry me. Say you'll live with me forever and have my children and watch my body sag and wrinkle and hold on–"

From my backpack, I took out a ring box. "I was going to wait until tomorrow at Chimney Top, but I just can't wait."

Maisy was sitting on her knees now and tears rolled down her cheeks. "Oh, my God! Yes! Yes, I will!"

"Do you know how much I love you?"

Maisy put the ring on her finger and held up her hand. "It's so beautiful."

I pulled out my camera.

"Wait. Let me get a tee-shirt on," she said.

"Hold up your hand."

Click!

In the photograph, Maisy's hand is next to her face á la Bob Fosse with a bright new diamond solitaire. And her face is flush with every moment from the night.

I had not seen the photograph since she died.

The intercom buzzed, and I got the impression it had been buzzing for awhile.

"Jack," said Sharon, "there's a Dewight Sanford here to see you."

"I'm not sure I know him. Is he an attorney?"

"No, he says he's Maisy's life insurance agent."

*

Dewight Sanford sat on the edge of the chair with a briefcase across his lap. He was in his late forties, tanned and free from the oval-shaped paunch of most over-worked businessmen. From his tailored suit accessorized with a matching tie and handkerchief to his tasseled Cole Hahn loafers, I got the feeling this guy never missed an alumni party at his college fraternity house.

He was probably more comfortable on the golf course pushing a universal whole life policy than in the office. And if he asked me for the names of five friends of mine he could call, I was going to punch him.

"I've left you several messages," Sanford said. "But you never called back."

I pointed to a three-inch stack of pink message slips. "As you can see, I've been taking some time off."

"Understandable, considering what you've been through. The receptionist told me you'd be in today, so I thought I'd drop by."

"What can I do for you?"

His hands tightened around the corners of his briefcase, and he cleared his throat. "I'm with Northwestern Mutual, and I apologize for not getting to you sooner. But with the irregular circumstances surrounding your marriage, you can understand that we spent some time confirming eligibility. But everything seems to be in order, and I thought so much of your wife that I wanted to do this in person."

I figured Maisy had a ten or twenty thousand dollar policy from working at the hospital. If I was lucky, that'd be a down payment on her surgery and funeral expenses.

"Frankly, I'm surprised you would come here on a standard employment policy," I said.

"Oh, I'm afraid I've given you the wrong impression. I was Maisy's personal insurance agent. I sold her this policy myself about six months ago."

"I was unaware that she even had a policy."

Sanford's head bobbed up and down. "Oh yes, she bought a million dollar term life policy. That also happens to be the amount of the certified check that I have made out to you in my briefcase."

"Excuse me, did you say one million dollars?

"That's right. I actually thought that figure was a little low considering her earning potential."

"One million dollars?"

"That's right, and as you probably know being an attorney, it's considered reimbursement of a personal injury, so this is a tax-free disbursement of funds."

Sanford snapped open his briefcase and brought out a sheaf of papers. "Now, if you could sign each of these forms where they are noted."

As I signed the forms, I glanced up and saw Maisy staring at me from the photograph. My cheeks burned a bright crimson. This wasn't right. I lose my wife, and a stranger shows up with a winning lottery ticket.

Sanford handed me the check. "So how's it feel to be a millionaire?"

"Lousy, Mr. Sanford. Just lousy. Now, if you'll excuse me."

I barely made it into the men's room stall before heaving. My hands shook as I turned on the water. My undershirt was drenched with perspiration. I splashed water in my face and peered at a pasty white face in the mirror. I wasn't any better than an O.J. lawyer accepting money from someone's death.

My fingers held the check up to the light. I could almost see blood stains smeared all over it.

Chapter 13

On Wednesday, Harlan finally gave me the nod to return to court, and I wanted nothing more than to lose myself in work. For the first time since Maisy died, I was doing something that felt normal.

When I arrived, I found the courtroom overflowing with people. Defendants were squeezed shoulder to shoulder along the benches and the back wall of General Sessions Court. The room was filled with defendants from that part of town where the average citizen prayed to God his or her car wouldn't break down.

I took a deep breath. *My people!*

In our county, Sessions Court was the crossroads of unoriginal sin: heroin-addicted prostitutes, department store grab-and-dash idiots, soured lovers who knifed each other, gang-bangers with pockets full of dope, housewives who kited bad checks to support a prescription drug habit, drunk drivers, number-runners, stalkers, country boys who thought their Mustang 5.0 was faster than a Crown Vic with a police package, homeless plastic-bag paint huffers and closet homosexuals fished out of the bathroom at Chickamauga Lake for performing public sex acts with strangers.

Wearing my customary game-face, I sat at the state's table as Judge William Dupriest called the docket. The padded shoulders of his black robe made him look small, but his disposition was tempered by the fact he was expected to handle 300 cases a day - so he showed up pissed off.

Harlan had assigned me to Judge Dupriest's courtroom, believing it would be less stressful than working a trial docket in Criminal Court. Of course, Harlan had not handled a Sessions docket in over a decade, so he had no idea what a little pressure cooker Dupriest was running.

After docket call, Judge Dupriest nodded to me. "You've got twenty minutes." Then he disappeared out of a paneled doorway behind his bench.

For Dupriest, speediness was next to godliness when it came to his docket. He was only giving me and the other lawyers 20 minutes to work out our cases. It is logistically impossible for a judge to hear 300 cases a day, so my job as a prosecutor was to work the docket like a triage surgeon and sort through cases to find those worthy of being taken to the trial courts.

The quicker the deals were generated, the quicker the docket moved. And to make the deal, you needed critical mass. Everybody involved had to be in that room – the arresting officer, the victim, the witnesses, the prosecutor and the defense attorney. It was meat cleaver justice, but what I liked about Sessions Court was that it was immediate. The victim's stitches were still fresh, the bandages still stained with blood and their emotions were only a few days off the street. And if I was lucky, I could do something today that meant something to somebody.

I took a stack of warrants from the judge's bench and waded through the cases with defense attorneys. Lawyer after lawyer came up for a brief round of negotiations using whatever they thought worked best: pleading, joking, begging, cajoling, needling, threatening or haggling.

I had worked through most of the stack when I looked up and saw Ned Wasserman waiting to talk to me. Wasserman was a giant pear of a man squeezed into a wrinkled gray suit and wearing a tie that was fashionable about the time the girl from Ipanema first walked by. His eyebrows were fuzzy white caterpillars squirming above his dandruff flecked glasses.

I couldn't prove it, but I personally believed that Wasserman had inspired all the really nasty lawyer jokes of the last two decades. Wherever he went, he spewed contention and bitterness, and he couldn't defend a speeding ticket without making a personal attack on the judge, the police officer and the prosecutor.

I braced myself. "What can I do for you, Mr. Wasserman?"

"General, how goes the persecution business? Enjoying trampling on the rights of the downtrodden and less fortunate?"

"Heady with power today, just like always."

"Well, thank heavens the great unwashed can look to me to protect their rights."

I usually don't respond to Wasserman's self-aggrandizing rhetoric, but today I was in too good a mood to ignore him. "I'm impressed to see you in court. Not all 'the great unwashed' can come up with your fifty-dollar retainer."

"Oh, I've got quite a client today. No retainer necessary."

"Don't tell me you're doing pro bono work?"

"Oh no, I'm representing a man whose civil rights were violated by the people sworn to protect them. Say, now that I think of it, maybe you know him. His name's Mr. Jimmy Ray McElvy."

My mouth fell open, and Wasserman grinned ear to ear.

"Consider yourself served, General." He chuckled as he slapped a civil complaint in my hand. "And just so you know, this isn't pro bono. It's contingency. This way, when all is said and done, I'll own a third of your house."

Sonofabitch!

I quickly scanned the document. McElvy was suing me, Harlan, the District Attorney's Office and the Chattanooga Police Department for ten million dollars for civil rights violations in federal court.

I flipped to the last page of the complaint and saw McElvy's signature on the last page.

"He murders my wife, and he has the gall to sue me!"

"My client has suffered greatly at your hands. You betrayed every oath you ever took as a prosecutor and personally violated his God-given Constitutional rights. We'll be taking more than your house. We want your car, your savings, your clothes and your income for the next twenty years!"

"He killed my wife!"

From the corner of my eye, I saw two uniformed court officers stand up.

"A jury's going to find that was self-defense," Wasserman said. "He believed that when that woman ran into the store she was going to attack him."

"He was robbing the place with a freaking shotgun!"

"You know as well as I do that self-defense can be valid even if the belief of impending violence is a mistake. So he was mistaken, but he believed in his heart there was a threat of impending violence. And I can prove that was a reasonable fear. A jury's going to walk him."

I threw the warrants and complaints to the floor and yanked off my coat. I started rolling up my sleeves. "Okay, Wasserman, what's your heart telling you right now about impending violence."

From behind me, a court officer's hands took my shoulders and gave them a firm squeeze. "Easy, Jack. Don't waste yourself on this guy."

Wasserman scurried behind the counsel's table, so I couldn't reach him. "Yeah, go ahead and attack me for no reason, just like you did my client!"

Lt. Stratten, the ranking court officer, stepped in between us. "All right, Wasserman. That's enough. Time to get out of here."

"You can't order me to leave. I'm an officer of this court. I'm defending the civil rights of a man who was savagely attacked by this man who bears the mantle of government."

I lurched forward to get Wasserman. "He killed my wife!"

The officer behind me jerked me back by the shoulders. Lt. Stratten pressed his meaty palm on my chest and pointed a finger at Wasserman.

"Mr. Wasserman, I'm telling you for the last time," Lt. Stratten said. "Leave! If I have to ask you again, it's going to be in handcuffs."

Wasserman held up his hands in surrender. "Sorry, I didn't realize zealous representation of my client was a crime in this state."

Yup, leave it to Wasserman, the only lawyer in the entire county desperate enough for business that he would represent McElvy. He was the lowest bottom-feeder from the plaintiff's bar.

Two officers were now on either side of Wasserman with firm two-handed grips above his elbows. They slowly began walking him toward the door.

Wasserman turned his head and yelled over his shoulders. "And, Henley, I'm going to have the grand jury bring charges against you for attempted murder!"

"Lt. Stratten!" Judge Dupriest had re-appeared on the bench. "Take Wasserman and put him in lock-up."

"Yes, sir!"

The officers spun Wasserman around and began forcibly marching him towards the back of the courtroom.

"But, your honor," said Wasserman, "I have a press conference scheduled in the hallway. I'm supposed to talk to them about my case."

"Mr. Wasserman, I'm holding you in contempt of court. You don't pull stunts like this in my courtroom."

"But, your honor! That violates my First Amendment right to free speech!"

"Another damn word and I swear to God, Ned, you'll never practice in Sessions Court again."

Wasserman shut up. As it was, he could barely eke out a living as a lawyer. He was already banned from Chancery Court, and if Dupriest cut him off from Sessions, he would never make it.

The scum in the gallery hooted as they took Wasserman away, and Dupriest banged his gavel until they were quiet. The court clerk approached the bench to tell the judge what had happened, and Judge Dupriest looked at me. "Jack, you all right?"

I nodded. Not able to find the words.

Tom Skerret, our number two man in the DA's office, came through the front doors of courtroom, and I could hear reporters yelling at him from the other side. I could tell from his expression that he had heard about Wasserman. I wasn't surprised; gossip goes through the court house quicker than a mid-sized junior high school.

"Officer," Dupriest said pointing to a deputy. "Tell those reporters to be quiet, or I'll have them removed from the building."

Skerret took the stack of warrants off the floor. "I got the rest of the docket, Jack. Sorry."

"It's all right, Tom. I can finish it," I said.

"But the hallway is *filled* with TV cameras and reporters," he said. "No telling how many were in court while you were served. Take a break. I'll handle it."

"I'd rather finish this docket."

"Not an option, I'm afraid. Harlan wants you out of here until the press clears out."

Right then I could have howled one of those primal, rage-filled screams that makes eardrums bleed and triggers labor in pregnant women: *Was there nothing in my life that could be normal again? What was it going to take?* I was breathing hard, and from the opened door to lock-up, Wasserman's loud voice boomed as he threatened to sue each of the officers. I was entertaining the idea of sprinting back there and slamming Wasserman's head onto the concrete floor.

"Jack."

I looked up to find Judge Dupriest off the bench. He put a hand around my shoulder and walked me toward the backdoor of the courtroom. He spoke in a low voice. "I'm going to order him held until after the eleven o'clock news is over."

"Thanks, Judge" was all I was able to get out. I slapped the metal door release with a bang.

I kept punching and kicking things down the back corridor and into the stairwell. I took the steps two at a time to the top and then scurried up the ladder to the roof. Only there could I be away from everyone. I pulled my phone from the pocket and hit the speed dial.

Weitzman answered on the second ring.

"To hell with all these bastards," I said. "I'm ready to do whatever it takes."

"What are you talking about?"

"Don't be coy. You know what I'm talking about. What you guys have been bloviating about for weeks...carefully planned surgical strikes...all three branches...making at least a third of them victims."

"Are you sure?"

"Tears without action is wasted sentiment."

"I can't wait to tell Tom and Bert. They'll want to get started immediately."

PART III
Full Contact Politics

Chapter 14

Outside the tinted windows of the Dodge Grand Caravan, the mountain landscapes of East Tennessee had given way to the rolling hills of middle Tennessee. From the looks of the topography, we were only about 30 minutes from downtown Nashville.

"So tell me, Weitzman," Cawood said from the front passenger seat. "How many boob jobs does did you do to pay for one of these babies?"

Weitzman frowned, checking his side mirror. "You got a problem with my ride, Cawood?"

Weitzman had bought the minivan under a fake name, so we could help build alibis by having our own cars parked in front of our homes or work. It was just a week since Wasserman had served me with papers, and the four of us had moved quickly to be ready.

"No, no," Cawood said. "I was just wondering how many boobs this represents."

"More than eight, less than 12."

"Breasts or pairs of breasts."

"Pairs."

Cawood let loose with a low whistle. "The men of Chattanooga owe you thanks. You must be one hell of a titty surgeon."

"Hey, listen to this," Lynch said, folding the newspaper over. "Looks like our target is quoted today in the paper."

Lynch was next to me in the back. All four of us had left work early to make our first strike.

Lynch began reading aloud: "*...and when asked if he would support strengthening sentencing laws, the Chairman of the Tennessee Sentencing Commission, Senator Mike Milligan said, "Of course not. This state has been burdened with heavy overcrowding for years. Think of the Titanic. They quit thinking about making their ship faster and stronger. After all, when the ship is sinking, you have to worry about getting the water out of the ship first'*."

"Get the water out of the ship," Cawood said. "And who cares if the water is drowning the public?"

"I wouldn't call the Sentencing Act the Titanic," said Weitzman. "It's more like a leaky rubber dingy."

"I heard Milligan speak last year at an open forum," I said. "I'll never understand how a defense attorney, a guy who takes money to keep people out of jail, can get put in charge of a Commission on how to put people in jail."

"Sounds like a conflict of interest to me," Weitzman said.

Cawood nodded enthusiastically. "Well, his ethics board is about to convene."

"All right," I said. "We're right on schedule, so when we arrive in Nashville, Milligan should be getting out of his meeting at the State Capitol and heading to a reception hosted by the Governor at the Renaissance Hotel."

I went on to outline the plan, just as we'd discussed a hundred times now. Lynch had originally been uncomfortable with my insistence that he do the actual mugging. But there was nothing more frightening to a guy like Milligan than a black man with a gun. If playing off stereotypes was what would scare him most, then that's exactly what we needed to do.

"Hey, I thought you said Milligan didn't have a carry permit," Lynch said after I reached into a black gym bag and tossed him a Kevlar vest.

I had checked to see if he had a license to carry a concealed weapon. "That doesn't mean he isn't packing."

"Yeah? Great."

Lynch pulled on dirty blue cover-alls over his gray slacks. He let them hang down from his waist and strapped the vest on over his blue button-down shirt. After the jump-suit was zipped, he slipped on a faded army jacket, opened a bottle of Mad Dog 20/20 and began dousing the coat. We had decided that if an armed robber was scary, a *drunk* armed robber was even scarier.

"Hey! Easy with that stuff," Weitzman said, "I don't want you stinking up the van."

"Here, let me have a hit." Cawood took the bottle and took a long pull before wiping his mouth with his sleeve.

"Lynch, those wingtips aren't going to cut it." I pulled out a pair of scuffed up Nikes and .9 mm Glock pistol. "You'll need this as well."

Cawood had purchased guns for our operation with fake IDs at a gun show in Atlanta, and then, still using the alias, filed a police report that they were stolen. Weitzman had then used surgical drills to mark out serial numbers. If the guns were found, we would never be linked.

Lynch frowned. "Is it loaded?"

"Yes, so be careful."

"But, if we are caught, wouldn't we be treated better if the guns were unloaded."

"First, we are not going to get caught, and secondly, the law makes no distinction between loaded or unloaded guns. Or between toy guns and real guns for that matter. If the victim thinks it's real and loaded, then the law punishes you as if it were."

"But, why—"

"Knock it off, Lynch," Weitzman said. "We use guns because they are a tool, and for this tool to work, you need ammunition. Do we ever want to fire it? Of course not, but the truth is we can't predict what will happen, so we want to be ready.

"I'll take it," Lynch said, "but I'm never firing it."

"And what ever you do," I said, "don't act like you're in the movies and constantly rack the slide. All you have to do is stick it in his face and let him smell the barrel and Milligan will know you came ready. Cawood?"

"Yo!"

In the front seat, Cawood was tugging on faded bib-overalls over his slacks and golf shirt. He pulled on a Tennessee Titans wind-breaker and ball cap.

"Here's your gun, and yes, yours is loaded too. You play a tourist nearby. If Milligan proves too tough to handle, you're there for Lynch. If civilians try to help, you're there for Lynch. If the wind blows funny, you're there for Lynch. Weitzman, your job is to stay close, but only just out of sight. Some of these downtown one-way streets will loop you several blocks away, but when this goes down, you've got to be able to get back in a hurry."

"Got it."

I reached in the seat behind me and pulled out a stainless steel briefcase. Earlier that afternoon, I had borrowed a key to the DA's surveillance locker out of Harlan's desk. The cabinet was filled with body mikes, infra-red cameras and tiny transmitters. In the briefcase, I had two-way com-links like those used by the Secret Service --tiny microphones for your shirt sleeve and clear miniature ear-pieces that acted as receivers.

I passed them around the van. "And since we're all amateurs, I'll remind you one last time not to use our real names over the radio."

Cawood cocked his head to one side as he crammed the ear piece in with his thumb. "That means we can use *code names*! Just call me *The Hammer*."

"Okay, ladies," I said. "Let's not get too cute. There's not a news agency in Nashville that doesn't monitor scanners, which can pick up police bands, citizens bands and sometimes cell phones. So if anyone hears us, I want them to think we're a taxi company."

*

Since I had to be in position first, Weitzman dropped me off at the corner of 7th and Charlotte Avenue at the hill below the State Capitol Building.

At 3:00 in the afternoon, people still swarmed the sidewalks. Wearing a two-button houndstooth suit, I looked just like another cog in the wheel of the State's business.

The afternoon sun was a bit warm, and to be outside working my leg muscles felt good after the drive. A few more weeks into November, and the jacket weather of fall would arrive.

The sound of Weitzman's voice crackled over my ear-piece. *"Yellow Cab, break for a radio check."*

With a gesture I had practiced for an hour the night before, I brushed my hand through my hair over my left ear bringing the microphone in my sleeve to my lips. "I copy you dispatch."

"We're inside the garage. Will advise on repairs."

"Copy."

They were searching for Milligan's car in the Legislative Plaza Parking garage. Step one would be to let the air out of his tires to ensure he'd be walking the three blocks to the Renaissance Hotel.

I jogged across 7th Avenue and began to take stairs two at a time as they lead up the hill to the State Capitol. Milligan's hearing was scheduled to last another 30 minutes, but meetings could end early.

At the top of the stairs, I paused to catch my breath and admire Tennessee's Capitol – a mammoth limestone monument to 19th Century architecture and convenient slave labor. The capitol was a hodge-podge of Greek themes - Ionic porticos, prolific columns and an elaborate tower with a colonnade and a cupola-like roof.

Construction of the building lasted 14 years, and I couldn't help but wonder how many slaves had been beaten and killed so our politicians could surround themselves with the physical reminders of the high ideals of ancient Greece.

Above the cupola flew the red and blue flag of Tennessee bearing the three white stars of the state's three geographic regions – East, Middle and West.

From the Smokey Mountains to the Mississippi River, Tennessee stretches into one of the longest Southern states. For crows, it's quicker to fly from Kingsport, TN to Canada than it is to fly from Kingsport to Memphis.

And each region is a world unto itself. There's no bigger insult to a Linden man than to ask how he likes living in West Tennessee. He'll tell with the jab of a finger in the chest that he lives in *Middle* Tennessee, *thankyouverymuch*. And never besmirch a Parsons resident by asking how life is in Middle Tennessee, when everyone knows that Parsons is in *West* Tennessee.

Now Linden and Parsons aren't 15 miles apart, but they might as well be in different states. And you better believe that all the people in Parsons and Linden thank God they don't live in East Tennessee, and all the people in East Tennessee thank God that people from Parsons and Linden don't live there either.

Yet the ambitions and desires of all these people were housed in this one gigantic stone building where all the laws that govern them are forged.

God help us all.

I walked into the building through a side door. A quick elevator ride, and I was on the top floor in the lobby between the House and the Senate. Although not in session, Tom Lynch had discovered that Milligan was scheduled to speak to "The Little Assembly," a group of students from across the state who met annually as mock legislators.

I was puzzled by the ashtrays bolted to the walls of the lobby. Enter any other government building, and you run a gauntlet of exiled smokers blowing a cancerous haze across the entranceways. But the capitol and the Legislative Plaza across the street were the only state buildings where smoking was allowed. A not so subtle reminder of the power of the tobacco lobby and legislators' beliefs that state regulations should apply to other people instead of themselves.

I headed towards the House, and the doors swung open as a student in a blue blazer slipped out. I caught a glance of Milligan at the podium. Black suit, matching maroon tie and handkerchief with a tortured paisley print. Maybe it was the puffy blond hair that was home to more mousse than the Adirondacks or the way he held the sides of the podium, but something about him reminded me of a bad televangelist. If you had to describe him with one word, it would be proud. He was just so proud of himself.

Today was going to be fun.

Again, I ran my hand through my hair. "This is yellow cab. I just picked up my fare at the house."

"We copy that."

I had just dropped my arm to my side when I heard a woman's voice behind me.

"Jack? Jack Henley? Is that you?"

Chapter 15

I spun around to face a slender brunette in her early thirties. She wore the unmistakable attire of an attorney – chartreuse skirt, cream colored blouse and a jacket with eel-shaped collars tapering down to a single brass button where her navel should be.

"Leslie Gilmore, how are you?"

I gave her an awkward one-armed hug and turned my left ear with the radio receiver away. The last thing I'd wanted to do was run into someone I knew.

Leslie had been in my study group in law school. When everyone else was about to self-destruct with anxiety the week before the bar exam, Leslie had been the Cool Hand Luke of the Uniform Commercial Code, tutoring me through the finer points of commercial transactions. I would never have passed the bar without her.

"Jack, it's Leslie Gilmore-Clark now. With a hyphen. I got married last summer."

"Congratulations. So how are things over Solomon & King?"

"I left about a year ago and opened my own shop. And get this, I'm a lobbyist now?"

"No way!"

"Yeah, I represent banks, insurance companies and the Methodist Hospital System in Memphis."

"That's great news. I always knew you'd do well."

A smile was glued onto my face, and I tried to act casual. But inside I was a complete mess. What did I do if Milligan left? Say *I'm sorry, Leslie, but I'm in the middle of an armed-robbery right now, can we catch up later?* And this wasn't a dumb woman whom I could blow-off with insincere cocktail-party chitchat. She knew me as well as anyone.

"Jack, here I am prattling on. Listen, I read in the paper about what happened. I'm so sorry."

"Thanks. I appreciate that."

"I understand she was a lovely woman."

"Yes, she was."

Leslie must have sensed that the topic was an uncomfortable one. And I could tell by the subtle tremor to her voice that it made her uncomfortable as well.

"So what brings you to the capitol?"

And there it was – the question where the only answer could be a lie. And for our entire operation, nothing was more dangerous. Lies take on an incredible life of their own and have an innate ability to come back and bite you in the behind. I had learned in court that an outrageous lie was better than a good confession any day. So I just couldn't drop a casual white lie. I had to pick a response that didn't engender follow-up questions and become quickly bartered gossip every time she bumped into an old law school chum. Whatever I said could reverberate for months in the University of Memphis legal circles. It was time to close this conversation down.

"Leslie, I'm here to..." I swallowed hard. "I'm here to meet with the medical examiner who performed the autopsy on my wife."

Her hands flew to her mouth. "Jack, I'm so sorry. I had no idea."

"No, no, that's okay. His office is a few blocks away, and I was early and had time to kill. So, I thought I'd walk around the capitol and get my thoughts together. This isn't going to be an easy afternoon."

"Yellow cab, we've made the necessary repairs."

My hand shot to my ear, and I cocked my head to keep it away from Leslie. I wondered how she could not hear Weitzman's voice booming in my ear-drum, but Leslie's face was a mixture of mortification and sadness.

"Jack, I'm so sorry. I didn't mean to pry."

"No, I don't mind telling you, but I'd appreciate it if you'd keep it in confidence. I don't want the prosecutors assigned to the case to find out that I'm poking around their evidence, but I've got some questions about Maisy's final hours. I'm hoping the M.E. has some answers."

I let all the sadness I felt inside bubble to my face. The words may have been false, but at least the emotion was real.

"Yellow cab, do you copy? We made the repairs and are headed to designated drop off points."

From inside the House chamber, I could hear applause. Milligan's speech must have ended.

"Well, it was good seeing you, Jack. And if you ever decide to move to Nashville, call me. I'll always have office space for you. If you hadn't spoon fed me search & seizure, I might not even be a lawyer."

"Yellow cab, do you copy?"

Leslie wrapped her arms around me and squeezed. I made sure my trick ear was on the outside and held my breath. From over her shoulder, students in matching blue blazers started filing out of the House. Milligan strolled out behind a clump of animated students. With a quick side-step, he jockeyed around them and headed down the stairs.

"Leslie, it was good seeing you," I said, breaking from the clinch.

"Yellow cab, advise of status!" Weitzman sounded as if he was addressing an incompetent scrub nurse. "Jack, stay in touch." With a wave good-bye, she walked to a nearby elevator, and I bolted for the stairs.

By the time I reached the bottom, Weitzman was yelling. *"Yellow cab, I have made the drop-offs. Advise of status!"*

"Standby," I said into my sleeve, scanning the hallway for Milligan. I could only hope Weitzman heard the adolescents swarming around me and shut up.

"What's all that noise?"

"I said *standby*."

Then came Lynch's voice. *"Dispatch, I'm in position."*

"Roger."

"This is red cab." It was Cawood. *"I want all my good buddies to know, I'm tanned, ready and rested and ready to go."*

"Roger."

Listening to all the voices in my head and the voices of about 100 high school kids echo off the marble made it hard to focus on the hunt. I swiveled around looking for Milligan's blond pompadour. He had to be there, but I couldn't trust what I was seeing. Maybe it was the noise. Maybe it was that I had just seen him upstairs, but Milligan had vanished.

Milligan could have exited a door on any side of the building, or he could have ducked into one of the offices to greet a constituent. Maybe there were secret entrances and exits for the politicians, so they could avoid crazies like me.

I had to move fast. I plowed through students running for the front door. Right now, everything came down to me.

Chapter 16

Where was he?

I pushed my way through the front doors of the capitol, and stepped outside, desperate for some sign of Milligan. By the time my eyes adjusted to the afternoon sun, I had made it all the way to the road that circles the front of the capitol, but I still saw no sign of him.

I ran across the pavement to steps leading around the statue of Edward Ward Carmack, a Tennessee statesman from the early 1900's. At the base of the statue was a rectangular balcony area that provided a semi-bird's eye view of Charlotte Avenue and the Legislative Plaza on the other side.

I hit the rail with my stomach and leaned over as far as I could to scan the pedestrians below. Traffic was getting heavier as workers headed home for a long weekend. I was concentrating on a throng of people at the crosswalk below, waiting for a break in the traffic.

"Yellow cab, advise of status."

Then I saw that hair - that blond moussed hair that looked like a sculpted motor cycle helmet bobbing across the street in a clump of people. We had been wrong too. He hadn't even tried for his car. Worse, I had no idea how Milligan had gotten down there so fast, and now there was no way for me to get down the hill without losing sight of him.

"I got him! I got him!" I said. Gone was any pretense of smoothing down my hair. "He's approaching the Legislative Plaza now. Red cab, can you spot him? He just passed the Bradford Pears at the top of the Plaza."

The Legislative Plaza is a mammoth public common spanning two full city blocks. Underneath its concrete patio roof is an underground network of committee hearing rooms, state offices and the personal offices of legislators. It's here where all the real work of state politics is conducted. The only edifice showing above ground is the War Memorial Building and the Auditorium, where every plaque, statue and courtyard commemorated war. I couldn't think of more suitable ground to take first blood.

"Black suit. Bad preacher hair?" It was Cawood. Positioned between the War Memorial and Auditorium, he would have good visibility.

"Affirmative."

"Then I've got him, all right. What a peckerwood!"

"Keep your eye on him, would you? Blue cab, proceed to Korea."

Tom Lynch would now head from the Tennessee State Museum to the Korean War Monument in the Plaza's south courtyard. From there, Lynch could intercept Milligan, or if necessary fall back to the valley between the buildings on Union and Church Streets.

Milligan moved down the Plaza in that no-nonsense, don't-mess-with-me gait that most urban dwellers believe makes them impervious to attack. Other pedestrians began trickling off to other areas of the Plaza, and soon the only other person in sight was Cawood, who had fallen about 50 yards behind Milligan. This window of opportunity wouldn't stay open long.

"Just tell me when," Lynch said.

"Dispatch, how's the scanners?"

"All clear."

"Things look good right now. Dispatch, I want you coming up Sixth in three minutes."

This was going to work perfectly. The Korean Monument was on the far side and below Milligan's line of vision. He was walking directly towards Lynch and didn't even know it. And this had to happen in the Plaza. The attack might be spotted from the one of the office buildings nearby, but that beat the passing traffic on Union Street, or worse, the odd passing patrol car.

"Okay, Blue, when I give you the Hi-Ho, come up the stairs ready for business. You'll be closing a distance of about twenty feet."

"10-4."

"Red cab, when I give the signal, just shoot past them and protect Blue's back. Go ahead and close your gap with the target."

Cawood didn't know where I was, but he held up his hand signaling okay.

"Smart ass."

Cawood nodded his head and jogged up a few feet behind Milligan.

I waited until Milligan was almost past one of the two fountains on the East side of the Plaza.

"Now! Do it now!"

What surprised me was Cawood's speed. I caught a glimpse of what he must have looked like between the hedges 20 years ago as an All-SEC defensive tackle for the University of Georgia. As if I'd said *hut*, Cawood swung around Milligan and bounded toward the stairs.

Milligan jerked his head up as Cawood went around, clearly realizing someone was behind him.

Lynch crested the stairs at a full clip with gun waist high like a 1940's gangster. His ball cap was pulled down low on his head, and he wore cheap drug store wraparounds and a Fu-Man-Chu moustache glued on with spirit gum.

He might have looked like a common street thug but I felt as though I was watching the University of Tennessee's star quarterback run out of the stadium tunnel.

I even pumped a clenched fist in a cheer. "*YES!*"

Lynch was on Milligan like a dog on fresh meat, like Mike Tyson on a date, like Madonna on a new look. He grabbed Milligan by the collar, jerked him forward so he was face to face with the barrel of the pistol. I saw

Milligan's head whip back, and even from a distance it was clear that he was almost frozen in terror.

"Don't forget the line," I whispered into my microphone. *"Hurry up and give me that wallet. I'm not going back to prison."*

Lynch backed Milligan up until the back of the senator's legs hit the fountain. Milligan took off his watch, Lynch reached into Milligan's back pocket and yanked out his wallet.

"I got pedestrians coming down Union from Seventh," Cawood said. "ETA one minute."

"Wrap it up," I said. "I also got people about thirty seconds from clearing the Magnolia trees by the War Memorial Building. Dispatch, I need you at the corner of Sixth and Deaderick now. Blue, exit on the stairs on the other side of the fountain to Sixth Avenue. Your ride will be waiting."

Milligan pulled his front pockets inside out. Coins, slips of paper and a comb fell to the ground as he held out little white-fabric rabbit ears. Lynch lowered the gun from Milligan's face. Milligan said something to Lynch, and from his demeanor, I got the feeling it wasn't very respectful.

Lynch must have felt the same way. With the flat of his hand, he shoved Milligan in the chest. With a frantic flurry of legs and arms, Milligan toppled backward into the fountain. Lynch raised his gun and fired five quick shots into the water. As the shots echoed across the Plaza, Milligan stopped writhing and stayed beneath the water.

Oh my God! Now every eyeball in every office building would be looking at Lynch, and somebody somewhere was going to punch in the numbers 9-1-1. There was no way Lynch could reach the minivan without the van being made. And if the van was made, none of us had a way out of town.

Lynch ran down the side steps toward 6th Avenue.

"What the hell was that?" Weitzman screamed.

"Change of plans. Abort pick up. We'll see you at the rendezvous point?"

"What?"

"Get the hell out of there!"

From my perch, I saw Weitzman's maroon Caravan speed past Lynch. Right now, Lynch was on the wrong side of the Plaza and closest to the guards who worked the parking garage on 6th. I had to get the hottest stick-up man in Nashville to safety.

"Blue, run to the State Museum. Tell the guard at the desk to call the police that there's a white guy shooting a gun at the Plaza. Then find a bathroom."

"For God's sake," said Weitzman, *"tell me! Did we just kill a man?"*

"Negative," I said. "He's coming up for air now."

Milligan was crouched in the fountain peering over the stone lip. His eyes were the size of egg-yokes, and a glob of blond hair clung to his forehead. People swarmed onto the Plaza from Union and Charlotte Avenues. Two security guards ran out of the War

Memorial Auditorium. A woman wearing jeans and a backpack started pointing in the direction Lynch had fled. All of a sudden, I felt exposed.

"Red cab," I said to Bert. "We'll see you at the rendezvous point."

"Roger."

I left my perch and made my way around Capitol Hill. Two minutes later I was walking down 6th Avenue and listening to the wail of approaching sirens. Metro police cars began to converge on the Plaza. Two cruisers blocked a lane of traffic on Charlotte Avenue as officers scrambled to the Plaza. I could hear an ambulance making its way down Union.

In another two minutes, I was inside the Museum gift shop. I paid $29.95 for a canvas tote bag, which to my thinking was the only real robbery of the afternoon.

In the men's room, Lynch was scrubbing his hands in the sink. The blue sleeves of his Oxford shirt were rolled up, and his rep tie was thrown over his shoulder to avoid the suds.

"I'm trying to get rid of gunpowder residue," he said.

"But you wore gloves?"

"I know, but I still reek of gunpowder."

"Where's your stuff?"

"In the last stall."

"How's your ears?"

"Clanging like the bells of Notre Dame."

I opened the stall door and was greeted by the smell of Mad Dog 20-20 - the smell of a good idea now turned lame. I cursed myself for not anticipating the problem.

I sifted through the clothing until I found the gun. I ejected the magazine from the handle, and with a quick tug of the slide, I cleared the Glock's last round. I didn't want it going off accidentally if I dropped the bag.

I wiped the gun down and stuffed it in the tote bag with the coveralls, hat, Kevlar vest, Fu Man Chu moustache, Milligan's Rolex watch and calf skinned wallet.

I was then next to Lynch rubbing that pungent, pink men's room soap all-over the jacket. "What did he say to you?"

"He said, 'Mister, you have no idea who you're messing with'."

"How conceited!"

"That's what I thought, so I gave him a crash course in Understand Who's Holding the Gun."

"Your shoes."

"What?"

"Your shoes. You gotta lose your shoes."

The Nike sneakers sticking out from below his gray flannel slacks were an incongruity and possible identifier he couldn't afford. I had once convicted an armed robber because the cashier remembered the turquoise stripe of his tennis shoes.

"So what am I supposed to wear?"

"Mine," I said kicking off my loafers.

I wrapped the jacket inside-out and stuffed it in the tote bag. I slipped on Lynch's sneakers, and they were big. Real big. I had to stuff brown paper hand towels in the toes.

"They're too small, Jack. I can't get my feet in."

"Just force them. We have to move."

"I'm going to stretch them out."

"I'll buy a new pair."

"You're going to have to."

"Will you just put them on!" I folded up my suit coat and stuck it on top of my bag. I loosened my tie and hoped that on the street the sneakers looked like a casual Friday fashion mistake.

"I tell you, Jack. I've done a lot things in my life that were a rush – jumping out of an airplane at 20,000 feet, singing *The Love Train* on stage with the O-Jay's at the Peabody Hotel, delivering a baby in a school cafeteria. There was even that one-time college experiment with grain alcohol and jello that ended up with me punching out a redneck at an all-night truckstop in Tupelo, Mississippi. But nothing I have ever done has given me a *rush* like this. Nothing! *Owww!*"

Lynch was cramming his heels down into the loafer. "What are these, Buster Brown's?"

"They are size 10."

His heel finally sank around the dark rounded leather. The fit was so tight I'd probably have to cut the shoes off his feet.

"So what next?" he said. "Do you go out first or me?"

"Police will be looking for a lone black man who runs when he see them. Not a pair of Turks who look like they just got off work from the brokerage house. So I say we stay together."

"Sounds good. Let's go."

"One more thing."

His hand was on the door, but he stopped with obvious agitation. "Look, my feet are killing me."

"That whole thing about a man's shoe size."

"Yeah?"

"It's a myth."

When we stepped out of the museum, two museum security guards stood at the corner watching all the activity on the Plaza. An eye-witness television news van was double-parked next to a police car, and up above, I spotted a news helicopter circling the area.

Incredible response time. This was going to play bigger than I ever imagined.

Lynch tugged gently at my sleeve. "Quit rubber-necking. We've got places to be."

Chapter 17

Metro police cruisers crisscrossed the area looking for a black male, wearing an army fatigue jacket and blue coveralls. Five blocks away from the Legislative Plaza, a cruiser slowed giving me and Lynch a once over as we walked down Second Avenue, downtown's main tourist drag.

We waved at the middle-aged officer behind the wheel. He nodded and then accelerated past the Hooter's and the trendy shops toward the Hard Rock Cafe.

At the first country and western shop, Lynch said, "Let's go get some boots."

"What?"

"Boots. My feet are killing me, and those sneakers look ridiculous."

"What, and cowboy boots won't?"

I had lived in Tennessee all my life and prided myself on the fact that I had never owned a pair of cowboy boots.

"Have you ever met anyone from Nashville that didn't own a pair?"

He had a point. Fifteen minutes later, we left the store chomping on victory cigars, an impulse purchase at the counter, and wearing a pair of matching black leather cowboy boots. Our old shoes – *evidence* the police would call it- were buried in the trash behind the cash register.

Lynch sucked on his cigar until there were deep pits in both his cheeks. "You're not lighting yours?"

"No, makes me nauseous." Instead, the unlit stogie dangled from between my lips like John Wayne in Rio Lobo.

"Then why'd you get it?"

"Goes with the boots."

Lynch and I were almost beside ourselves as we strutted down the street. We were so hopped-up on adrenaline that goofy dialogue popped out of us like teenage girls at the mall.

"Jack, we should go line dancing?"

"Line dancing?"

"That's right."

"I don't think cowboys are supposed to dance with each other."

"That's the beauty of line dancing. Nobody can tell who's dancing with who."

"As strobe lights are to the epileptic, so is line dancing to me."

"You're telling me you've never done the Amos Moses?"

"Now you're really showing your age."

"Line dancing ain't nothing but a white boy's soul train. The remedial electric slide. The hustle for people in boots. I figure we're in boots, we're in the country music capitol, so why not?"

"Listen, mister, this town's not big enough for the both of us right now, and we need to be on that stage coach out of town before sun down."

"It's those boots making you talk that way," he said.

"You're right as rain, pardner."

"I was surprised they even had boots that small. What size are those? Hobbit?"

"You don't want to mess with me, cowboy. I know Isaac Weitzman."

For the first time since Maisy had died, I was having fun. On one level I felt guilty about it. For months, I had deprived myself of pleasure as if that somehow proved my love for her. But the undeniable reality was that a connection with another person felt good. Our jubilant parade was incredibly stupid. What if I ran into Leslie Gilmore-Clark again? Or someone else I knew? I'd look like an idiot. Of course, our celebration was spontaneous, but to strut down the street like a couple of cowboys – well that was delusional. We were as far from being desperados as Fred Rogers was from being a bouncer at a dive bar.

A few blocks down, Lynch and I turned the corner onto Commerce Street and made our way to the rendezvous point - the San Antonio Taco Company. Started by a couple of Vanderbilt students, the restaurant encompassed all the great aspects of a college hangout – a comfortable casualness, buckets of iced down beer, hot wings, authentic Tex-Mex fajitas and fresh-cut Pico de gallo.

Cawood and Weitzman were sitting in a booth next to a fake cactus. One look at Weitzman's face, and I could see how hard it had been for him not to have a bigger role in the day's activity. Although all of us probably believed we were the alpha-male of our foursome, Weitzman really was. It was his vision and daring that glued us all together, along with his Yankee know-how of just when to kick us in the pants. To be the wheelman and still not know what was happening had to be driving him crazy.

Weitzman wore a casual but expensive looking V-necked Italian sweater and olive slacks, but tension had sent ripples of skin into his bald head. The anxiousness of unanswered questions burned in his eyes.

Lynch and I ordered from the counter and made our way to an out of the way table. I got a large order of wings and two chicken fajitas with beans, peppers and guacamole. My nostrils flared in pleasure at the smell of the hot sauce, and the steam rose from the individually foil-wrapped tortillas. The afternoon's events had left me famished.

Cawood was squeezing a lime in his Corona when we sat down. In front of him was a mountain of food. He must have ordered one of everything. "Glad you could make it, boys."

"Good to be here," Lynch said.

"Who did you guys have to mug to get those boots?" Weitzman said.

"Operational decision," I said. "We had a shoe problem we hadn't anticipated."

"Apparently, there was a lot we didn't anticipate. Like the response. Lynch stirred up quite a hornet's nest when he started shooting like that. I was afraid he'd been arrested."

"I was too," said Lynch. "We need to work on our exit strategy."

Everyone nodded.

After making sure no one was within earshot, Weitzman said, "From the top. I want to hear everything."

For the next 20 minutes, Weitzman debriefed us on every detail of the operation. He not only asked the *what*, but he probed us for the *why* in every decision made – especially in Lynch's decision to start shooting.

"You fellows want my opinion?" Weitzman said.

"Hardly ever," Cawood said with a wink to me.

"Today, we were sloppy. Henley can't go on surveillance without making it homecoming week and losing the target. Cawood's giving hand signals to the sky and jogging behind the target like he's about to pull off some college prank. And Lynch escalates this thing cutting off his escape. We should have anticipated using a getaway car that could be seen."

"All good points." I said.

"Even Ray Charles can see that," Lynch said.

"Boys, you're missing the point," Cawood said. "Tonight we made a Tennessee state senator and the Chairman of the Sentencing Commission piss in his pants with fear, and when the General Assembly goes into session that peckerwood may do some good for the first time in his life. And the best part is that any time one of those politicians steps onto the Plaza they're going to think about what happened to their buddy Milligan. So maybe this wasn't pretty, but it was our first time out, and we got the job done. Our first time out! That's like clearing the fence at Wrigley Field on your first swing."

"I agree," Weitzman said, "but we have to learn from our mistakes because we can't always count on being so lucky."

"We've got to stay and watch the news," I said throwing a chicken bone into a paper basket. "The fallout is going to be incredible."

"I'm sure it will," Weitzman said, "but we don't have time. We need to be in Memphis before midnight."

"Memphis?"

"There's someone we need to visit," he said.

Cawood, Lynch and I looked at each other. This was news to us.

Tom Lynch wiped his mouth with a napkin. "Hold on. I thought the plan was to slip back to Chattanooga and see how this thing shakes out. You know, lay low and beef up our alibis before we ride again."

"That's right," I said. "We didn't plan for anything else. We don't want too be hasty."

"Why not?" Weitzman said. "We've got to cover the whole state, and we need to use speed and decisiveness for our advantage."

"Exactly." Cawood said.

"Jack, you've already given us the basic four-man frame work for each operation. We're only going to get better," Weitzman said. "Next time out, Cawood's the barrel man, Jack's backup, I'm the eyes, and Lynch is the wheelman."

"But do we even know who and where our target is?" I said.

"I think I can find him," Weitzman said.

"Why didn't you mention anything earlier?"

"I wanted to see how today went. Look, let's not over-analyze this. We hit and move, racking up believers and building a consensus. We have 49 targets left on the list. If we can't find one, I bet we can find another. It's just hit and move on."

"Who are we going after in Memphis?" Lynch said. "Justice Peggie Cook?"

"Are you crazy?" Weitzman said. "She's got a black belt in karate. We're steering clear of her."

"And she's a good egg," I said, "law and order all the way."

"Then who?"

"Speaker of the House."

Smiles slowly spread across the table. Cawood raised his beer into the air. "To the Speaker of the House," he said.

"To the Speaker of the House," we all said, clinking beer bottles.

Cawood polished off his beer and slapped his bottle on the table. "May that lousy no-good peckerwood finally see the light of truth."

"Here, here," Lynch said.

"But for the moment, we have a bigger concern" said Weitzman. "Does anyone know how to hotwire a car?"

For some reason, every head rotated toward me.

Chapter 18

A fat moon hung in the sky above the tree-lined streets of Jackson, Tennessee. By 9:00 pm, I was jogging down Northwood Street, which cut through one of Jackson's older and more affluent neighborhoods. I wore nothing but running shorts, a sweat shirt and a UT Vols ball cap. This was not a district for street disguises.

About an hour before we had reached Jackson, I had thrown the museum tote-bag with the gun, wallet, watch and clothing off the bridge into the Tennessee River. During a coffee stop, Milligan's money, $172, had been stuffed into a Ronald McDonald House donation box outside a McDonald's drive-thru.

Since we needed a getaway car in Memphis, Weitzman pulled off I-40 into Jackson. "I bet Appellate Judge Walter Simpson has a nice car."

"We want to use a judge's car?" Lynch said.

"We've got to increase the perception of crime running rampant at every level," he said pounding on the steering wheel. "Stealing a getaway car isn't a problem, it's an opportunity!"

That was fine with me. Simpson's liberal prose had been stinking up the Court of Criminal Appeals for years. He saw rights for criminals behind every tree and viewed all police action as a necessary evil to be tolerated. He was one of the rare idiots who believed that police should have to Mirandize someone before asking their name or driver's license.

I didn't mind making his car an impromptu target, but I was nervous about what it would take to pull it off. I had prosecuted 12 year-olds in Juvenile Court who could handle something like this in 20 seconds, but I had never hotwired a car before. The risk would be huge, and I was not sure if I wanted to take such a big chance to make a point with Simpson.

My backup was parked three blocks away, and if a police car wandered into the neighborhood, they'd let me know. If there was trouble, Weitzman was only one minute away, but a lot could happen in the course of a minute.

As I turned the corner onto Simpson's street, I saw a neighborhood watch sign. If this was like most neighborhoods, the "watch program" was just a polite way of saying "We're not organized – just really, really nosy."

From the numbers on the mailboxes, I knew I was getting close to Simpson's house, and then I saw the magic numbers 523 on a black mail box with dogwood blossoms hand-painted on the side.

Simpson lived in a brick Tudor home set back on a lawn that looked like a putting green from Augusta National. The lawn wasn't just well-manicured; it was like perfect low-pile carpet. Colorful flower beds hugged the house and front walk. Under a weeping willow tree in the front yard, a small two-foot high statue of Jesus guarded a ground-level bird bath.

I slowed my pace as I ran past Simpson's house, checking out the level of activity. From a bay window, the blurred lights of a television danced through sheer curtains. Two houses down, a dog barked, and the next street up, I heard some kids playing basketball.

Simpson's house looked as if it was built about 75 years ago when garages weren't that important. There was a concrete driveway that went up to steps leading into the side of the house. A brand new mint green Chrysler Sebring was parked next to the door.

Just as I was about to enter the driveway, a figure moved in Simpson's den. In the bay window, an elderly woman slowly got up and leaned on a walker. She gripped the metal sides tightly getting her balance. Her cardigan slipped off her bony left shoulder and hung half-way off her arm.

I acted as if I was stretching out a cramp, as she worked her way out of the room...*thunk...drag...thunk...drag*. I had no idea who she was – wife, sister, aunt – but she was someone who probably needed that Chrysler along with the feeling that this quaint home was a sanctuary from a crime-ridden world.

Great. Now I'm stealing from the handicapped.

The butterflies in my stomach now seemed engaged in aerial combat. From here on out, Simpson would never write an opinion about police traffic stops without wondering the cops were speaking to the guy who stole his Sebring.

I trotted to the Chrysler, letting a large screwdriver drop out of my sleeve into my hand. The flat-head screwdriver was the tool of choice with car thieves because it so was easily concealed and not a bad defensive weapon if discovered by an irate owner.

When I got to the car, I lifted the handle and slid the screwdriver into the thin insert between the door skin and the handle mechanism. I leaned back on the screwdriver trying to feel for the mechanism and - *POP*- the door opened right up.

With a quick glance toward the house, I got inside the car and gently shut the door. I ran my hand underneath the steering column looking for a leverage point. I found what I was looking for and attacked the column with the screwdriver. The cheap metal around the steering column was no more than an eighth of an inch thick, and pieces of it broke off easily in my hand.

Car thieves call this *peeling the column*. After I exposed the left half of the column by the turn signals, I would find a slide that unlocked the steering and start the ignition. In court, I had presented testimony on more than one occasion to juries on peeling the column. Any kid could do it.

I could always judge a car thief's experience by how well he had accessed the slide in the column. The pros had a special tool that drilled into the column and pulled the slide up. The kids just ripped the turn-signal arm off. I was shooting for somewhere in-between. I didn't care if I exposed the column, but I wanted to save the turn signal arm. The last thing I wanted was to be stopped as I left the neighborhood for making a turn without a signal.

I was encouraged by how quickly the column was coming off, but the metal proved stubborn around the turn signal. Being right handed it was hard to make backhanded jabs through the wheel itself.

"Be calm. Be calm."

I tried again to pry the metal. Then again.

I grabbed the turn signal arm and yanked it downward. In three swift tugs, it was hanging by its wires. More pieces of the column fell off, and my left hand fumbled among the jumble of wires searching for the slide. My head moved around like a gyro to see if anyone was looking, and the back of my sweat shirt was wet with perspiration.

Then the tips of my fingers felt the outline of what could only be the slide. With a flick of my forefinger, the car started, and the alarm was bypassed. I backed out of the driveway with a grin. From the door to ignition had taken only three minutes. In the future, I could cut that time in half.

As I drove away, I looked in the rear-view mirror. No one saw me except a stone-faced Jesus standing beneath the weeping willow.

Chapter 19

"Can't be much longer," Cawood said. Seated next to me in the Chrysler passenger seat, he banged out the drum solo from *Wipe-Out* on the dashboard.

"Any time now." I cracked the window to let in the cool night air of Memphis. We were parked in a handicapped spot on the north side of the Pyramid, a silver-plated sports arena built on the banks of the Mississippi River. Fashioned after the tombs of ancient Pharaohs, the pyramid was built when I was in law school. I always thought the city should move Elvis's grave there. What a perfect spot to bury "The King," but instead, powers-that-be designated the Pyramid home of the University of Memphis basketball team.

"How long is he going to be?"

"I don't know," I said, looking at my watch. "The game was over half an hour ago."

Cawood was wearing a black cowboy hat and a fake goatee. We had decided he was too heavy to look like a crack addict, so we were going for more of a white trash look. He had on a Lynnard Skynard jacket and a huge WWF belt buckle. In his coat pocket was a .357 Magnum.

"Nice outfit."

"What are you staring at? You look like a roadie for the Nitty Gritty Dirt Band."

Actually, I looked like a roadie for almost any Southern rock band in the seventies. My shoulder length brown wig was pulled back in a ponytail, and I wore an open flannel shirt over my black tee shirt of an airbrushed marijuana leaf. On my feet were the boots I'd bought in Nashville yesterday, and tucked into the top of my left boot was a Walther PPK.

At six that morning, we had left our hotel, the Ridgeway Inn out on I-240, and driven to a parking garage next to a retirement high-rise off Poplar Avenue. We had stolen a handicapped license tag off a Chrysler Sebring and put it on Simpson's car; then, we cased the Pyramid and parked the Chrysler in the handicapped space.

Parking the car next to the Pyramid had been smart on Wetizman's part. When Lynch dropped us off at eight that night, we had a place to keep out of sight. Like teenage car thieves, we had covered the stripped steering column with a towel. Although the plan was flexible, it was pretty much the same as in Nashville. Wetizman would direct us in when the time was right. The big difference was we now had a disposable getaway car. My job was to protect Cawood, and I was nervous about living up to the task.

Over the ear piece came Weitzman's voice. *"Target's leaving the locker room and now glad-handing in the hall. Be alert."*

Weitzman was inside the arena bird-dogging the Speaker of the House, Democratic State Representative Bill Nichols of Memphis.

And anyone who knew anything about Bill Nichols knew he was a basketball fan and on the Board of Trustees for the University of Memphis. In less than 10 minutes, Weitzman had found Nichols sitting center court at the Tiger's season-opener.

Weitzman: *"Okay, girls. Target's leaving through the North exit. You should be able to spot him."*

"Jack, do you see him?"

"Not yet."

A few vendors were packing up tee-shirts, sweat shirts and stuffed tigers. Concession stand workers carried out stacks of cups. Parked in front were television news trucks with their microwave antennas stretched skyward. In less than half an hour, their sportscasters would go live from the Pyramid for the 10 o'clock news. If all went well, they would be featuring quite a different story than they planned.

"There he is!"

Speaker Nichols now stood in front of the Pyramid chatting with two other men in suits. Nichols was about six foot three with a healthy head of graying black hair and thin black moustache. Although in his late forties, Nichols had none of the paunch that usually strikes middle-aged men. He was probably only about 20 pounds heavier than when he played basketball in college 25 years earlier.

Most men would kill to weigh only 20 pounds more than they did at age 21, and from the care he took of himself, you could tell Nichols was still an athlete.

Under his gray suit coat, he wore a blue sweater vest topped off with a brightly colored bow-tie.

Nichols was telling his friends a protracted tale of some sort. His hands were highly animated, and if the attention of one of his friends strayed, you could see Nichols grip their arm above the elbow and pull them closer. This was a politician who knew how to work people. He was going to be a great convert for the cause.

Then, I got the call from Weitzman. *"Check for cops north of your 20."*

"10-4"

"How's your scanner?"

Parked a block away, Lynch said: *"She's just fine and doesn't whine."*

"10-4."

A quick jog half-way up the walkway didn't show me anyone who could be a problem. Not surprising. This was not a part of town you wanted to be caught in late at night.

But in case anyone was watching, I reached both my hands back to adjust my ponytail and spoke into my mike. "Back-door's all clear."

"10-4. Our shipment's on the move. His buddies have peeled off to their cars. I do have a cop cooling his heels by the front door, but he's not going to be a problem if we work fast. Standby to go."

"You shake the trees, and I'll rake the leaves," Cawood said.

"Back-up, standby to move into a support position. Now here he comes....And go! Go! Go!"

With his feet Cawood kicked opened the door of the Chrysler Sebring right as Nichols was about to pass. The door caught the legislator square in the knees, sending him stumbling backward.

Cawood was out of the car in seconds, and for Nichols, it must have been like watching dough explode out of a popped biscuit tube. Fully unfolded Cawood was about the size of Elvis, circa 1976, but unlike the later Elvis, Cawood had speed and agility that was always underestimated.

"Hey, watch it!" Nichols said rubbing his knees.

"Shut your mouth!" Cawood's long arm pointed the .357 at Nichols. "And hand over your wallet."

Nichols blinked twice taking it all in, and for a split second as I jogged back toward them, I thought Nichols would be as big a cream puff as Milligan. But I thought wrong.

Nichols pivoted to his left whipping his right leg around in a perfect roundhouse kick that would have made Jet Li proud. When his tasseled loafers struck Cawood's hand, the pistol flew out, and Cawood's big hands fumbled in the air for the gun. But Cawood was never meant to be a ball carrier, and the revolver clattered over the sidewalk skidding to a stop next to an empty malt liquor bottle in the grass.

Nichols used the momentum of his kick to complete a full spin, and as he came around, his key chain was outstretched in his hand. He squirted a small but concentrated stream of pepper spray directly in Cawood's face.

I was still too far away to do a thing about it, and Cawood doubled-over gagging. His hands clawed at his eyes.

Nichols turned and began running toward the Pyramid. "Help! Help! I'm being robbed!"

Great, we had decided to mug the guy who graduated suma cum laude from his YMCA self-defense course.

"Target's running in your direction," I radioed to Weitzman.

I stopped and searched the grass for the .357. After I picked it up, I looked up and saw Cawood in a dead run for Nichols. Tears streamed down Cawood's cheeks and vomit ran down his neck and jacket. This was a guy who knew how to play hurt.

Nichols was fast, but Cawood was faster. Cawood leaped and wrapped his arms around the Speaker taking him hard to the pavement in a perfectly executed tackle. I found out later it was the move that made Cawood All-SEC.

Nichols lifted his head and screamed, "Help!"

Big mistake.

Still on top of him, Cawood grabbed Nichols by the ears and slammed his head into the concrete sidewalk.

"Shut up!"

"I-"

"Shut up!"

Cawood bounced his head again on the side-walk, and then he began punching Nichols hard in the kidneys.

Nichols squirmed in pain, so Cawood got on his knees and rolled him over to get a better grip. As Nichols was turned, he jabbed Cawood hard above the sternum with his knuckles. Cawood gasped for air and his head jerked back in agony, but he didn't budge off Nichols.

Cawood responded to the jab with a backhand across Nichols's face. The sound of flesh smacking flesh echoed off the side-walk. Cawood seemed startled by the sound, and then, suddenly, Cawood was like a frightened boy. With his left hand, Cawood grabbed Nichols' neck above the Adam's apple and slammed his torso flat on the pavement. With his right hand, he worked-over the Speaker's stomach and ribs.

After a moment, he didn't even have to hold Nichols down anymore; his fists just pounded again and again into Nichols' midsection.

By then, I was inside the Chrysler with my fingers searching inside the column for the ignition slide.

"Cop headed your way. Get out of there."

As the car started, I lurched out of the parking space and drove about 50 feet ahead until I was alongside Cawood. Now, he was punching Nichols' face.

I grabbed the microphone in my sleeve and yelled. "Wrap it up! The cops are coming."

Cawood's head jerked up, and he peered down the sidewalk towards the ramp leading up into the Pyramid. His eyes were nearly swollen shut from the pepper spray, by this point I wondered if he could see anything at all.

I rolled down the passenger window. "Come on! Let's go!"

With a handful of Nichols' coat and belt, Cawood flipped him and leaned all his weight onto Nichols' shoulders. With his left hand, Cawood searched Nichols' back pockets for a wallet.

The tight skin in the center of Nichols' forehead was torn in a ragged star-burst. Blood flowed into his eyes and busted mouth. His nose was now a mess of twisted bone and cartilage, and a puddle of blood began collecting below his face on the walk.

Cawood lowered his lips until they were next to Nichols' ear: "In prison, I always loved turning pretty boys like you into one of my bitches."

And then Cawood slowly licked the side of Nichols' bruised face. "Yum yum."

Nichols' face recoiled in horror. His cracked bloody lips moved but no sound came out.

"Don't you worry. I'll never go to prison again. The doctors say I'm *crazy*."

Cawood slipped the wallet from Nichols' hip pocket, and then gave Nichols' butt a gentle pat.

I laid on the horn. "Come on!"

At the foot of the north ramp, a police man unholstered his pistol and ran toward us. "Stop. Police!"

Cawood was in the Chrysler in a second, and before the door had shut, I had mashed the accelerator to the floor, scrunched down in the seat half expecting the officer to shoot, but we passed him in a draft of blue exhaust skidding towards the exit. No shots. The officer had no idea what he had stumbled into.

"Bert, what in the hell were you doing?"

"That SOB maced me!"

"Yeah, but the cop was right on top of us."

"He wasn't fast enough to catch me."

"Really? You think you're faster than his two-way radio?"

Cawood's head jerked up. "I didn't think about that."

Chapter 20

Cawood squinted as he looked out the car windows. "Turn on the bridge. We'll be in Arkansas in 60 seconds."

"Wrong. That's the first place they'll look," I said, turning left on Front Street going away from downtown.

As if he was reading our minds, Tom Lynch's voice crackled over the radio. *"You guys are about to be swarmed with cops. I've got three cruisers headed north on Front. According to the scanner, two units are taking positions on the bridge. They got a pretty good description of your ride complete with license tag."*

"10-4." I could hear other sirens now and shot through a red light. "How bad are your eyes?"

"Bad."

"Can you see at all?"

"Not really."

"Can you get out of those clothes?"

"I can do that."

With Cawood's eyes, there was no way we could slip into the bar at the North End Café and blend in with the locals as we had planned. Nor could we mix with the tourists on Beale Street to the south. We were running out of options.

Lynch: *"They've called in a bear-in-the-air to help with the search. ETA 2 minutes."*

"He's talking about a helicopter, isn't he?"

I nodded as I spoke into my sleeve. "We need your eyes on our front door. What's your 20?"

"I just passed St. Jude's."

"We're a block north of the Pyramid."

"10-4"

"Why don't we just ditch the car in an alley," Cawood said. "Then we can hook up with Lynch and find some other way out of here.

"What are you nuts? With our DNA all over this car?"

"Then we'll burn it – inside out."

"Why don't we just use flares to signal the helicopter? Besides that looks too smart. We need to just disappear like cockroaches when the light's turned on."

Lynch swerved off a side street a half block ahead of us. We flashed our high beams, and he sped ahead acting as our eyes. About five blocks up the road, we could cut back onto Mud Island and ditch the car in the river, but I wasn't sure we could make it. Too much distance to travel with too much attention all around us.

Up ahead, the road curved away from the river into a rundown residential area.

Lynch had just made the turn: *"Boys, I got two cruisers heading in your direction with their rollers on. ETA yesterday."*

"What do we do?"

"Go faster," I said spinning the wheel around and hooking the Chrysler down a dirt drive-way by the Levi Garrett Tobacco factory.

The car shook as we bounced along the gravel and across railroad tracks. We shot through an opening in a concrete flood wall and down a hill. I saw blue strobes flash by in my rear-view mirror as we headed down. We'd missed them.

"Bert, time to do a little off-roading."

"You gotta be kidding."

We spun through the gravel around a microwave tower and plowed into the undergrowth. I put the car into low gear and floored it. We sailed over an embankment, bouncing over rock and concrete until we reached to the sandy banks of the Mississippi – or at least that slender finger of Mississippi water that flows between Mud Island and Memphis.

The Sebring lurched to a stop. "Time to go."

Cawood and I got out of the car and finished changing clothes. I threw my wig, boots and marijuana tee-shirt in the back seat and put on a white button-down and khaki slacks with a pair of beat-up loafers. No socks.

"What about the guns?" Cawood was now wearing a navy golf shirt with a crest from the Honor's Golf Course and cream-colored gabardine slacks.

"Keep them," I said. "The crime's just terrible in this neighborhood."

He tucked his .357 into the front of his pants. I put the .380 in my waistband and tied an L.L. Bean navy wool pullover around my waist to hide the handle.

Across the dark murky water, lights burned brightly in the upscale residential homes on Mud Island. Three-story town houses shoe-horned together to take advantage of water front exposure and a view of Memphis. In the summer, they had to have the worst mosquito problem in town.

After Cawood finished wiping the car down for prints, I put the car in gear and threw a cinder block I found mixed with debris and broken liquor bottles on the accelerator. We watched from the back as the Chrysler crashed off the bank like a bull sea lion heading for the waves. There was the sound of rocks tearing metal, branches snapping in two and two tons of Detroit steel hitting water, then the liquid rush of the river as it was sucked into the open windows of the car.

Finally, there was just the sound of crickets as Cawood and I stood in the darkness watching the water from the Mississippi cover our getaway car. Neither of us said a word until I could no longer detect the mint green of the Sebring below the swirling black water.

We turned and trudged up the bank toward the tobacco factory.

"Bert, what happened tonight?"

"What do you mean?"

"Just what I said. We went out to scare the bejeebees out of a politician, and we ended up leaving a bloody pulp half dead on the sidewalk. What in the hell was going on?"

"It was self-defense."

"Give me a break. You attacked the man plain and simple. No one ever said anything about trying to hurt anyone."

"I know. I know. But a fat lot of good you did as back-up. I thought you were supposed to help me contain him?"

"If it hadn't been for me, you'd be in the Memphis City Jail right about now."

"Yeah, but—"

"And his face, Bert. You licked his face! What was that all about?"

"Cassius Clay and Sonny Liston."

"What?"

"Cassius Clay and Sonny Liston. In 1964, Muhammad Ali, back when he was Cassius Clay, fought Sonny Liston for the world heavyweight title. Before the fight, Ali knew that the toughest man in the world couldn't scare Liston. But Ali also realized an important aspect of human nature - everyone is scared of a crazy man. You never know what a crazy man will do, right? So at the weigh-in, Ali acted insane and tried to take a few swings at Liston. Of course it was all staged, and Ali's trainers held him back, but Liston didn't know that. And it worked. Ali got into his head and won the fight."

"And by licking the face of the Speaker of the House you accomplished what?"

"Nothing in the world will scare Bill Nichols. He's a powerful man in this state, and so what if an armed robber detains him for five minutes? As soon as the robber's gone, Nichols' world is restored to its proper balance with him at the center of power. So I started thinking about what would really scare him long after I was gone. And my answer was the same as Ali's – a crazy man."

"Well it obviously worked. The guy was terrified."

"And it didn't hurt knowing that he was the chairman of the House Oversight Committee on Mental Health. He regulates those so-called state doctors that found Kyle Burnette insane. I know Kyle Burnette better than his momma knows him, and when he cut my wife's neck 14 times, he wasn't insane. He just wanted to settle the score."

"Is that what you did tonight, Bert? Settle the score?"

"You got a problem with that?"

And there it was. Cawood had planned all along to play rough. It didn't matter whether Nichols had rattled his cage or not. Cawood would have found an excuse. I had to warn Weitzman about this.

"Remember what you told me the first time I met you?" Cawood was leaning over with his hands covering his eyes.

"What was that?"

"I asked you if it felt good beating the crap out of the man who killed your wife. And your response was that you beat up the wrong guy. Well, I just gave an ass-kicking to the guy who needed it most, and I promise you it wasn't half as bad as what you did to McElvy."

"Yeah, but—"

"Listen. The Speaker's not going to end up in a coma tonight, so don't become a girl scout on me now at the first sight of a little blood. What I need from you, Henley, is more back-up when the play goes down and less sanctimonious questioning afterwards. You got that?"

My mouth opened to deliver an angry reply when I heard the loud blast of a locomotive around the bend. I could see the lights from the train engine as it was coming around the curve heading right for us. Amtrak's nightly run to St. Louis. Cawood and I scrambled to the other side of the flood wall.

Cawood held onto the back of my belt as if I was his seeing eye dog and yelled, "We've got to get a better exit strategy!"

I was careful to get us far away from the tracks. I'd always heard that if you're too close to the tracks the train forms a vacuum sucking you under its wheels.

Maybe that was my problem, I thought as I coughed up dust kicked up by the train. I always lived life too close to the tracks.

Chapter 21

That night at the hotel I dreamed of Maisy. Wearing a flowing white toga, she cradled a sword in her arms, and sported a black sash tied across her eyes in a stylish blind-fold.

I was in pajamas with my hand in the small of her back leading her down the path next to a railroad track.

"Nice jammies," she said. "Chickens?"

"Ducks. Any idea where this road goes?"

"No. I can't see anything because of the mace."

"Are you Lady Justice?"

"No, I'm Maisy. Don't you remember me?"

"How could I not? You were and always will be the love of my life. But I can't help but wonder why you were dressed like Lady Justice? And what's this about mace?"

"I'm not Lady Justice. I'm Maisy. Don't you remember how I look! Your memory of my face is becoming hazy, isn't it?"

"NO!"

"I bet you can't even remember the color of my eyes."

"Blue. They're the most amazing blue in the entire world. Take that sash off and let me see them."

She caressed the flat edge of the sword as if it was a baby and gave it a gentle kiss. "Oh, I'm not wearing a sash. This is a bandage. See."

With a quick dip and nod of the head, she flicked her rich blond mane out of her face and yanked off the blindfold. Where her eyes should have been were dark bloody sockets, and small thin lines of blood started trickling down her cheeks like tears.

I screamed and accidentally gave her a quick shove out of shock. She fell forward onto the railroad tracks, and then out of nowhere - a train flew down the tracks running right toward her.

I started to jump in front of the train to save her when the hands of three shadowy figures grabbed me and held me back.

"Hold on, buddy," said one of them. "Do you really think a man in duck pajamas is faster than a speeding locomotive?"

By then, the train was grinding her body beneath the wheels. White fabric from her gown became caught in the wheel arm and fluttered like a kite tail behind the engine as it sped down the track.

"You did what you had to do," said another.

"And it made you rich too," said the third voice.

That's when I woke up covered in sweat. I had never had that dream before. Usually it was me at the Golden Gallon urging Maisy to run inside the store to her death.

The clock radio bolted to the night stand read 4:23, meaning I had been asleep for four hours. I usually averaged about three, so this wasn't bad. But of course I'd paid a price for it with that awful dream.

I climbed out of bed and changed into my running clothes in the bathroom. I didn't want to wake Weitzman in the next bed. On the floor of the bathroom were Weitzman's blood-stained clothes from the night before.

After Cawood and I had sped away, Weitzman had played Good Samaritan and stepped out of the crowd forming around Nichols to look him over. Weitzman told us in the van afterwards that Nichols had three or four broken ribs, a broken nose and a concussion.

"With those bruised kidneys, he's going to piss blood for about three days," he said. "His breathing seemed okay, so I don't think he has a punctured lung or anything."

As we rode back to the hotel, I kept waiting for the moral outrage, but I never heard it. I thought as a doctor Weitzman would be the one person in the group to agree with me about Cawood's excessive use of force.

So I had to ask: "Will he be okay?"

"Oh yeah. His face might need some plastic surgery, but Nichols needed that long before tonight?"

Everyone laughed but me. "Did he say anything?"

"No. Nothing."

When I came out of the bathroom, Weitzman was sitting up in bed with the light on. He was plugging the telephone cord into the back of a laptop computer.

"Couldn't sleep. I haven't been able to get a straight eight since Fran died."

"I know the feeling."

"I'm checking the web pages for The Commercial Appeal and The Tennessean. They may have something on Milligan and Nichols."

I sat on the carpet and began stretching. "You should have seen Bert. For a moment there, he was totally out of control."

"He really did a number on that guy, that's for sure. I've triaged a lot of bar fight losers in my day, but I've never seen one beaten as skillfully as Nichols. Cawood did a professional job on him."

"Professional? Are you kidding? Bert totally lost it. We agreed that no one would get hurt, and then Bert goes postal on the guy and puts him in the hospital. You're all right with that?"

"Ah, he's not hurt that bad..."

"Listen, Doctor, I've always been straight with you, so I'd appreciate it if you wouldn't piss on my leg now. Bert Cawood seriously injured that man in an unprovoked attack that we helped carry out. So I'm putting you on notice that he's a liability. He enjoys it too much."

"Is that why you didn't help? Because you were scared?"

"*What!* What do you mean didn't help? I got the gun before his victim could use it against him, and I got his ass out of there before the police nabbed him."

"Nichols wasn't going for the gun. He was running in the other direction while Cawood was vomiting up pepper spray, and instead of backing him up, it sounds to me like you were looking for a gun that had been knocked out of play."

"First off, I wasn't close enough to help. If you'll remember, it was you who sent me away to act as a lookout. And that gun wasn't out of play."

"Come off it, Henley! As soon as Nichols turned and ran, you should have been all over him. Instead it was Cawood, half-blind and unable to breathe, who had to chase him down and take care of business."

"Well, if taking care of business is beating people within an inch of their life, I don't want any part of it."

"Are you kidding me? You knew when we started this that things might get rough. None of us wanted to hurt Nichols, but that was the way the play went down. It's spilt milk."

"We went too far. That's all I'm saying."

"Don't ever underestimate the power of a good ass-kicking. That's the problem with civilized adult life - we can't kick the asses of the people who need it most. You watch, Jack Henley. When we're through, this will be a better world, but only if you step up to the plate."

"That doesn't mean damn near killing someone."

"You know, growing up in Boston, I used to see guys like you on the corner all the time. They had all the answers. They were the kind of guys whose schemes got everyone else in trouble because they never had the cahones to stand behind just one of their own ideas. And I'm telling you right now, Princess. Get on board and do not wuss out on us again."

"Sorry, I didn't know having a conscience would be a problem for you. Okay with you if I continue to stay within the bounds of humanity?"

"Listen," Weitzman said, "I wanted you in because in the courtroom you're one hell of a fighter. Now I want you to do it on the street. But more importantly, we need to know you're here for us, and that you won't let us down again."

"What a bunch of crap." I stood up and began strapping on my running watch. "I've given nothing but one hundred percent for this entire operation, and I don't appreciate being second-guessed in deciding to cover a loaded gun versus a fleeing politician."

"I'm not trying to —"

"And don't ever question my loyalty again. Because if you sorry SOB's haven't realized it yet, you're all I got. Pathetic I know. But even you have to realize there's a line in what we're doing, and from what I hear you saying, that line is death. Well, I'm saying that line is somewhere in front of substantial blood loss, broken bones and making a guy piss blood for a week. And if you have any doubts, put me in the barrel for the next job. You'll see how I do."

"Oh, don't worry, Jack. You're in the barrel for the next job, and if you don't deliver, then I'm personally applying my boot to the seat of your pants."

"Don't worry, old man. You'll see. Jack Henley can deliver."

Chapter 22

Results from our weekend road-trip came in sooner than expected. Weitzman called me at 6:30 Monday morning, just as I was scraping a congealed low-fat paste masquerading as butter onto my toast.

"Are you watching channel three?"

I punched the remote. "Hey, that's Milligan."

A raw bundle of anger, Michael Milligan was perched on the steps of the state capitol surrounded by television cameras. "I promise each and every Tennessee citizen that in the coming legislative session I will ask for tougher sentences on violent offenders. How can we expect this state to be a leader in education and commerce if we can't keep people safe on the way to school and work?"

What struck me immediately was how sincere Milligan sounded. For perhaps the first time in his life, this windbag of political energy had an issue of substance that he really believed in. To me, the look of conviction on his face suited him well.

"Can you believe it?" Weitzman said.

"I hate to admit it, but you're right. A good ass-kicking made him a better person."

"Whoa, look at this guy."

On the screen, Bill Nichols was lying in a hospital bed. Despite the tubes, bandages and a metal splint down the center of his nose, his voice was strong as steel. "...

Parole must be abolished. What started as a mechanism to give prisoners incentive to behave has turned into an entitlement used by state officials to control overcrowding. The average citizen is paying the price for a state that is incapable of running its prison system."

"And you know the best part," Weitzman said. "They haven't linked the two crimes. The media's just accepted that they both could be the victims of random violence."

"Sounds good, doesn't it? Calling Milligan and Nichols victims." In some odd way, I was already starting to respect them; maybe because they were more like me now.

"But, Jack, I'm getting a sense they don't know quite what to do. How do we keep them from lashing out with no real direction."

"Simple. We hire a lobbyist."

Weitzman thought for a moment before answering. "That's a damn good idea, Henley. You got anyone special in mind?"

I laughed and reminded him of when I ran into Leslie Gilmore-Clark, right before we got to Milligan. "She's smart as a whip and from what I remember from school, incredibly persuasive. She'd be the perfect one to spoon-feed these guys a little common sense on how to effect some real change."

"Doesn't she have to say who she's working for? The press starts connecting the dots and that might make us suspects."

"Okay, how about if we hire her through a legislative committee from the support group?"

"But we don't have a legislative committee."

"We will after Tuesday night."

Weitzman laughed and then said, "Okay, paisan, you're on."

*

When I got to work, I found a yellow slip on my desk chair informing me that Harlan wanted to see me. I made my way to his office, found him standing behind his desk talking on the telephone. When he saw me, he nodded his head to the chair in front of his desk.

Sit.

"No, Dan, what I'm saying is that if The Chattanooga Times wants to rely on information provided by Ned Wasserman as *factual*, that's your prerogative. But I'm also saying that may open you up to a lawsuit down the road. Nothing the man says is true." Harlan was talking to Dan Alderman, managing editor of The Times. "So what if he says he has tapes? The man will say anything. Remember when he sued the chief of police for being a part of a Colombian drug cartel?"

I fidgeted in the chair. Like everyone in the office, I was not protected by civil service laws. I served at the pleasure of the district attorney, and right now, he didn't look pleased. The reality of working for an elected official is that on some level they are always a politician, and their survival depends on being reelected.

"Dan, come on! Wasserman's milking the high-profile murder of the wife of one of my assistants. I can understand why the television stations are biting, but you?"

Over Harlan's shoulder, I noticed a new picture hung on the wall. It was an 8x10 photograph of Tennessee Supreme Court Justice Barbara Briggs with a laser-printed piece of paper taped across the bottom: "Know the Enemy."

Since the Rawlins case had been overturned, Harlan had worked the phones to drum up support among other district attorneys across the state for going around the opinion legislatively. With our current legislature, their efforts could take years. After my weekend, I thought their efforts were naïve. How could they not see that violence was a resource?

"Okay, thanks."

Harlan hung up the phone and rubbed his jaw with the look of someone trying to decide where to begin. He took a deep breath and focused his full attention on me. "Jack, I've been meaning to talk to you about last week. I heard you showed your ass in court."

"What do you mean?"

"It sounded to me like you were getting ready to go toe to toe with Wasserman."

"I did kind of lose it for a minute there, but can you blame me? The guy had just slapped me with papers."

"Yeah, me too." Harlan leaned over his and looked at me like I was crazy. "But, I didn't threaten to kick his ass."

"Easy for you to say. With you, it is not personal."

"Jack, what would be easy is for me to ask for your resignation. Now that you've gotten that insurance check, I could fire you right now and not miss a moment's sleep worrying about how you'd eat. So let me tell you, allowing yourself to be baited in open court by Ned Wasserman with a gaggle of media around is not helpful to anyone."

"I'm sorry, General. I didn't mean to cause any problems for the office."

Harlan paced back and forth behind his desk. "My gut tells me that you're too eaten up with anger and your wife's murder to see things objectively. That's okay if you sell cars, but you're a prosecutor who's going to have to handle murder cases every day. I'm paying you to make tough decisions, and right now, it appears to me that your judgment's pretty well shot."

"General, that's not true. If you'll only-"

"Don't worry, Jack. With this lawsuit pending, I'm not going to fire you. But I am going to tell you exactly how this is going to work. First, you're going to get a lawyer."

"I don't want a lawyer."

"Too bad. You need one to counter sue McElvy for the wrongful death of your wife. The only way you can beat the civil suit is for that jury to hear exactly how Maisy died. And since I'm personally a co-defendant in that lawsuit facing triple damages, I'm damn sure going to see to it that fight this with everything you've got. Play your cards right, and you can generate a lot of sympathy with that jury."

I had already decided not to sue McElvy for wrongful death, thinking him a dry well. But Harlan was right to recognize the strategic advantage of such a suit.

"What's the saying?" he said. "Even a blind hog occasionally finds an acorn. Well, that's what Wasserman's got--an acorn with a little meat on it."

"What's that make me, General?"

Harland shook his head dismissively, obviously in no mood for jokes.

"Secondly, we need to document your emotional state for the jury. Show them how you're suffering from PTSD or something like that. After all, you were right there when she was shot. We'll get your attorney to hook you up with a high priced expert who testifies well in court."

Fair enough, I thought. *I can live with that.*

"And last, if you want to keep working for me, you are going to get help. And not this support group that meets once a week. You're going to see a counselor at least three times a week."

Finally, I couldn't hold it in: "But I don't have a *problem*! It's the state Tennessee that has the damn problem."

Harlan started laughing. "Oh, you've got a problem. Your problem is me, and if you don't like what I'm saying, you can leave. I've tried to give you space, but I can't have you physically attacking defense attorneys in the courtroom."

No one had ever threatened to fire me before, and Harlan was only forcing me into counseling to protect the political currency of the office. It would look good for him to support the prosecutor whose wife was murdered, but I resented the whole tack he was taking just the same.

"Is that all, General?"

"No, I set up a meeting for you after lunch with Tillman Raines at Milton & Martini. Tillman use to be a prosecutor, and he should understand the ins and outs of this thing better than anyone."

"Tillman Raines? Awfully expensive, isn't he?"

"Five hundred an hour, if you can believe that," Harlan said. "But you can't afford not to hire him. Also, I called Father Humphreys and set up an appointment for you. He'll be a good person to meet with regularly, and since he's a priest, there's no way Wasserman can claim he's entitled to anything you tell him."

Ouch. This really was all about Harlan.

"And whatever Humphreys says goes. I'll be checking in with him weekly on your attendance and progress."

*

Back in my office, I picked up the phone and called Leslie Gilmore-Clark in Nashville. She was delighted to hear from me again but was paid by the hour, so we quickly got down to business.

"Leslie, you probably don't know this, but I'm a member of the Greater Chattanooga Victims of Crime Support Group. I'm wondering if you might be interested in doing some lobbying for us in the legislature."

"Well, this is quite a surprise."

"I know you're busy, but this is for a good cause.

"Sure, why not? I'd be happy to make a few calls for you."

"Leslie, I'm not calling to ask a law school buddy for a little professional courtesy. Our group has deep pockets and deep convictions. We desperately want to reform sentencing laws here in Tennessee, and what we want you to do is lead a full court press on the Capitol."

"You're serious about this?"

"You bet. We'll do whatever it takes to retain you for however long you think you will need."

"That's quite a vote of confidence."

"Well deserved, from what I'm told." I had done some asking around after running into her. "Word on the street says you're already one the most powerful lobbyists in the state."

"Well, I am interested. Especially after what just happened. Did you read in the papers about Mike Milligan and Bill Nichols?"

"Yeah, I did."

"It's weird. Even before you called, I had this funny feeling that we just might be seeing crime legislation creep onto the agenda."

Something in her voice threw me. Surely she couldn't suspect anything.

"Leslie, this may sound crass, but is what happened to Milligan and Nichols something we can take advantage of?"

"For Pete's sake, we're lawyers. Of course we take advantage of their personal tragedies. Judging by the press conference Nichols gave this morning, I'd say the man is already putty in your hands."

"Good. So you will represent us?"

"Yes, but I'll need to run a conflict check with my other clients before I can give you a hard yes. And I'd like some idea on exactly what you're pushing."

"No problem. I'll send you a package of proposed legislation. Before we finalize this, I have to put this before the group for approval, but that's just a formality. I've already told some of the members about you. They know you're terrific."

Then she brought it up again. "You know Milligan and Nichols will be very interested to see these proposals."

"Have the police made any arrests?"

"No, but I gather they have a suspect. I saw some fliers posted around the Plaza with a police sketch of the gunman who robbed Milligan. But it's so odd, Jack."

"What is?"

"That both these guys got attacked on the same weekend. I know it's probably just a coincidence, but I don't really believe in coincidences."

"You don't?"

"It might sound silly, but my mother believed that there was no such thing. That coincidences were really the hand of God. So maybe these guys both fell prey to random violence so crime could be on the legislative agenda."

"That's one way to look at it," I said, trying to keep the discomfort out of my voice.

"Yeah, it's funny how God works sometimes."

I opened my bottom left-hand drawer and started rummaging for my Pepto-Bismol. "Yeah, funny."

Chapter 23

After Tuesday's support group meeting, I wove through the crowd to Chenester Jones. Sitting in a fold-out metal chair in the front, she was putting on her jacket when I sat down next to her.

I don't know if it was because her daughter had been killed with Maisy or because she had this peaceful presence about her, but I never went to a support group meeting without speaking to her.

"How are you, Mrs. Jones?"

"I'm fine, sweetie. Just fine."

"Pretty exciting, isn't it? The group hiring a lobbyist."

With a motion from Weitzman and a second from Lynch, a legislative committee consisting of Weitzman, Lynch, Cawood and me, was formed to hire Leslie Gillmore-Clark.

"For me, that kind of thing doesn't matter."

"Doesn't matter? If those idiots in Nashville had been doing their job, Jimmy Ray McElvy would have been in jail, and both Katrina and Maisy would be alive."

"I wouldn't know about that," she said, "but I know enough to not get worked up at those folks in Nashville about what happened."

"What do you mean?"

"Folks waste a lot of time getting mad at other folks because they're not perfect. Liberal people don't like conservative people because they're not perfect, and conservative people don't like liberal people because they're not perfect. As far as I know, only one person was ever perfect, so I'm not surprised they're not perfect up there in Nashville either. And I can name you plenty of people who aren't perfect right here in Chattanooga - beginning with me."

"But doesn't it bother you that if these particular people had done their job, Katrina and Maisy might still be with us?"

Mrs. Jones gave me a sad smile and whispered confidentially. "That's not for us to say. Only God knows when it is someone's time."

Inside, I was livid. You couldn't tell me Jimmy Ray McElvy was an instrument of God carrying out divine will. He was the lowest of humans exercising free will, and I hoped that the State of Tennessee took McElvy's life for the choices he made. After all, Jesus said to render unto Caesar what is Caesar's, and the way I saw it, Caesar wouldn't be satisfied until they unstrapped McElvy's dead body from the electric chair. Let God sort out his portion afterwards.

She could see I was troubled and patted my hand. "I'm praying for you."

I wanted to say don't waste your time, but I nodded my head in polite thanks. "How are the kids?"

"They're working through it. Nights are still real bad, and they're also having trouble adjusting to the new school."

"New school?"

"Their old one was too far away for me, so I moved them to a school closer to my neighborhood."

"That reminds me. The media attention over this case flooded our office with donations for the kids." I reached in my pocket and handed her a cashier's check for $50,000. "I'm sure they could use this."

With a knotted finger worn from years of labor at a downtown car wash, she counted the zeros. Twice. "And you say this is from donations?"

"Yes, ma'am."

"You are such a bad liar."

"I've lied to women before, but I swear I'm not lying to you now."

She didn't believe me for a second.

"Please take it," I said. "I know those beautiful children could use it."

Her hands trembled as she folded the check and put it in her purse. "For the children. I'll keep it for the children."

*

In the back corner, I found Cawood, Lynch and Weitzman huddled around the table with the doughnuts and coffee. From the way Lynch's hands kept slicing the air when he talked, I knew he was angry.

"What's going on?" I said grabbing a white powdered off the table.

"They want to hit another target tonight," Lynch said.

"It's time," Weitzman said. "We've got to strike while we have momentum."

Tom Lynch reached inside his suit pocket and brought out a folded piece of paper. "That's what concerns me. Did you see the picture of me this morning on the front page of *The Tennessean*?"

He unfolded the paper to reveal the police artist composite based on Senator Milligan's description of his attacker. There were two different mugs – one with the hat, sun glasses and Fu Man Chu moustache and one where the police artist guessed what he might look like without those things.

Cawood let out a low whistle. "Say, that's pretty good."

"You're not kidding," I said.

"Let me see." Weitzman grabbed the paper and in a series of quick takes looked at the sketch, then back to Lynch. "You're nuts. This doesn't look a thing like him."

Cawood and I started laughing.

"Will you guys knock it off." Lynch grabbed the paper and looked around to make sure no one else saw it. "My point is we need to let things settle down a bit. Let Milligan's memory from the weekend fade a bit, so I'm not so ripe for picking out of a line-up."

"We've got to keep them stirred up." Cawood said. "The last thing we want is for that peckerwood to feel safe. We hit them tonight, and we keep on hitting them."

"What are you worried about, Tom?" Weitzman said. "No one will even see you tonight. It's Henley that'll be in the barrel. What do you say, Henley? You up for it? You got what it takes to do this on a school night?"

"Where would we be headed?"

"Nashville. I was thinking Wally Cochran would be an ideal target."

"Good choice."

Cochran was the Governor's chief policy advisor and one of the Governor's closest friends. He was also the lamebrain who had come up with the idea of naming work release centers "Community Service Centers." In reality, these were corrections day care centers where convicted murderers, robbers and drug dealers bunked down at night after working unsupervised in the community during the day. For the prisoner, it counted as jail time and was usually the last stop before parole. The big insult was that somebody like Cochran would call that "community service" and use that handle to sneak the facilities into unsuspecting neighborhoods.

"Will we be back by morning?" I said.

"I don't see why not," Weitzman said. "We haul ass up there. Hit him hard and fast, and then we're back home."

"Think about this, Jack," Lynch said. "We need to think about this."

"Do you know where he'll be?"

"Oh, yeah," said Weitzman. "He teaches a political science class every Tuesday and Thursday night at Vanderbilt."

"That's in central time," Cawood said. "So if we leave right now, we can catch him on the way out. I got the mini-van right outside."

"No, fellows," Weitzman said. "We're not going. Jack's apparently not interested in saving lives."

Weitzman was still needling me for my performance in Memphis. I stared Weitzman in the eyes. "Do you have to be a jerk all the time? If you could shut your yap for two seconds, you might hear what I'm saying."

"What are you saying?"

"I'm saying, let's do it. From what I understand, no one in the state is closer to the governor. It will be a sincere pleasure to put the mojo on this guy. Who's with me?"

I held my hand up and got high-fives from Weitzman and Cawood.

Lynch crumpled up the police artist sketch and shot it into a waste basket next to the wall. He started walking toward the door. "Well, let's get it over with, then. I got to be at work early tomorrow."

Chapter 24

"Wait by the steps." Weitzman pointed to the glass doors of a huge red brick building. "When the class is over, Cochran should be heading for his car. Jump him and run like hell."

"No way," I said. "I'm not taking any chance of someone interfering. The last thing I want is to have to out-run college students."

"They shouldn't be a problem. You have a gun."

"Forget about it."

"What are you going to do?"

I stuck a screwdriver up my shirt sleeve. "An old fashioned car jacking."

*

Tom Lynch dropped me off next to Cochran's Ford Expedition in a parking lot off West End Avenue. I jimmied the passenger door and climbed into the dark shadows of the back seat.

Hiding in the car, I was blind to everything outside, and the cramped conditions began to hurt my back. I was starting to regret my boldness, wondering why it was important for me to show everyone else I had hair on my ass when Cawood's voice came over the air from inside the building. *"Everybody stand ready. Class is dismissed."*

I stuck my gym bag under the back of the driver's seat and pulled the black ski-mask over my face. Scrunching down on my knees, I held the .380 automatic with both hands. "I'll need some eyes to tell me exactly how he's getting in the car."

"Copy that," Weitzman said.

"Target's yakking it up with some students," Cawood said. *"Okay, he's on the move. He's mid-thirties, wearing an olive colored suit and a purple tie. Also got a black briefcase. Approaching the parking lot, but he keeps looking around. I'm afraid to get too close."*

"I see him," Weitzman said. *"Pull back if you need to."*

"Did you see that?" Cawood said. *"He just made eye-contact with that coed on the side-walk."*

"Which one?"

"The brunette with the legs from here to eternity. Tight argyle sweater and the micro-mini."

"I see her."

"I would hope so. She was sitting in the front row of his class. Check out his head-tilt toward the car."

"Oh, he's smooth."

"I can't believe it! We got us a Yoko!"

"Expect company in the car. Standby on locks."

The Expedition's horn chirped, signaling that the doors had been unlocked. Despite the warning from Weitzman, I almost jumped through the roof.

Then the front door opened, and I held my breath as Wally Cochran slid into the leather driver's seat, swinging his briefcase onto the back seat. He missed my head by inches.

With the interior light on, he would see me for sure, but Cochran reached up and turned off the dome light. He was in a hurry to get the light off before the passenger door opened, and he beat it only by seconds.

The passenger door opened, and with the quiet rustle of her skirt, his student popped inside the Expedition and shut the door. Her finger tapped the armrest instantly locking all four doors.

From their coordinated motions, I had the feeling they had done this before, but what got me most was her smell. Even in the back seat I could smell her, and she smelled good. It had been months since I'd truly smelled a woman, and I don't know if it was her perfume or pheromones or the rapid breathing from her dash to the car. But she was ripe, almost too ripe, and hanging heavy on the vine ready to be plucked. And from the way Cochran's hand traveled up her thigh, I knew he was about to pluck her brains out.

"Anyone see you?" he said.

"No, I was careful." Her voice sounded soft but excited.

"You know, I can't afford for us to be discovered."

"I know, I know. And I know we didn't plan for tonight either, but I was desperate for you to give me my *exam*?"

"Did you write your answers out on your panties like I asked?"

"Oh, yes, and let me just say this is the *longest*, *hardest* class I've ever had. I just hope I can be on top when the semester ends."

"Oh, baby, you will. You're my straight-A girl."

The girl pulled her sweater off over her head. And Cochran removed her panties, pulling them slowly down her long, long legs. He stuck the crotch of the raspberry colored panties to his nose and took a deep drag. "Oh yeah!"

"They should smell good. I've been wet since you called roll."

"Oh, this pair's a keeper," he said taking another sniff and tossing them in the back seat.

She giggled and leaned across the seat kissing him on the mouth. "Do they smell better than your wife's?"

On the word *wife*, the girl unzipped Cochran's pants.

"You know I haven't smelled her in years. If it wasn't for the kids, we'd be divorced."

I bit my lower lip hard. Here I was with three men who would do anything to be with their wives again, and this guy was stepping out on his family to make it with a girl about 15 years his junior.

A purple-striped tie sailed into the back seat, followed by an olive coat and a small pleated wraparound skirt. It landed on the floor right in front of me. My God it was tiny. And about the only way you could consider it tasteful was if you took it off with your teeth, which is exactly what Cochran had done. Three tugs at the snap and a growl.

The front clasp on the girl's bra snapped, and I peeked up in time to see her breasts spill from raspberry colored lace. They hung firm above her rib cage, and she arched her back for effect. She had large brown eyes and a heart-shaped face. She was pretty but young. Eighteen, nineteen tops. Probably a freshman. She had none of the sorority beer weight that's symptomatic of the sophomore year and above.

I would be lying if I didn't say I was aroused, but there was no way I would sit there and listen to this creep have sex with a well-developed teenager on the make for a 4.0.

I rose to one knee and reached over the seat grabbing Cochran by the hair. I wrenched his head against the back of the seat and screwed the .380 into his ear.

"EVERYBODY FREEZE!"

Both of them shrieked. I had surprised them good. The girl screamed grabbing at her clothes, and Cochran lurched forward. "What the-"

I yanked his head back again and shoved the gun underneath his chin.

"Nobody moves, or I'll kill both of ya." To disguise my voice, I spoke in a thick Appalachian accent. I hoped it made Cochran think of the movie *Deliverance*.

The girl's bottom lip trembled, and her eyes were moist with tears.

"Now, don't you worry, little sister. You put your things on while pops here zips it up. Do just what I tell ya, and we'll git along fine."

After Cochran zipped up his fly, he reached toward the ignition switch, probably to try and scare me off with the alarm button on his key chain.

I whacked him hard on the head with the barrel of my gun.

"*Please!*" he yelled, putting his hands up as high as the ceiling would allow. A small trickle of blood began to drip from behind his right ear. I must have hit him harder than I thought.

"Did I tell you to move? I don't think so! Put both hands on the wheel." I handed a pair of handcuffs to the girl. "Cuff his right hand to the wheel."

She had gotten her sweater back on and was trying to stretch it down past her hips. She got on her knees and snapped the cuff on Cochran's wrist and the steering wheel.

"Now put this on." I tossed up her skirt.

She fastened it quickly around her waist. "What do you want from us?"

"I want you to do just like I tell ya before this here gun goes off in your boyfriend's head."

"Damn, did my wife send you?"

I popped him in the side of the head again. "Listen, mister, if you was so worried about your wife, you'd be at home, wouldn't ya? But, no, you're just like my daddy. Never home and humping everything that moves. Did ya ever think how that makes a little kid feel? Did ya? And I want you to know, mister, that's the same question I asked daddy 'fore I kilt him dead."

Cochran and the girl exchanged looks.

"I caught him humping my fifteen-year-old cousin – just a might younger than this girl here. So, I'm telling you, don't piss me off. Now, little sister, reach in his pockets and give me his wallet, cash and anything else he got."

She did as I instructed handing me a worn leather tri-fold, a Palm Pilot and a wad of cash.

"Well, well, well," I said looking at the cash. "Looks like someone could have afforded a motel room."

I then instructed the girl to sit up straight and tied Cochran's purple tie around her neck and the head rest of her seat. It was tight enough to keep her from jumping out at a red-light, but not tight enough to restrict breathing.

"Put your feet up on the dash. If pops here stops suddenly, I don't want you to choke."

"Where are you taking us?" she asked.

"To his wife's house."

Both their eyes got real big.

"I'm just kidding. We're going to an ATM."

"What?" Cochran said.

I scooted up and stuck the gun in his crotch, and with my left hand, I triggered my radio with the button behind my ear. I wanted all the guys to hear this.

"I said we was a goin' to your ATM machine. Now git this buggy started and git it pointed to First Tennessee Bank."

Cochran had to reach through the wheel and start the car with his left hand. We pulled slowly out into the West End traffic.

"Take it slow, mister. I don't want to see that speedometer go past 40."

Cochran was trying to adjust to driving with one arm handcuffed to the wheel. I was squatted down in between the two seats with my gun on Cochran.

I heard Lynch's voice in my ear. *"There's a drive-thru First Tennessee ATM one block down on the right."*

"Okay, mister, there's an ATM one block down on the right."

My eyes constantly checked every movement of my two passengers. It wasn't easy covering both of them from the backseat, and I couldn't afford any mistakes.

Cochran made the turn and pulled up next to the ATM. The Expedition was so high that you could barely make out the top of the keyboard and screen from the driver's window.

"What's your pin?"

"I don't know. I never use that card."

"Wrong answer. Try again."

"I swear. I never use that card. It's my wife's account."

"Wrong answer!" I smacked him again in the head with the gun. Blood began to flow more freely down his ear and cheek. Ruby specks splashed onto the shoulder of his blue dress shirt.

"For God's sake, Wally," the girl yelled. "Tell him!"

"I swear to you. I don't remember!"

"WRONG ANSWER!"

I half-stood and fired the pistol between his legs into the driver's seat. The sound was deafening in such a small space, and Cochran jumped high.

"*Wally!*"

He wiggled and squirmed to get away from the smoking hole in the leather seat. Gone was his brave face for the girl. The reality was that I wasn't afraid to use the gun.

"It's 1487! 1487!"

I started removing the tie from the girl.

"You could have killed him."

"Yeah, without a second thought, too. My prison psychologist says it's unresolved daddy issues. Me? I think it's because I enjoy the work."

After I freed the girl's neck, I handed her Cochran's ATM card. "Lean across pops there and git the money out of that machine. And smile pretty for the surveillance camera, so the cops can show your picture to his wife."

From the back seat, I watched her half-lean out the window and punch the ATM buttons. Her long brunette hair fell across her face. Considering the circumstances, she was handling herself fairly well. Much better than I could have at 18 or 19.

"I want a balance first. And pops, don't try to cop a feel or nothing while she's working."

She worked quickly, and it didn't take two minutes to withdraw $500, the maximum withdrawal allowed per transaction.

So we did it again, but this time at a couple of ATM's in Green Hills, then a couple in Bellvue. I just kept us heading west and kept us close to I-40. There wasn't much conversation in the car, just street directions that Lynch would occasionally speak into my ear.

As we pulled away from the last ATM in Bellvue, I heard Lynch's voice again. "There's a police cruiser up ahead on the right."

I saw Cochran's left hand slide down the steering wheel to the signal arm. His movement was too casual.

I tapped his thigh with my gun. "If you even think about flashing your headlights at that cop, I'll blow your nuts off."

Cochran's eyebrows arched with surprise and a new sense of fear. This was a situation he was unable to control. "What are you going to do with us?"

"Whatever the hell I want."

I didn't give a specific answer because a detailed description of terror would be nothing compared to what Cochran's own imagination could conjure up.

I zipped up my gym bag which was lined with $2,500 of Cochran's money. "Drive to the Bellvue Mall."

The mall was a dark fortress with no signs of life except hazy light from the parking lot lights.

"Pull up in front of the food court entrance."

When the car stopped, I had the girl unlock the cuffs. Then to Cochran: "Slowly, and I mean slowly. Take your pants and shirt off."

"What?"

"Take them off!"

With trembling hands, he undid his shirt buttons and then his pants. He kicked off his shoes and dropped his pants on the floorboard.

"Boxers too."

I untied the girl again. "Come on. Time to go."

At gunpoint, I made Cochran and the girl climb out of the driver's door and walked them to the entrance of the mall. I tossed the handcuffs to the girl. "Cuff him to that light pole. Hands behind his back, and I want those cuffs tight."

I reached in the girl's purse and took out a tube of lipstick, tossing her the bag. "Now git out of here. The only thing I'm keepin' of yours is your lip stick and panties."

I pulled her panties out of my pocket and dangled them next to my mouth licking my lips. "*Oh, Yeaaaah!*"

A wave of revulsion washed over her face, and her nostrils flared with nausea. Good. Maybe in the future, she'd think twice about where she took them off.

"Now, git! And don't look back!"

She staggered off into the parking lot heading for the main road. There were convenience stores a couple of blocks in either direction, but it would take her at least five minutes to reach them on foot. I waited until she was about halfway through the parking lot before turning my full attention to Cochran.

He was pulling forward, so his rear end wouldn't have to touch the cold metal of the pole. His hair was matted with blood on the right side of his head, and he was rubbing one foot on top of the other to generate warmth for his toes.

With the girl's lipstick – a nice red shade called Nymph - I wrote *a big scarlet* A on his chest. "You know, you're probably going to burn in hell for cheating on your wife."

"Then I'll see you there," Cochran said, "I'll see you there."

I rolled my eyes and pulled the girl's panties over his head. The elastic was stretched tight stopping just above his eye-brows. He looked like a mutant chicken.

"Tell the cops about me, and I'll kill you in your sleep."

And in a heartbeat, I was back in the Expedition speeding toward I-40. In my rearview mirror were the lights from the mini-van, my posse of widowers close behind.

Chapter 25

"Are you out of your mind?" Weitzman said. "What you did back there was completely out of line. Completely!"

Even in the dark, I could see he was angry as he drove the mini-van back towards Chattanooga. Lynch sat next to me in the back staring out the window, and Cawood was fiddling with the locks of Cochran's briefcase in the front seat.

"We don't want him to lose his job. We need him in his position if he's going to be of any use to us."

"Isaac, he won't lose his job. I doubt if he'll even tell the police the whole story."

"You don't think they'll be suspicious when they find his SUV abandoned in Dickson County with a bullet hole in the seat?"

"I'm sure he'll report it stolen. But you better believe, he'll never mention the girl or the ATMs."

"The police won't believe him."

"Who cares what the police believe? He's close friends with the Governor, so the police will have to accept whatever he tells them. The media will never even hear about this."

Lynch turned his head into my direction. "What happened to making this look like an ordinary street crime committed by an ordinary criminal? What was with the whole psycho mountain boy routine?"

"Yeah. And how come you got to wear a ski-mask, and I didn't!" said Lynch.

"Jack, you did great. And the team did great. We were fast and flexible," Cawood said. "But I do take issue with you on the affair business."

"What?"

"Come on, Jack, lots of people have affairs. You don't know anything about his wife or their situation at home. No one can make any assumptions on what goes on behind closed doors. He may have been having trouble at home, and this may have been his way to work through something."

"Work through something? Are you serious?"

"Sure, everybody's got a little life crutch they fall onto now and again, whether it's booze, golf, gambling, or women."

"Let me get this straight. Putting a target into intensive care is okay, but putting a target in Dutch with his wife is not? Give me a break," I said. "I read the situation and did what I thought was best."

"But you left us out," Weitzman said. "We had no idea what was going on. Our plan has always been to strike fast, but you're driving all over Nashville with this guy and playing wounded-psycho marriage counselor. Meanwhile, Lynch is driving a van all over Nashville while every Metro officer has a sketch of his face. In the future, how about you include us in, so we're all on the same page."

"Wait a minute," Lynch said. "I thought you said that picture didn't look like me?"

"None of us mind taking risks," Weitzman said, "but I'm sure we'd all appreciate a chance to calculate them on the front end."

"You know, Isaac, I'm going to start calling you Goldilocks. In Memphis, I didn't do enough. In Nashville, I did too much. And you're looking for the situation where I did just right. Well, this all boils down to your lack of control, doesn't it? You can't control every little thing that happens, and it drives you crazy."

"He may have a point there," Cawood said.

"The beauty of our team structure is it anticipates what we can never anticipate and adapts to the situation," I said. "Tonight, we created another pissed-off victim of crime, and I'd call that a victory."

"I call it a freakin' mess," Weitzman said. "We just needed to rob this guy and take his money. But you were overcompensating for dropping the ball in Memphis. You didn't need to brand him with a scarlet letter because he offended your own sense of decency. So he was banging a student. So what? Some guys would call that a perk of the job. We always said our targets would be politicians, not puritans. For all we know, this may have been the one and only time he ever cheated."

With a final twist of the screwdriver from Cawood, the brass latches on Cochran's briefcase sprung open.

Cawood leaned back and roared with laughter.

"What! What!" Weitzman said turning on the dome light.

Cawood held up the brief case up and shook. Panties of every shape, size and color imaginable cascaded from the briefcase.

"Oh, momma!" said Cawood spinning a bright yellow thong and around his index finger. "This guy's a player."

*

Weitzman didn't say another word until we stopped about 30 minutes outside of Chattanooga to throw the panty-laden briefcase in Nickajack Lake. We were waiting in the van at a rest area while Lynch and Cawood disposed of the evidence.

"Everything has to be perfect, Jack. We can't afford any mistakes."

"I know. I know." I sounded like a teenager receiving a lecture from a parent.

"And we have got to find a way to hit more people more quickly. We've spent days driving all over the state, and we've only hit three people."

"Isaac, have you ever gone fishing?"

"Sure."

"When you go fishing, you can't expect to catch *all* the fish."

"You can if you fish with dynamite."

I started to say something, but I kept my mouth shut. I was never quite sure with Weitzman what was bravado and what was not.

I gazed outside the van window at the black water of Nickajack Lake. For a second, I thought I saw hundreds of dead fish floating on their sides reflecting light from a barren moon – bobbing silver pixels of trout, bass, blue gill, crappie and gar. Just how much dynamite would that take? And would anything be left but dead fish? I didn't know.

PART IV
The Tennessee Waltz

Chapter 26

Father Nick sat behind his desk fiddling with his glasses. With his thumbnail, he tightened the screw that held his ear-piece to the black frames.

On his beige desk blotter were stuck about ten or so post-it notes; in the hands of Father Nick, one square of yellow paper with a few hastily jotted words could bloom into a ten minute sermon on Sunday.

I sat on the hard-backed wooden chair before his desk staring at the worn bindings of the Greek and Hebrew Bibles that Father Nick always kept on the corner of his desk. I was in the same chair I had sat on a few months earlier to discuss how I had failed my marriage compatibility test.

Neither of us had said a word for over a minute. We had just been sitting, looking at each other. It was almost as if were waiting for Maisy to breeze in the door late from the hospital, anxious to get our marriage counseling rolling.

This was our second counseling session, and despite my respect for Father Nick, he was pissing me off. Harlan had told him about my run-in with McElvy and had managed to convince him I had a problem.

The silence didn't bother me; it was the straight-backed chair. Finally, I tossed aside my pride for the sake of my lower lumbar region. "May I at least sit on the couch?"

He didn't hesitate. "No."

"Why not?"

"Because we haven't discussed your problem."

"Just because Harlan's misread my situation doesn't mean you have to.

"So what do I tell Harlan when he calls? That we just sat here and stared at our toes?"

"Tell him that in your professional opinion I'm fine."

Father Nick slipped his glasses back on. "Would that be truthful?"

"Look, I'm telling you. I don't have a problem."

"This reminds me of when I went to the Honda dealership, have I told you this yet?"

I sighed. "I don't think so."

"Well, I had just bought a brand new Honda Accord, and a month later, the air conditioner goes out. Well, the guy in the service department sees my collar and thinks I must be an easy mark. He's trying to tell me that the air conditioner's not covered under the warranty because it's an extra. But I insist he do the work. Finally, he becomes exasperated and says, 'Preacher, I thought you was suppose to be born again?'

"And I say, 'I am, but I wasn't born again yesterday'."

I don't know if Father Nick was expecting a laugh, but I slowly began massaging my temples with my fingers.

"So, my point is, Jack. Don't treat me like a patsy because I'm a priest. Your wife was murdered, and I can't imagine anyone not having difficulty with that. The fact that you savagely beat the man who did it suggests what I would call a problem."

"That's why I go to my victim's support group. Every Tuesday night."

"Yes, Harlan told me you were going there for the same reason you're coming here - you'd be fired if you didn't. But are you getting anything out of it?"

"Some of the closest friends I've had in years. Guys who've gone through the same thing I have and would do anything for me."

"Guys who are probably as angry as you are."

There it was again. This reference to anger as if it was a bad thing. But the truth was that I loved anger. In the courtroom, I often tapped into my rage like Pop Eye peeling back the lid on a can of spinach. My passion made the difference in close cases, and juries had rewarded me for unleashing the self-righteous beast within. Anger cleansed the squalor of human depravity off the courtroom floor and acted as a moral compass pointing the jury towards guilty.

"Father, if you believe that I'm angry because Maisy was killed, you're absolutely right. But if you're telling me that it's wrong to feel that way--"

"I'm saying your resentment is a natural reaction, but anger is the path toward self-centeredness. Face it, every time we're angry as human beings it's because an expectation went unfulfilled. We get mad at the guy who cuts us off in traffic; we expected him to stop. We get mad at politicians who lie; we expected them to tell the truth. We get mad when our loved ones are killed; we expected them to be with us forever. But Jack, there are no guarantees in life except death. Our time is not our own; it's a gift from God."

"Father, now you're treating me like I just got off the boat. I'm no stranger to death. Death was at my high school graduation in the two empty chairs where my parents should have sat. Death was waiting for me in the DA's office where its victims' loved ones camp out at my doorstep. And death was waiting for me at the altar of marriage. My whole life has been surrounded by death.

"Did you know that I can name every victim in every homicide case I've ever handled? Father, I'm always waiting for death. I never know when it will send my career spiraling towards the black hole of an O.J. Simpson Case or a Jon Benet Ramsey or a Columbine High School. I make a living off him, and I've learned that death is not part of God's master plan. Death is a predictable and preventable phenomenon. How many lives did I save the first time I put Jimmy Ray McElvy in prison?"

Father Nick pulled on his ear lobe as he looked thoughtfully out the window.

"Name them for me."

"Who?"

"Your homicide victims," he said meeting my gaze. "Name them?"

I shook my head.

"Why not?"

"Too personal." In reality, I didn't think I could get through it without breaking down, and I suspected that's exactly why he wanted me to recite them.

"You're in so much pain, Jack, and you don't have to be. I could help you accept what's happened. Acceptance is the road to serenity."

I looked at my watch. "Are we done?"

"Why haven't I seen you in church since the funeral?"

My only answer was a shrug and another deliberate checking of the watch.

"Do you have plans for Thanksgiving? My wife and I would love it if you could come by the house after the service for dinner."

"I appreciate the invitation. But some of the guys from the group and I are going camping at Abrams Creek up in the Smokey's. For most of us, this is the first Thanksgiving without our wives." I stood to leave. "I'll see you Monday."

"Here's something to consider before I let you go. Something about death that even you don't know. Fact: there's a higher premature death rate for men who've lost a spouse than women who've lost a spouse. Do you have any idea why?"

"I have a feeling I'm about to find out."

"Men tend to repress their grief through an obsessive need to occupy their every waking moment. That way they don't have to feel anything, but hyperactivity along with anger only blocks the pain, letting the grief and pain build like an abscess."

"So what are you saying?"

"I'm saying you have a choice. Stay hyper and pissed off and die early, or let me help you find a way to get through this and live a long time."

I blinked a couple of times at his answer. "Okay, right now, I'm not sure which is the best option, but I'll get back to you on that."

Chapter 27

Alibis are tricky things.

On Wednesday before Thanksgiving, Sessions Court ran late, and I couldn't get out before five o'clock. Saul Jenkins caught me in the hallway on the way to the parking garage, a big grin strung between his ears.

"Great news, Jack. Jimmy Ray McElvy was booked about half hour ago on two counts of first degree murder."

"Really?"

"Lt. Shane personally went to Erlanger and took him into custody. And you'll love this, Shane tipped off the media. They had an impromptu perp walk with the TV cameras in the hospital parking lot."

"That's great, Saul. How'd McElvy look?"

"Not too bad, if you ignore the permanent press marks across his face. DuPriest set a $75,000 bond in each case, but McElvy's mother was waiting for him at the jail with a bondsman."

Those were high bonds – even for a murder case. That meant McElvy's family had managed to pony up $15,000 to get him out, probably with a second mortgage on the home where I'd attacked him.

"So he's already out again?"

"Yeah, but his arraignment is set for next Monday."

"Thanks, I'll be there."

"I figured you would be. Meanwhile, what are you doing for the holidays?"

"Just a little camping with Weitzman and some of the other guys in my victims group."

"With Weitzman you say?"

"That's right."

"Well, wonders never cease." Saul scratched his head. "Isaac Weitzman strikes me as the kind of guy who thinks roughing it is drinking Bloody Mary's without Tabasco sauce. I can't imagine him adapting to using the bathroom in the woods."

Damn, Saul was sharp. It shouldn't have surprised me he'd sense the pieces didn't quite fit.

"He's going to be just like the bears," I said. "He should provide us with good entertainment."

I kept my tone light, but mentally I was anything but relaxed. His questions about camping with Weitzman had caught me off guard. I needed to be better prepared to discuss my alibi.

Yeah, no one was better than Saul Jenkins.

*

Our plan for Thanksgiving weekend was to hit as many people on our list as quickly as possible, this time with property crimes. Cawood had wanted to keep up the armed robberies, but Weitzman and Lynch recognized that we could expand our circle of influence with a series of burglaries and thefts. This suited me fine; Cawood wouldn't have a chance to put anyone else in intensive care.

Our first stop was Kingsport, hometown to the state Supreme Court Justice Louie Rice. The house was dark when we got there, so we assumed Rice was out of town for the holiday weekend. With the help of a crowbar, the back door popped open as easily as a box of Cracker Jacks. No alarm either. We quickly ransacked the entire house and left with a good haul of stereo and computer equipment.

The next stop was the ritzy home of John Knapp, the Senate's Republican Party Chairman. His house was a veritable Fort Knox, so I drove away with his most vulnerable possession--a brand new Lexus--and ditched the car behind a church in downtown Kingsport. We broke out all the windows, poured beer over the interior and spray painted gang graffiti on the sides. I used a gang intelligence circular from the office and copied the pitch-forked insignia of the Folk Nation.

Our next stop was Johnson City. We tossed the loot from Louie Rice's house into a Salvation Army donation dropbox and bunked down in a Hampton Inn off the highway.

On Thursday, as the sun rose over Bristol, we broke into the deserted law office of Representative Janice Westbrook, who was also Chairman of the House Judiciary Committee.

"What the hell are we going to do with a copier?" Lynch whispered.

"Just shut up and get the damn thing in the van," Weitzman said. "And Jack, find the petty cash box."

We reached Knoxville around noon on Thursday, had Thanksgiving dinner at Sam & Andy's on Cumberland Avenue. Later that afternoon we drove down Cherokee Avenue and cased the home of state senator David Norton. The driveway was packed with cars, so we headed on to our next target, Paul Hazlett, of the Finance, Ways & Means Committee.

Hazlett's house looked good. He lived in an 80 year-old mansion off Kingston Pike. While there we no signs of life from inside, we waited until dark to make our move.

With years of working as a contractor, it took Cawood only a few minutes to disable the alarm. The ceilings inside were easily fifteen feet high and a suit of armor standing in the foyer was only one of many distinctive decorative touches. But what really got our attention was the oil painting above the mantle.

At first, I thought it was an expensive reproduction of Leonardo Da Vinci's *The Last Supper*. But then I saw something was wrong with Jesus.

"Who is that?"

Lynch shined his light on the Jesus. "That's Paul Hazlett. And judging by the other pictures in the house, I'm guessing that's his family he's had painted in as the disciples."

We all laughed.

"Now I know there's a lot us Jewish folks don't understand about Christianity," Weitzman said, "but was Smokey even at the Last Supper?"

Sleeping under the table close to Jesus/Hazlett's feet was Smokey, the blue-tick hound and mascot for the University of Tennessee Football team. Smokey wore his traditional big orange dog blanket with "Tennessee Vols" on the side.

"This is just too creepy for words," Lynch said.

"You're not kidding."

Weitzman nudged me with an elbow. "Then take it."

Lynch and I cut the picture out of the frame while Weitzman went through the rest of the house. Weitzman had quite the eye for antiques and knew just what to pinch.

"This guy really has some nice stuff. Check out this '77 Barolo I found in his wine cellar."

Thirty minutes later, we were on our way to Nashville, with the finest of Hazlett's possessions and the worst of his art.

Earlier in the week, it was Cawood who had came up with the most creative idea for the weekend. Using fake IDs, he had opened two bank accounts in the name of the Lt. Governor and Speaker of the Senate Charlie Goodson.

"Are these for real?" I held one of the checks up to the light and studied them.

"They're for real, all right," he said. "Thanks to you. If you hadn't gotten me their driver's license info from the state computers, I couldn't have pulled this off. But, that's his name, his address, his social security number and everything. I put $500 in each account when I opened them. Of course, Goodson doesn't know they're his, but he will soon enough."

We dropped Cawood off at the Greyhound bus station. He strolled through the terminal letting a few checkbooks fall to the floor. He dropped a few more in a couple of run-down liquor stores in the neighborhood, and then the rest in a parking garage next to the unemployment office.

"Jack, how long you think he's got before the bad check warrants start rolling in?" Cawood said.

"I'd give it a week or so," I said. "Goodson is going to learn firsthand how easy it is to be ripped off on paper."

By nightfall on that same Friday, we had reached Union City in the upper west corner of Tennessee. After a quick dinner at Dairy Queen, we pried open the back door of a three-bedroom ranch with wall to wall soft pile carpet and plastic runners going room to room. It was the home of Cathy Cole, the Senate's Democratic Party Chairman.

"Watch the dirt on your shoes," I said to Cawood. "We don't want to leave any footprints behind."

In her bedroom, we found a signed picture of Cole with Hillary Rodham Clinton and a closet lined with hundreds of Beanie Babies encased in plastic boxes.

"You really got to wonder who these people are making our laws," Cawood said, shaking his head at the discovery. He began scooping the Beanies into a trash bag. "I can't stand the way people leave the tags on their ears. It's just so Minnie Pearl."

Just then Weitzman's metallic voice crackled into all our receivers. *"We got trouble, Gentlemen. A Mercury Marquis just pulled up in the driveway. Driver's in her late fifties with curly white hair."*

Lynch nearly dropped the television he'd just taken from a bedroom. "That's got to be Cole. What do we do?"

"Out the front door," I said. "Quick!"

"Hold on," Cawood said, throwing more Beanies in a trash bag. "I'm not leaving here without these guys."

Lynch shot me a look as if Cawood was insane.

"Come on, Bert," I said, "it's time to go."

But Cawood's eyes were wild with determination. To force him to leave would have been like trying to wrestle a chicken leg away from a dog.

I heard the kitchen door open and the click of heels on linoleum. A beat of silence followed and then a shriek, presumably meaning Cathy Cole had spotted her ransacked living room.

Lynch and I looked at each other, grabbed the blue quilted bed spread, ran into the living room, and threw it over the hysterical senator. I wrapped my arms around the bundle and with the sweep of my leg knocked her feet out from under her. I caught her and lowered gently her to the floor keeping one hand on her as Lynch pulled Cawood and his booty out of the bedroom.

"Take anything you want," said a muffled voice from under the blanket. "Please don't hurt me!"

When Lynch and Cawood were out the door, I ran for the back door and grabbed the purse off the kitchen table. Thank God she hadn't had the presence of mind to use the Lady Smith & Wesson I later found inside.

Cawood had managed to steal 348 Beanies. "It's a good thing I liberated them. Now, let's get them into the hands of some real kids."

We left the bags at the back entrance of Memphis's St. Jude's Children's Hospital with a note reading: 'For the children'.

It was a great way to roll into town, especially since Memphis was, by far, to be our most challenging city. Residents there expect their cars to be stolen and homes to be broken into. Crime in the city had made the wrought-iron bars covering doors and windows chic. But we had come prepared. Cawood brought a crow bar that worked wonders on the bars on the Germantown home of Patrick Costa, the most senior and influential member of Shelby County's 16 representatives. Costa was a master at delivering the Shelby County block vote on the House floor.

I signaled Weitzman who was a lookout at the

corner, and the three of us went inside. Everything went smoothly until we discovered a collection of rare first-edition books.

"Let's leave those," I said when I saw Weitzman loading them into a pillowcase. "That's a first-edition *To Kill A Mockingbird*."

"So?"

"So, it's completely irreplaceable," I said. "Not something you just take from someone."

"Keep it personal, Jack. We've got to keep it personal."

He had a point, but I felt lousy about it just the same.

Next, we broke into the home of Sharon Powell, a brassy, tell-it-like-it-is Senator from the black community and a majority leader in Memphis. We took the usual electronic stuff again but also included her underwear.

"Isaac, you got some kind of panty fetish you want to tell us about?"

"Just keeping it personal, Jack."

Next, we went to the home of Representative Mickey Litton off Massey, but before we could make it around back, Lynch noticed the lawn jockey in the front yard. The small statue of a horse jockey with an extended arm and ring was common on the horse farms in Tennessee, and like a good politician, Litton had painted the face white instead of black.

But before anyone could stop him, Lynch had picked up the statue and flung it through the plate glass living room window of Litton's house.

As the glass shattered, Lynch ran back to the van leaving the statue tangled in chintz drapes. "I don't give a damn what color they paint the face," he said. "A little white wash don't hide their point."

That night we sat in the van outside the house of Arvin Pearlman, the vocal and annoying Chairman of the Senate's Oversight Committee on Sentencing. He often led the charge for restructuring prison sentences to relieve overcrowding.

We followed Pearlman and his wife in their dark green Cadillac Seville to the Racquet Club. From the way they were dressed, it looked as if they were there for a long dinner. Seville entry time: 23 seconds. I left the Seville unlocked with the engine running in the parking lot of the Mall of Memphis.

By the time we rounded Moccasin Bend on our way back into Chattanooga, I could make out Christmas lights outlining some of the buildings downtown. After spending 25 hours in the minivan over the last four days, it was certainly a relief be home. Better yet, with the exception of one missed target and a close shave at Cathy Cole's, our little crime spree had gone off without a hitch.

My town house was dark and empty when I returned. My answering machine had only two messages: one from Maisy's parents wishing me a happy Thanksgiving and one from Harlan Griffin.

"Jack, I wanted to make sure you're doing okay this weekend. I heard you went camping, but if you get in early, why don't you come on up to the house. We'll watch football and grill some steaks. I also wanted you to know that McElvy's going to be arraigned Monday. I called and let Mike Steelman in Rhea County know about it."

I turned out the lights and fell into bed, and for the first time since Maisy had died, I slept - hard, deep and refreshing. I dreamed Maisy and I were at our wedding reception dancing to *The Tennessee Waltz*. The song was our first dance as a married couple, and I held her tight in my arms and buried my nose in her neck and hair as we spun around the room. I just couldn't figure out why everyone in the band was naked.

Chapter 28

One great thing about being an American is that everyone is entitled to hire their own son-of-a-bitch to fight for their rights. And for Jimmy Ray McElvy, that son-of-a-bitch was Ned Wasserman.

I sat in the front row behind the State's table for McElvy's arraignment. Wasserman was wearing the same rumpled gray suit he had worn when he served me with the civil papers, and McElvy sat at the defense table, wearing a yellow knit shirt buttoned to the top. His hair was slicked back with something oily and showed the streaks from the teeth of a jail issued comb.

"Judge, I want the court to know that General Steelman has refused to allow me to look at his case file," Wasserman said, "and as this court is well aware, I'm entitled to discovery so my client can be afforded his constitutional right to adequate assistance of counsel at the preliminary hearing. I demand that he desist in this unethical behavior."

"Absolutely absurd!" Mike Steelman shot to his feet. Steelman was tall with short curly blond hair, and his accent and plaid tie bespoke of a jury practice in a more remote county. "As your Honor also knows, the defendant is not entitled to any discovery before a preliminary hearing. All that is required is that a minimally competent, licensed attorney sit next to the defendant. I did call the state board, and I was surprised to learn that Mr. Wasserman's license is currently valid. A remarkable feat when you consider the number of his past suspensions."

Wasserman's face turned the color of braised chili peppers. "Your honor!"

"And I take personal offense at the idea that by following the law I've done something unethical," Steelman said, raising his voice above Wasserman's. "But I suppose personal attacks are the only defense that can be mustered for this murdering thug."

Wasserman exploded, and he charged the bench yelling. Steelman was at his elbow bawling back. They were going toe-to-toe like enraged bulldogs yapping at a UPS delivery man.

Judge Dupriest pointed his fingers at the lawyers. "That's enough! In my courtroom, we're all going to be nice to each other. Do you hear me? We're all going to be *nice*."

Ordinarily, I would have enjoyed watching such an exchange, but not today. Maisy used to say that there was no telling what could be accomplished if lawyers quit being jerks and pursued more noble endeavors. "Pyramids could be built or planets explored or maybe all those over-educated minds could produce the world's most sublime haiku." So, in Juvenile Court, I wrote Maisy a haiku entitled *Recess - Nine millimeter,/that baby sure fits my hand;/ teacher won't notice*.

"That's not quite what I was talking about," she said.

"Well, none of the other lawyers would help me."

There was no denying that Maisy would have been disgusted by today's display, but then Wasserman detonated his secret weapon.

"Your honor, we have a unique situation that entitles me to discovery. You see, my client is unable to assist me in preparing his defense. He can't remember anything about the incident. I have here the sworn affidavit of Dr. Delores Byrd that Mr. McElvy is currently suffering from *retrograde amnesia*."

"Retro what?" Dupriest asked.

"*Retrograde amnesia*. Proof will show that my client has suffered an unprovoked and unlawful attack at the hands of Assistant District Attorney Jack Henley. Those attacks created an aggravated head injury for my client. As we speak, he has no memory of the events of the day in question, and he is unable to assist me in the preparation of his defense. How can I adequately prepare his defense in a preliminary hearing if he is unable to remember anything?"

So Wasserman had switched from his hail-Mary self-defense argument to planting the seeds for a mental defense down the road. And I'll be damned, this one had a shot at working.

Dupriest turned towards the prosecution table. "General Steelman, what do you say about this?"

"Biological speculation. Or what we call up in Rhea County - pure B.S. And even if what he's saying is true, he's not entitled to any discovery at this point."

Dupriest nodded his head. "I agree. Mr. Wasserman, can you be ready for a preliminary hearing in two weeks?"

"Impossible, your Honor. With my client's condition, I have no idea when we will be able to proceed further. Perhaps we could reset the case three months from now and come back and see if Mr. McElvy's mental condition has improved."

"Your honor, if counsel's representing to the court that there is an inability to move forward because of his client's mental condition, then I move the court to immediately take the defendant into custody and have him evaluated by State psychiatrists."

"But we're not claiming he's incompetent to stand trial," said Wasserman, "only that we're experiencing a temporary set-back that temporarily suspends the legal proceedings."

"He can't have it both ways," Steelman said. "The defendant is either ready to move forward with his case or he isn't. So, now that a serious question of competency has been raised, the court should determine for itself whether Mr. McElvy can stand trial."

"But this is only temporary!" It was beginning to dawn on Wasserman how unhappy his client would be if Judge Dupriest ordered him into custody for psychiatric evaluations.

"Enough," Dupriest said. "Your client's got two weeks to get better, or I'm ordering him into custody and having him held until the evaluation is completed.

Now, do you wish to be heard on bond, General? It's currently set at $75,000 in each murder case."

"Your honor," said Steelman, "at the time these two women were murdered, the defendant was on parole. Obviously, he's a danger to the community, and we beg the court to revoke his bond before he murders two more women."

"The claim that my client killed two women is only an *allegation* at this point." Wasserman threw his pen on his desk. "This man is presumed innocent until his case is decided by a jury of his peers. A parole revocation was filed that will address any parole issues, but since these charges are the only basis for the revocation, the Department of Corrections is postponing their hearing until there's a disposition in these cases. And furthermore, bond is to guarantee the appearance of defendants in court, and my client did not fail to show today, nor will he fail to show in the future, and...."

"That'll do," Dupriest said. "The court finds that it needs more in front of it before determining the defendant to be a danger to the community, but I believe it is undisputed that the defendant was on parole at the time he was charged. Therefore, I'm ordering him placed in the pre-trial community corrections program, and as a condition of bond, I'm ordering weekly drug screens. If he violates any condition of the community corrections program or fails a drug screen, I am revoking his bond.

"General Steelman, you can be heard again on bond in two weeks after I've heard the proof in the preliminary hearing. Let the defendant be taken into custody. Court stands adjourned."

McElvy's head whipped around to Wasserman. "What did you do?"

Wasserman draped a fat hand over McElvy's back and whispered violently in his ear. McElvy shook his head side to side. "No!"

Three court officers edged up to the defense table surrounding McElvy. When Wasserman and McElvy were through talking, the officers nodded at McElvy to come on.

McElvy knew the drill and pushed back from his chair. He mumbled expletives under his breath, and red blotches burned up his neck to his face as he walked to jail.

I enjoyed the sight of this scrap of human garbage being escorted from the courtroom, even though I knew he would be released before the day was over. Dupriest had split the baby, placing him in community corrections or what was called "house arrest." You could only be processed into the program from jail where electronic bracelets were strapped above your ankles.

The house arrest program was another one of those insane, wet-brained ideas of former Lt. Gov. Otis Whitaker. The idea of prisoners paying for their own incarceration was attractive to the legislature. So under the law, a day spent in house arrest was considered the same as having sat in the worst cell in Brushy Mountain prison.

Unfortunately, there was no legal distinction between prison time and bracelet time.

The program wasn't like some science fiction movie where a team of soldiers stared intently at a giant screen tracking criminals: "We've got an absconder in sector four. He just stepped off his porch to sell crack. Deploy the take-down team." In reality, a police car wasn't even sent to look. House arrest employees would check a computer printout in the morning, and if the people were gone, they would have a warrant filed with the court to pick them up. In the best cases, that was a 24 hour turnaround just to get paperwork filed.

So now McElvy was getting credit toward his sentence on house arrest. *Whoopee!* He was still living at home, and it wouldn't take him long to figure out how to get around the monitoring. They always did.

But Dupriest had also telegraphed that in two weeks McElvy was going to be in custody one way or another, and I couldn't fault him for being careful in a double homicide case.

Steelman came back to me on the front row and whispered, "I'm laughing my ass off at retrograde amnesia. That's a new one on me."

"Have you dealt with this doctor Wasserman's hired?"

"Dee Dee Byrd? Yeah, she's a defense whore out of Memphis," he said. "A real publicity hound, which is probably how McElvy got her. In high profile cases, she's been known to offer her services for free."

"How is she on the stand?"

"Not bad, but I'll get some transcripts of where she's testified before."

"Let me know what I can do to help. Research. Leg work. You name it."

"All I need you to do," Mike said, sliding onto the bench next to me, "is stay the hell away from Jimmy Ray McElvy. That stunt you pulled at his mother's house is really going to cause us some problems."

"Look, I know as a trial lawyer you focus on the weaknesses of a case, but I'm telling you this is a strong, strong case. You've got surveillance video--"

"Let's see how his mental condition shakes out. This may be an up hill battle of experts, but I'm serious when I tell you to stay away from him. They asked me to review bringing criminal charges against you for the incident at the house."

"They're looking at charging me criminally? With what? Assault?"

"Aggravated assault and attempted second degree murder."

"*Whoa!*" If I was indicted on a felony, I'd be lucky to keep my law license let alone my day job.

"Since you are the victim in this case, I have a conflict of interest. So the DA's Conference has appointed Phil Ottoman, the DA up in Kingsport to review the matter.

"Look, I'm not telling you anything you don't know, but I don't enjoy the idea of putting a witness on the stand who is under indictment for a felony."

"Mike, do you really think they'll indict me for aggravated assault?"

"I do. Or maybe even attempted second degree murder or attempted manslaughter. What happened in that house will be your word against his medical records, and I know those aren't pretty. The bottom line is that things are just too personal between you and McElvy. That's going to affect your credibility."

"Well, of course it's personal, Mike, he murdered my wife. But I can beat the criminal charge. Get the Kingsport DA to let me testify before the grand jury."

"You've got to be kidding."

"Talking to a jury is what I do best. If I can just sit down and tell them why I did what I did, they might no-bill the case."

"That would take some string pulling."

"I promise you, Mike, just get me in front of that grand jury, and there will be nothing Wasserman can use against me on the stand."

"We'll see." Total non-commitment in his voice.

I might have been pushing too hard, but everything depended on it – my job, my law license, my career. And I found myself surprised that I even cared about those things, and after all the felonies I had committed in the last few weeks, I couldn't believe that hitting Jimmy Ray McElvy with an iron could be the one that took me down.

"I know I'm a pain in the ass to work with," I said, "but my wife was a beautiful person who helped other people. She didn't need to be gunned down for buying ice. I don't want the fact that she was married to a hothead to get in the way of McElvy's prosecution. So please, get me in front of that grand jury."

Mike's expression softened. "I'll see what I can do, but you've got to be a choirboy until this trial starts. Wasserman is trying to dig up all the dirt he can on you. He's already ordered a transcript of your armed-robbery trial against McElvy, and he's looking into everything you've touched the last seven years."

"Are you kidding? I'm the original choirboy."

Steelman smirked. "Yeah, right."

Chapter 29

Back in my office, I sifted through the stack of papers on my desk: motions to suppress, motions to continue, a memo on vacation policy, fliers from the National District Attorneys Association advertising seminars, a pro se motion from a prisoner entitled, "Motion to Get Me Up Off the Floor." According to the fifth-grade letters scrawled on notebook paper, the prisoner had been sleeping on the floor of the crowded county jail, and he wanted a bed. Best paper lawyering I had seen in weeks.

I heard a soft knock and then the face of Ron Close poked in the door. Close was a special agent of the Tennessee Bureau of Investigation. A tall black man with an athletic build and easy smile, he was called "The Closer" because he closed more open investigations than any other agent with the TBI.

"General Henley, you got a minute for a hard-working detective."

"Well, I'll be," I said taking to my feet. "Ron Close, it's good to see you. How long has it been? Two years?"

"Something like that."

Close was originally based out of Nashville, but two years ago, he had been assigned to our office to investigate the death of a black man who died during an arrest by five white sheriff's deputies. On its face, the incident looked horrible, but the reality was the man was obeying the voices in his head that told him to cut the hearts out of the police officers with a butcher knife. With an officer riding his back, the lunatic almost got one deputy's heart. The fight ended with 32 slugs in the man's chest and five officers on suspension left to nurse their knife wounds and broken arms.

Close managed to pull off an investigation that didn't alienate the law enforcement community or the black community. Everyone respected him because he was committed to the truth and not the perception of the truth.

Close hadn't changed much in two years - a few pounds heavier and the eyes had a few more lines. Last I'd heard, he was the right-hand man for the director of the TBI.

"So what brings you back to Chattanooga," I asked after pulling up a chair for him. "Rock City?"

"Nothing as fun, and let's just say, if anyone asks, it's nothing official."

I didn't think anything of Close being cagey. Most detectives were pathologically secretive about anything they worked on.

"So what have you got?" I expected he was working a big-time narcotics reverse or corruption in the jail's bonding office.

Ron looked out in the hallway to see if anyone was listening and closed my door. "Jack, I'm mixed up in the damnedest thing, and I trust what I tell you will be kept in confidence."

"Absolutely."

"Well, you're really going to think this is hair-brained. But you know Wally Cochran? Governor's chief guru on policy?"

"Yeah, I've heard of him." In fact I had handcuffed him nude to a light pole and drawn a scarlet letter across his chest in lipstick.

"Well, he was carjacked outside of Vanderbilt."

"Is that so? I didn't hear anything about it."

"You wouldn't have. He kept it all hush, hush because he was with a coed, who let's just say was not his wife."

"I see."

"Well, he had the Governor call in the Director of the TBI to discreetly investigate the matter. Of course, we came up with zip. But then Cochran points out that other politicians in the state have been attacked too, and Cochran wants the TBI to give them protection. He's trying to get the governor to turn the TBI into Tennessee's version of the secret service."

"What?"

"I know, I know. It's crazy. The last thing we want to become is babysitters for politicians too stupid to keep their pants zipped. After all, how many of these politicians are victims of crime? But here's the weird part – quite a few people who work in Nashville have been victims of crime lately. I started crunching the numbers so the Director could show the Governor it isn't necessary, and if you look at the numbers for the last 10 years, it's not. But I found a spike."

I swallowed hard. "A spike?"

"In the last few months there has been a huge jump in politicians that have been attacked. You should see my numbers for last week alone. And it's not just politicians, but others connected to the criminal justice system itself."

"Isn't that sort of a leap?"

"I thought so at first. But I expanded my search definition of public officials hoping it would lower the average, but it didn't. The numbers showed the opposite for people involved with criminal justice. Believe me, I've twisted the data every which way looking for a pattern."

"I'm still not following you. Are you saying there's some sort of statewide conspiracy out there?"

"I'm not saying it, but the numbers seem to suggest it. Of course, the facts of each crime don't. Different perps in different cities wanting different things. That's what's crazy. Everything is unrelated."

"It's been my experience that conspiracies are far and few between."

"Mine too."

"So why me? Why drive all the way down from Nashville to tell me?"

"You are one of the first victims of the trend. And I apologize for reducing what happened to you and your wife as a statistical number. You know how awful I felt about your loss."

"I do. I appreciated your note. But you think her death was part of some conspiracy?"

"I don't think anything, but things are stirred up right now. Cochran is needling the Governor who is needling the Director who is needling me for answers. And I don't have any. So when your name came up, I thought it would be a nice excuse to leave town and talk to you about it. Is there anything that you've discovered that might connect McElvy to any organized group?"

"None." I stared at Close for a long time. I was trying to see if he was playing me. Was I his number one suspect or was he genuinely befuddled? There wasn't a hint of guile behind his dark brown eyes. "You might want to check with the Department of Corrections. I don't know if he was in any type of gang in prison."

"None, I already checked. Do you mind telling me what happened?"

I took a deep breath and let the air out slowly, as much for effect as for time to think. I did not want to have this conversation with Ron Close, but he could smell an evasive answer at a 100 yards. "It's still not easy to talk about, Ron. Get Lt. Shane to show you his file. The video of what went down would do a better job than I could, anyway."

"Do you actually think the Homicide Division of the Chattanooga Police Department would share anything with the TBI? Shane's more territorial than Palestinians. I don't need a lot of details just something that could help me figure out if McElvy was working an angle or working for someone else."

"Trust me. Jimmy Ray McElvy's your garden-variety, dumber-than-dirt armed robber. If he had any help, he would have done a much better job."

"Do you think that McElvy was getting even with you for putting him in jail?"

"I doubt it. He was already in the store when we got there, and until thirty seconds before we pulled in, even we didn't know we'd be there."

"Do you think he saw you and made his play?"

"No, I was outside getting ice. He had never seen Maisy before. What about suspects in these other crimes?"

"That's just it. No one else has been arrested. We've come up empty on every single case. The most we have is McElvy and a police artist sketch of a guy who mugged Senator Milligan."

"Oh, yeah, I heard about that."

"I'm chasing a statistical shadow, and we all know how statistics can give the snap shot of events."

"It's like every time you hire more police officers the crime rate goes up because you have more people making arrests."

"Exactly, but my problem is these statistics are attached to powerful politicians that can make my life miserable." Close stood to leave. "If you think of anything, call me."

"Absolutely, and I hope you don't take this badly. But I hope your spreadsheet's wrong. It's been hard enough to deal with Maisy's death as it is. I don't think I could handle it if it was part of some great pay-back conspiracy among criminals. But did the Director cave? Is the TBI protecting politicians?"

Close nodded. "The ones who need the most ass-kissing. Now you understand why the Director's the Director and I'm not. He's one helluva a politician."

"The overtime on that's got to be incredible."

"It's not like we're going 24-7. It's more of a dog-and-pony show for Cochran and the Governor. We just show up at certain events and act conspicuous."

"Sounds real productive."

"It's a living."

Close and I said our good-byes, and I waited a good five minutes to make sure he had cleared the lobby. Then I hurried out of the office to a pay phone next to the third floor bathrooms.

After what felt like an eternity, I heard Weitzman's voice: "What's so important for you to tear me away from a patient."

"We've got to meet."

"What's going on?"

"Not on the phone. Meet me in half an hour at Sticky Fingers Barbecue."

"But I got patients."

"Reschedule them. And get the others."

"That bad?"

"*Oh yeah!*"

Chapter 30

There's an expression among Chattanooga's crack addicts called "Geekin' & Peekin'." That's when crackheads are extremely high, *geeking*, and so paranoid from prolonged cocaine use that they're constantly *peeking* out the window for police.

Geekin' & Peekin'.

I finally understood what they were talking about as I walked down Market Street towards Sticky Fingers Restaurant. I was as close to geekin' & peekin' as a man could be without the assistance of cocaine. My visit from Special Agent Ron Close was like mainlining paranoia. At that moment, my panic-driven delusions made me actually believe that every person I saw on the street was a TBI agent. I was out of my head and convinced I was the subject of surveillance.

But then I really had no idea.

I cut through the parking garage of the old Sears building to Broad Street. I stopped and pretended to shake a pebble out of my loafer and carefully scanned the people on the streets. No one looked like a TBI agent, but then again most TBI agents would be hard to peg as TBI agents, especially if they were on surveillance.

Damn it! How much did they know? Did they suspect me? Could there already be taps on all our telephones?

My mind started replaying highlights from our take-downs. What could someone have picked up on? Was Lynch I.D.'d off that sketch? Was one of us recognized? What if one of us was talking? That gave me pause. No, no one in the group would be talking, could they? I was overreacting, getting all paranoid, acting like a damn defendant.

Worse, if the TBI was watching me, I was playing right into their hand, leading them right to an accomplice.

So rather than going inside Sticky Fingers, I kept on walking. I needed a way to reach Weitzman without being followed and without benefit of his cell phone. I was already pretty close to the Tennessee Aquarium, and as I looked at the funky brick edifice of Chattanooga's premier tourist attraction I had an idea.

An incredible multi-million dollar fish tank filled with fresh-water exotics and salt-water standards, the Aquarium almost single-handedly turned around Chattanooga's downtown area. While other downtown areas across the country fell into decay, Chattanooga crawled out of a cocoon of decaying industry and metamorphosized into a hip, trendy and environmentally friendly city. The building itself was a work of art capped with four triangular glass peaks.

Even at the start of the Christmas season, the plaza was filled with buses and tourists. Dodging the lines, I found the members-only entrance on the side and showed my charter member card at the desk. No

TBI agents would be following me through that door unless they also had paid the yearly membership fee or took the risk of breaking cover by flashing a badge. I called information from a payphone in the lobby and was soon describing Weitzman to Sticky Fingers' bartender.

It took only a moment for Isaac to come to the phone. "Jack? Where the hell are you?"

"At the Aquarium."

"Why aren't you here?"

"I was afraid I was being followed, so I came straight to the aquarium."

"Followed? By who?"

"The TBI."

There was a long pause on the other end of the phone. I could hear the loud music in Sticky Fingers, and a customer shouting a drink order at the bartender.

"Isaac, did you hear me?"

"Hell yeah, I heard you. What's the skinny?"

"We'll get to that I promise, but right now you've got to do what I tell you. Did Tom and Bert show up?"

Neither one of them could make lunch on such short notice, and under the circumstances that was for the best. So I told Weitzman to meet me on the upper deck of the aquarium's mountain cove in ten minutes and to make sure he wasn't being followed.

On the top floor of the Aquarium, underneath the hypotenuse of a glass steeple, is a gigantic room constructed to be a self-contained environmental display. Sort of a bio-dome with right-angles. A waterfall cascaded into a clear mountain pool inhabited by river otters. Song Sparrows and Evening Grosbeak flew from sculpted tree to sculpted tree, and indigenous snakes – orange corn snakes and timber rattlers - were displayed safely behind glass in hollowed-out, man-made logs. The room was like walking into a beer commercial where a guy in a flannel shirt talks about the purity of the mountain spring water.

Most tourists stop to look at the river otters and miss a set of stairs leading to a small deck above the otter pool. Weitzman found me sitting there alone on a bench in the highest point in the room.

"Why here?" was the first thing he said.

"It's public and private."

"For what?"

"Sorry. For this." I ran my hand down from the top of his sweater to his belt. With my other hand, I felt down his back.

He started to resist, but then he saw the look on my face and almost smiled. "Don't worry, Henley, I'm not wearing a wire."

"I didn't think you were, but I'd be a fool not to check." I patted down his coat pockets and ran my hands around his legs.

"Enough already. What the hell's going on, anyway?"

I told him about Ron Close's visit.

For once, Weitzman didn't say much of anything. He just listened intently, only interrupting for clarification.

When I was through, he said, "You want my take on this?"

"By all means"

"I think you're overreacting."

I looked at Weitzman as if he hadn't heard a word I'd said. "But he knows it is people connected with the justice system. It's time to pull the plug."

"I don't see it that way. He may have connected a few dots about what connects the crimes but that was bound to happen. Nothing you've told me suggests he knows squat about who committed them. That's why he was down here talking to you. And if you don't keep your cool and keep playing spy games, you will get people suspicious."

"You can't be too careful."

"Careful, my ass. If you'd met me for lunch that would have looked a lot less suspicious than meeting me here. Two friends from the victim support group breaking bread together. What's the big deal? Now we just look gay, especially after that rub down you gave me when I got here."

"Don't flatter yourself."

"Henley, I know you respect this Close guy, and that's got you shook up. But he's done us a tremendous favor by tipping us off to his thinking. We always knew our hits would be investigated. So we lay low for awhile. Big deal. But when our lobbyist needs an assist, we'll do some assisting."

Weitzman's words washed over me like the cool mountain mist billowing in the air around us. Everything he said was making perfect sense.

"You're right. You're right. We're probably doing just fine. There's just been an awful lot of talk about indicting me this morning, and a visit from Ron Close didn't help."

"It takes a hard man to do what we're doing, Henley."

"I know. Not everyone understands that robbing and stealing can be for the greater good."

"Don't be flip. I'm being serious here. It takes a hard man to do what you're doing, and I recruited you because you're a hard man. Now I know you've been through the wringer these last few months, but I need you to keep being tough for a couple of more. Then, this'll all be behind us. Meanwhile, let's not get spooked away just because the things we did to get noticed got noticed."

Neither of us said anything for a moment. In a tree above, I listened to the mournful song of the Yellow-breasted Chat and wondered if the bird was fooled by the man made habitat around him. Did it even know it was in a cage?

"Face it, Jack, you're still tired from our road trip. Who wouldn't be? Here..." He reached into his breast pocket and pulled out a sheet of white paper. "I took the liberty of writing you a prescription for a few valium. Get a decent night's sleep, and we'll talk again about this at group."

I nodded.

"And one more thing, Jack, I'll never betray you. Ever. If there's one quality I hold above all others, it's loyalty. So sticking together is the most important thing we can do. Do you understand?"

"I do."

"All right. So if you pat me down again like that, I'll break your fucking hands."

Chapter 31

Over the next few weeks, the four of us laid low, keeping to our usual routine of victims' support meetings and late dinners at Jimmy's with guarded conversations. During the day, it was off to the office, court and counseling – the holy trinity to Harlan Griffin's happiness and keeping my job.

My counseling sessions with Father Nick had dissolved into 45 minute sessions that I expect we both knew were pretty useless. I was cordial, at times responsive, but for the most part very guarded, and I couldn't decide if Father Nick kept seeing me because he liked the challenge or that he couldn't stand to see me lose my job.

Two weeks after my visit from the TBI, I sat in a hard back chair in front of Father Nick's desk. He kept pecking away at me like an angry Blue Jay.

"So why won't you speak to Anna and Frank Gillespie?"

"Because I don't want to."

"Anna's worried about you, and I am too. Don't *you* think it's a little strange that you've cut yourself off all your close friends?"

"What are you talking about? I spend a lot of time with my friends."

"Your new friends, sure, and that's great. But it seems like everyone you were close to when Maisy was still alive is almost completely out of the picture now. Frankly, it makes me wonder what you're running from and what you're hiding?"

I looked sideways at Father Nick. "What do you think I'm hiding?"

His words were slow and measured. "Pain. Fear. Anger. You know, your life's not over. There's still a happy ending out there for you, but you're not going to find it unless you take the sign down."

"What sign?"

"The one around your neck that says *'victim'*." Father Nick put those annoying two-fingered rabbit ears around the word.

"I appreciate your concern, Father, but some things take time. Can't you understand how seeing all of my old friends only reminds me of Maisy? This is just something I have to work through."

"When your parents died, you didn't act like this way. What's your excuse now?"

"I expected to outlive my parents. Maisy was supposed to be with me forever."

"And now she's not, so what are you going to do about it? The reality is human beings need intimate relationships to function. At some point, you will have to develop another relationship. Have you thought about dating again?"

"I would, but my boss has forced me into mandatory counseling three times a week with a cranky Episcopal Priest. But for that, I'd be placing personal ads and going to MatchMaker International."

That's when Father Nick pulled his usual trick. It was what he did whenever I got too smart-alec. He would drag me into prayer. "The Lord be with you."

And with the speed that only comes with years of serving as an acolyte, I mumbled, "And also with you."

"Let us pray. Oh Lord, Father of all mankind, we pray to you to help Jack Henley see that you still have a plan for his life..." And then Father Nick would basically use the prayer as an opportunity to tell me off (as though he was the bad cop and God was the good cop). "...please help him accept the loss of his dear wife and get on with his life. Help him learn to acknowledge his anger and help him learn acceptance is the only road to serenity..." Blah. Blah. Blah.

So ended another productive session.

Back home, I scrounged in the cabinets for food. Gone were the bereavement rations from the months before. My refrigerator was stocked with a few condiment jars – mayonnaise, mustard, blackberry preserves. On the back shelf was an opened box of baking soda that Maisy had put there last summer.

Maisy and I often walked from the townhouse to the Mudpie Café on Fraizer Avenue for turkey and avocado sandwiches with a cream cheese spread. But I couldn't go back; the girl behind the counter might ask where Maisy was and what would I say?

In a cupboard above the microwave was a can of processed cheddar cheese and two heels from an old loaf of bread. Falling back on a recipe from my law school days, I toasted the heels, sprayed cheese in the middle and smashed the bread together. *Voila* a "grilled" cheese sandwich.

God, these were getting old.

And so was sitting around the townhouse wondering if the TBI was watching. I realized more and more that I needed the action. I needed to feel as though I was doing something about Maisy's death. *Tears without action is wasted sentiment.* And more than anything else, I desperately needed something to fill the hours after I left the courthouse and before I returned.

Despite Weitzman's protest of over-reaction, I had the unmistakable feeling that our operation was unraveling. On the surface, everything looked fine. The response from our Thanksgiving forays was good. As anticipated, the events had provided modest to exuberant motivation for legislation. Leslie had been amazed with our progress on Capitol Hill, and many key bills were anticipated to sail through in January.

But here I was waking up at three in the morning and wondering if we had set things into motion that we could never imagine and if those things would somehow, some way, be our ultimate undoing – like Ron Close. His presence in my office had been an unforeseen wild card, and no matter how hard I tried I couldn't shake the idea that the TBI was nipping at our heels. If everything he had said was true, the man had driven from Nashville to talk to me for five minutes. Why hadn't he used a phone? There could be only one reason he had made the trip – to see my reaction. I didn't think I had given him anything, but then again I didn't have a mirror in front of me either.

I washed down my sandwich with warm tap water and fired up my laptop. The phone rang before I could get on-line, and I heard the tense voice of Leslie Gilmore-Clark.

"Jack, I've got some bad news."

That, I didn't expect. "But I thought things were going great."

"They were. But the funding for new prisons is log jammed in the Legislative Affairs Committee. That's the committee where all proposed legislation has to pass first. Apparently, the Chairman of the Committee is sitting on it."

"Who's that?"

"Jason Face."

"Figures." Jason Face was a power-hungry state senator from Ripley, Tennessee. "Did he say why?"

"He's still mad at the District Attorneys' Conference for using their influence to get step-raises during last year's budget crisis. He swore then that he would never approve any legislation recommended by the Conference, and now it looks like he's sticking to it."

I remembered the crisis. Unable to balance the state's budget in one of the best economic years in decades, the legislature had cut all pay increases for state employees. That was not supposed to affect prosecutors. After all, our salary increases were guaranteed by state law, but it was Face who wanted to get around the legal requirement to pay by changing the law. He created a new pay scale for prosecutors that paid us the same as kindergarten lunch room assistants. Prosecutors across the state rallied against the bill, which was barely defeated by three votes in the House.

But I still didn't get how Face linked the legislation our Victims' Support Group was pushing with the DA's Conference, and I told Leslie so.

"It's pro-law enforcement," she said, "and it's got the DA Conference's stamp of approval. That's why Face is so dead set against it."

"Doesn't he realize this is victim driven?"

"He did when I got through with him. I cornered him in the hallway this afternoon and reminded him of that. But when he realized what bill I was talking about, his face went from politely paying attention to visibly pissed-off. Obviously this is something personal between him and the conference, and there's nothing I can think of to change his mind. I think he believes our proposals are a put-up job by the Conference."

"I can't believe this. We've come so far. What's this guy like, anyway?"

"He's always been hard to deal with. Moody, incredibly arrogant. A real godfather complex. When you meet with him, you have to genuflect a lot. Workaholic who is perpetually divorced."

"No surprise there."

"As far as I know, the only person he really gets along with is his daughter. In fact, he dotes on her. She's a senior in the business school at UT Knoxville, and if you don't believe me, you should see the increase in funding UT's business school has received the last four years."

"What's the daughter like?"

"She works for him here in the summer. At first, she seems like your typical goody-two-shoes daddy's girl, but I've heard some talk. She can be pretty wild at times."

"You did say she went to UT."

Leslie went on for about 10 more minutes on the different strategy and methods her firm would be conducting on behalf of our group. But everything seemed to stop with Jason Face.

"If you were a regular client instead of a dear law school friend, I wouldn't put this so bluntly, but Jack, my professional opinion here is that we're dead in the water. Unless the DA's Conference is abolished or Face rolls over dead from a heart attack, there's probably not much we can do."

"Well, you never know what might happen, Leslie. Face might change his mind."

"Given what I've seen, that's as likely as the moon falling from the sky. But I'll keep an open mind. Talk to your people and get back to me with whatever you'd like me to do."

I punched the cordless phone off and threw it onto the couch. Building more prisons was the linchpin to our proposed legislation. After all, what's the point of tougher laws if there's no place to put dangerous offenders? If Face didn't approve funding for their construction, everything else would have been in vain, but to go after Face now was riskier than ever. If Face knew other legislators were getting TBI protection, he would demand it for himself too; otherwise, he wouldn't be nearly as important as he thought.

And speed was everything. If we didn't act fast, his committee could kill the bill before Christmas break, and the General Assembly wouldn't even be able to consider building more prisons for another year.

I grinned and speed-dialed Weitzman. I wish I could say I was sickened by the dark plans brewing in my heart, but all I felt was the sheer delight of getting together with the guys and trying to fix the world. Maybe that's why I was so unprepared for what happened.

Chapter 32

First thing the next morning, I made another call.

"University of Tennessee's Career Planning and Placement Center, may I help you?"

"Yes, ma'am, this is Joe Finch," I said from the pay-as-you-go cell phone Cawood had gotten me under a fake name. "I'm the vice-president of human resources at Chattem in Chattanooga."

"Oh yeah, you're the makers of Flexall 464."

"That's right and Corn Silk makeup and Bull Frog Sun tanning products to name a few. This is a little embarrassing, but I'm scheduled to have an interview next week with one of your business students. We're quite interested in her, but I'm afraid I lost her resume."

"Oh, dear, that is embarrassing."

"I'd hate for her to know that we misplaced it. Do you mind faxing me a copy?"

"Not a problem. What's her name?"

"Rebecca Face."

Sixty seconds later, Rebecca's resume was faxed to my lap top. Not surprisingly, she was an impressive student: president of the Finance Club, Student Orientation Assistant, research assistant for a well-regarded finance professor, Alpha Delta Pi Sorority president. Her long term goal was to manage her own mutual fund, and at the top of her resume in bold print was her school address and phone number.

Easy.

*

Twelve hours later, Tom Lynch, Isaac Weitzman and I sat in a stolen full-sized paneled van watching the red brick house of Rebecca Face in Knoxville. We were parked in a neighborhood of old houses between the west side of the university and Cumberland Avenue.

Locals referred to this stretch of Cumberland Avenue as "The Strip" - several blocks of businesses that catered almost exclusively to the college kids – book stores, delis, music stores, T-shirt shops, copy centers, pizza joints and bars. Lots of bars.

We were on South 22nd street, a block behind The Strip, wedged in between the cars stacked along the sidewalk. Even a couple of blocks off campus, parking was a rare commodity.

I had stolen the van from a parking lot behind Andy Holt Tower. No one would miss it until tomorrow, and with the official seal of the University of Tennessee on the side, the van blended into the neighborhood where the school used a number of the old houses for office space.

Up the hill on the right, Rebecca Face lived in a 1930's red brick house that had been carved into a duplex to provide more student housing.

"*All clear in the rear,*" Cawood said from the minivan next to tennis courts behind the house. His job was to listen to the scanners and let us know if she came in through the back.

Weitzman shook his head with disgust. "Does he always have to rhyme?"

Lynch leaned back behind the wheel. "I wish we'd gotten her class schedule. Any idea when she'll be coming home?"

"None," said Weitzman. "All we know is she lives in the left half of that duplex."

So we sat. And waited. And sat.

"I've got to stretch my legs," I said. "I think I got a cramp."

"Stay close by."

"You got it."

The street was darker than I expected - heavy with the growth from older trees and poor lighting designs of the 1930's. Perfect.

I wore jeans and a heavy olive green sweater with hiking boots. I walked up the hill past Face's duplex. At the top of the hill, I turned and looked back. No sign of her. Nothing.

The cool December air felt good after being stuck in the van, and I readied myself for the old fashioned bag job that lay ahead. At Weitzman's insistence, we were abandoning the pretext of random street violence for the maximum impact of an organized kidnapping.

"It's a bigger shock," Weitzman said. "A rinky-dink mugging could be too easily dismissed as a foreseeable risk of living near The Strip. To make this man do a one-eighty on every political position he's taken this year, we have to kidnap her."

I walked back down the hill toward the van, my boots crunching dried leaves with each step.

A candy-red BMW zoomed up the hill and turned into the driveway, damn near taking me out in the process. On the back of the car was the official license tag for a member of the Tennessee Senate.

A girl with long brunette hair popped her head out of the car door. "Sorry, I didn't see you in the dark."

She stepped out of the car wearing tight black stretch pants, calf-high black leather boots and a bulky sweater with a small oval purse hanging from her shoulder. On her sweater was pinned a small jeweled fraternity crest near the collar.

I recognized the pin and decided to make a play. She had seen my face, but if Weitzman followed along, it wouldn't matter.

"I'm sorry I was in your way," I said giving her my best smile. "I've been wandering around here for the last half hour. Do you know where the Phi Delt house is? I was supposed to meet my little brother there, but I think I'm turned around."

"Oh, your brother's a Phi Delt?"

Her cheekbones glowed from the cold and her brown eyes looked wet. A definite looker. I was pleased to see the ADPi's were keeping their standards up.

With a hand cupped to my ear as if I couldn't hear, I stepped closer: "Excuse me?"

"I said is your brother a Phi Delt?"

"Yeah, he pledged this fall."

"Really? My boyfriend's a Phi Delt. What's his name?"

"I'm sorry, I don't know your boyfriend's name."

She laughed. "No, not *my* boyfriend."

"Well, I don't have a boyfriend."

"I mean *your* little brother."

"Oh, you want his name?"

"Yes."

"Well, why didn't you say so?"

She laughed, clearly enjoying our banter, so I edged up to the end of her car and leaned on the trunk. Down the hill, I heard the van engine start. *Come on guys.*

"How about I start with my name?" I stretched out my hand. "I'm Jake Seymour."

With cool slender fingers and a firm grip, she shook my hand. Not a half shake, but a real shake. She was a true politician's daughter.

"But I don't know any pledge named Seymour," she said.

"We're half brothers. Same mother. Different fathers."

"Oh."

"I'm sure you've seen him around."

Behind me, I heard the roar of an engine and the sound of tires crackling through dry leaves onto the driveway.

Rebecca Face stunned. "What the--?"

I spun around and saw Weitzman and Lynch jumping from the van with ski-masks over their faces and guns in their hands. I grabbed Rebecca's wrist and pulled her behind me. She would perceive the move as if I was shielding her, but I didn't want her running away.

"Don't worry," I said. "Let me take care of this."

And then, they were on us, pushing and shoving us up against the side of the van.

"Look I'm not surprised you found me," I said. "But leave the girl out of this. She's just a--"

"One yell, one shout, one scream," Weitzman said, "and I'm capping a round off in your knee."

"But I'm telling you. She has nothing to do with it!"

Always quick on the uptake, Weitzman backhanded me with his left hand. "Shut up! You expect me to believe your girlfriend doesn't know anything."

"She's not my girlfriend. I was just stopping to ask for directions."

"That's right!" she said.

Lynch had a firm grip on her arm just above the elbow, and a gun stuck in her ribs. "Both of you in the van."

They sat us side by side on the first bench seat. Rebecca closest to the door. Weitzman sat in the front passenger seat with the gun pointed at us as Lynch backed out and sped down the hill. Rebecca's breathing was heavy and rapid, and she was whispering. "Please, oh please no."

Weitzman jabbed the barrel of the gun toward me. "You should have paid the money. We front you a fucking kilo out of the kindness of our hearts, and what do you do? Skip town with our dope."

"I'll get you your money, I promise" I said. "I just need a little more time."

"This is the same bullshit you tried to pull last time. We find you shacked up with some little coke whore. Probably half the inventory is up her nose."

"That's not true!" Rebecca yelled. "He's not my boyfriend. I just met him. All I know is his name is Jake something. I can't even remember his last name."

Weitzman chuckled. "It doesn't matter if you do. It won't be his real name."

"I swear," she said, "look at my sweater. I'm pinned to someone else. Would I wear the pin of someone else if I was dating him?"

"She's got a point," Lynch said.

"It's true," I said. "I just met her. I saw her in that BMW, figured she was well-heeled, and thought I'd make a play. You can't blame a guy for trying."

Weitzman laughed. "Always the hustler."

"Look, I'll get you your damn money, but just let her go."

"Oh, so now you've got the money."

"Yeah, but you won't see a penny of it unless you let her go."

"How much do you have?"

"Fifteen K."

"Fifteen. You owe us at least twenty-five."

"But the price was fifteen."

"The vig goes up when you're on the lam. But you may be on to something. The girl looks like she's got some dough. How much do you got in your purse there, darling?"

"About $130," she said.

"Then who pays for that pretty red BMW."

There was a long pause. "Daddy."

Weitzman and Lynch started laughing and both mimicking her by saying "Daddy."

"I said let her *go*. She's got nothing to do with this!"

"Shut up, dog breath. And ask yourself, has anything you have said since you got in this van helped you?"

Weitzman rummaged through her purse retrieving Rebecca's cell phone. In a series of rapid beeps, Weitzman scrolled through her digital phone book. "Here it is. *Daddy*." Weitzman pushed send and waited. "Hello, Senator Face? I'm calling about your daughter, Rebecca...Yes, that's right...something bad has happened to her...No, no, she's okay for *now*, but she need's your help immediately. You see, we kidnapped her.... and unless you deliver us $100,000 at dawn, she's dead. It's just that simple. If you don't believe me, I'll let her tell you about it."

Weitzman held the phone to her ear. "Daddy," she said between fanatic breaths. "It's for real. I'm so sorry. They had guns. Help me! Please!"

Weitzman jerked the phone away, and I could hear Jason Face shouting.

"It's gonna cost you $100,000 if you want her back in as-is condition. I'll call you back with instructions. And remember – and I'm as serious as a heart attack about this- no cops, no feds or no daughter."

Weitzman looked down to turn off the mobile, and Rebecca Face saw her chance. She seized the handle of the van's sliding door and yanked the door back until it clicked open. Blacktop rolled by at an easy 40 mph, and Rebecca Face crouched looking like she was actually ready to jump.

Chapter 34

Weitzman grabbed a fist full of wool from the back of Rebecca Face's sweater and yanked for all he was worth, just as Lynch slammed on the brakes. The van skidded to a stop, and Rebecca came flying sideways, landing violently on top of me. A tangle of wool, brunette hair, elbows and feet searching for purchase.

The scent of her perfume lingered for a moment while we got disentangled, my brain frantically searched to place it. Then with a rush, the memory came on stronger than an Amway salesman meeting new neighbors.

"Maisy, what do you call this?"

She had just come out of the hotel shower wearing a towel tucked under her arms. Her wet hair was brushed away from her face. I was standing over the vanity sniffing a glass vial I'd taken from her makeup bag.

"What are you doing?"

"Trying to find out what makes you smell so good. Is this your perfume?"

She nodded. "Happy."

"Yeah, I'm glad I found it, but what's it called?"

"Happy."

"Oh, you mean that's its name."

"That's right, college boy." She took the bottle from me and expertly dabbed it behind her ears and along her neck. "It's Happy from Clinique."

"Is that from their Seven Dwarves Collection? Let me see," I said rummaging through the bottles. "Where's that Grumpy you use at end of the month?"

"Stop it."

"Oh, wait, here's a bottle of Sneezy. You wear that in the cold and flu season."

Maisy picked up a hand towel and swatted me with it. I did the rope-a-dope and then drew her toward me, began nuzzling her neck from the nape to that soft spot behind her left ear - inhaling perfume all along the way.

"I shouldn't tease," I said. "It really is the perfect name for what life is like with you. Promise me you'll wear this after we're married."

"I promise, but Jack, if you don't quit nibbling my ear, we'll be late for dinner. They're expecting us."

"Who cares?"

She raked through my hair with her fingers. "We could see if your new cologne is working."

"Really? What's it called?"

"Ridden Hard & Put Up Wet." With a laugh, she yanked open her towel, and with a wild naked leap, she tackled me on the bed. And I was so happy.

But, as I struggled to push 21 year-old Rebecca Face off me, I wasn't so pleased. She was scratching, screaming and kicking. Weitzman kicked back at her as he struggled to shut the van's door.

"Pull over into that alley," Weitzman said to Lynch, through clenched teeth "and get me the duct tape."

Weitzman was livid, and next thing I know I watched his boot connect with Rebecca's cheekbone.

"Don't ever do try anything like that again," Weitzman said.

I helped put Rebecca up on the bench seat and sat beside her. Her check was already turning purple and her lower lip was trembling like crazy. Whatever fight she had in her was gone.

"Here." Lynch held up a roll of duct tape.

When Weitzman leaned over to grab it, I drove my shoulder into his chest, pinning him into the back of the front passenger seat. "Run!" I shouted to Rebecca, who was already scrambling to open the side door.

"How dare you--"

I slugged him hard. The force of the blow caused his head to smack the back of the passenger window. "*Oooff.*"

"Oh, that had to hurt," I said. "Just like a kick in the face!"

Rebecca bolted out the door, and Lynch started to follow. With knuckles full of shirt collar, I wrenched him back and turned his ski mask side-ways, so he couldn't see. Then I jumped out into the alley and ran to catch up with Rebecca.

At the end of the alley, she started to turn left toward the main road, but I grabbed her hand and pulled her towards the right. "This way," I said. About half a block behind us we could hear Weitzman and Lynch pounding pavement. Weitzman was unleashing a list of expletives that would make Larry Flint blush.

We ran around the corner and down a hill between two buildings, and straight into the old World's Fair Site.

We dashed across the common area and over a bench behind the bushes.

"Over there," I said pointing to the Butcher Shop, a steak place at the edge of the park. "Get over there as fast as you can and call the police. I'm going to draw these guys out and head toward the Sunsphere."

"But they were going to kill us."

"You okay?"

She nodded gulping for air and pointed.

The van crept out of the alley, and Lynch and Weitzman headed at about 10 mph toward the Sunsphere, the most remote part of the park. It was the only place Weitzman thought I would flee.

"Ok, now go!"

"What about you?"

"I'll be fine, but run and don't stop until you get to the restaurant."

"Come with me. You saved my life."

"Sorry, I'm on parole. But if you want to do me a favor, don't mention me to the police. Or if you do, at least give a misleading description."

"Okay."

"And one more thing."

"Yes."

"I am truly sorry for what has happened to you tonight, but those guys in the van should never have been let out of prison. I heard them say your Daddy is a Senator. Maybe he can do something about keeping them locked up. Now, go!"

With a quick shove, she darted out of the bushes for the Butcher Shop. I watched her until she made it in the door, and then, I broke cover to find the boys.

I found them in the road by the Sunsphere turning around. Weitzman leaned out the window and pulled off his mask. Underneath his right eye was the beginning of a great shiner. "Where is she, Jack?"

"Oh, come on!" I said. "What do you need her for? We did what we came to do."

"I said where is she?"

"Inside that restaurant over there calling the police."

"What?"

Lynch got on the headset to Cawood, who was listening to scanners.

Weitzman's mouth had trouble forming words, but he finally sputtered, "You hit me, you asshole!"

"You kicked her."

"Damn it, Henley! We've been over this and over this. That was something I had to do. She's part of the machine."

"No, she's not. She's just a college kid that doesn't deserve your boot in her face."

Lynch curbed the van, and both got out, abandoning their stolen vehicle for police forensic teams that would be there within the next half hour. Cawood pulled up in the minivan, and Weitzman opened the door for Lynch.

"Get in," Weitzman said.

"Sorry, this is where it ends for me."

"Let's go, Jack" Lynch said.

"Not on your life." I started laughing. "I'm serious, I'm done with this shit. It ends for me here and now."

"Then what's so damn funny?" Cawood said.

"This is. All of this." I said spinning around with outstretched arms. "Just look at us. Here we are, four people who hate crime more than anyone, and look at what are we doing? It's pretty funny. And for this prosecutor, a bit too rich. I love and respect you guys, but you can count me out, starting now."

In the distance, police sirens wailed.

"You don't have anything to worry about. No matter what happens, I swear I will never mention a single one of you. But, like I said, this is it."

Weitzman didn't say a word, but his face was as easy to read as a Dick & Jane book. He wanted to kill me, but as sirens got louder, he slammed the mini-van's sliding door and slapped Cawood on the shoulder. And then they were gone.

I giggled as I walked through the shadows of the park towards UT's campus. I was going to grab a beer at the Copper Cellar and sort through some of this. I could either cry or laugh, and for the first time in a long time, laughing was easier. I had to be getting better.

Chapter 35

The next morning I ground through cases in Sessions Court, fighting back the image of Weitzman kicking Rebecca Face. People like me just didn't get involved in things like that, no matter how valid the cause. Not to civilians. Not to true innocents.

When I was eight, I watched my father put lobster into tepid water and slowly turn up the heat over the next half hour. He saw the puzzled look on my face and said, "Throw a lobster into boiling water, and they fight like mad. Now, I love to eat lobster, but I hate to see them suffer. So I put them in warm water and slowly turn it up. By the time it's boiling, they don't even know it. They are swimming around having a good time."

When Weitzman had kicked that girl, I realized I was swimming in water that was boiling. How had things gotten so crazy? While I was in love with how we started, I was not in love with who we had become. I had to leave or forever lose myself to the slow escalation of violence and the potent rationalizations that we were no different from common street thugs.

In court, we worked well past noon and recessed with only 25 minutes for lunch before the next docket began. I grabbed a turkey and mustard sandwich from the snack bar and barricaded myself in my office. Defense attorneys were already piled up in the lobby, wanting to talk with me about cases for that afternoon.

The intercom buzzed. "Jack, General Steelman from Rhea County on line eight."

"Afternoon, General."

"Jack, you won't believe it. I called in a few favors, and Phil Ottoman, the DA up in Kingsport, has agreed to let you speak with the grand jury regarding that aggravated assault on McElvy."

"That's great news."

"I called in a huge favor for you, so don't screw it up by not showing up. It's your only shot at beating an aggravated assault charge."

"I appreciate all you've done for me, Mike. Well done."

"I didn't do anything for you. I did it to protect my first degree murder case against Jimmy Ray McElvy. So do me a favor and don't be a wise-ass in there. Play it straight. Show lots of contrition. You can count on a lot of automatic sympathy because of your wife, so don't blow it by coming off like a know-it-all jerk."

"Fair enough. What time should I be there?"

"Friday morning at nine a.m. sharp. Don't be late."

I hung up the phone and had just taken a bite of my sandwich when Sharon buzzed in again.

"Jack, it's Ron Close with the TBI on line seven."

I about choked. "Could you please tell him I'm in court? I don't have time to speak with him right now."

"Sure thing."

That excuse might buy me 24 hours before I had to return the call. I lifted my sandwich halfway to my mouth when there was a knock on my office door.

"What!"

Harlan Griffin stuck his head in. "Bad time?"

I put my sandwich down. "Never a bad time for you, General. What's up?"

"I need a favor."

"Anything."

"I'm suppose to give a speech at the DARE graduation tonight at Big Ridge Elementary, but I've got to go to Nashville this afternoon for a meeting at the DA's Conference. Do you mind covering for me?"

"A speech?"

"You know, the usual stuff about how they are the cavalry coming to the rescue in the war on drugs and until there's no demand we can never win. You know the drill. You'd only have to talk for about five minutes, then hand out certificates and shake hands."

"What time?"

"Six o'clock."

I looked at my watch and grimaced. I really didn't want to do it, but in Harlan's own way, this was an olive branch. He was letting me know he still trusted me to represent the office in public.

"Sure thing. I'll be there with bells on."

"Thanks, Jack."

The afternoon docket moved a little more quickly than the morning's, and I wrapped it up in respectable time, in part due to my gift of the necessary bluntness required in hastily evaluating the cases – *Yes, ma'am, I understand you were cut. But are we talking about a paper cut or were you opened up on the table?...So how much crack had you smoked?... You realize if you don't testify he'll cut you again and maybe next time you won't live?*

When I returned to the office, Sharon waved me over.

"Oh, you're in luck. He just came in the door," she said into the phone.

"Who is it?"

"Ron Close. He's been calling all afternoon."

Nothing I could do now but take the call. I hurried to my office, grabbed the phone. "What's up, Ron?"

"I need your help. I got a lawyer down there from one of your banks tying me up in knots. He's refusing to honor one of our subpoenas for records. Do you think you could give the guy a call and straighten him out?"

"I'd be happy to try. What's the case?"

"Same one we talked about last week."

"No way."

"Yeah, get this. A couple kids fishing on the Mississippi River snagged the bumper of a Chrysler we'd been looking for. It was the same car used by the guys who beat the hell out of Bill Nichols."

"You don't say."

"But here's the weird part, the car was stolen from Judge Walter Simpson."

"I'm not sure I understand."

"I'm not sure I do either, but I do know that both men have ties to the justice system."

"Interesting. So what's the bank got to do with all this?"

"We found a pair of black leather boots in the car, which had the name of a specialty store in Nashville stamped inside. According to their records, a fellow from Chattanooga bought them there with a credit card."

I think Ron was waiting for me to respond, but I didn't say anything. I couldn't.

"Anyway, that's why I'm calling," he went on. "I'm trying to get the guy's credit card records from his bank, but I'm getting a run around you wouldn't believe."

"...Ah..." I cleared my throat trying to find my voice. "Who's the guy?"

"What?"

"The cardholder?"

"Thomas Lynch. Ever heard of him?"

Like a lawyer, Ron Close leveled a question at me to which he already knew the answer. And my lies of convenience would not pass muster with this man. I had to stick as close to the truth as I possibly could.

"You don't mean Dr. Tom Lynch, our county school superintendent?"

"Yeah, that's the one. I think that's why the bank is giving me such a hard time about it."

"You don't think he's involved in this conspiracy idea of yours, do you?"

"I have no idea. His card wasn't reported stolen, but he may have an explanation. But before I approach him, I want to see his credit card records. Maybe they'll show he was in Jackson or Memphis too."

"Well I don't envy you, Ron. Dr. Lynch has a tremendous reputation in this town. You better get your ducks in a row before you do anything, or he'll sue you and the TBI faster than you can say subpoena-for-your-bank-records."

"Well, I don't know if he is involved or not. Maybe he bought the boots for a son or daughter. They're kind of small. I just want a peek at his records to see how he shakes out. Can you get on the horn this afternoon and put a little pressure on the bank for me?"

"Can it wait until tomorrow? Harlan's out of town, and I've got to cover for him on something."

"No problem. I'm swamped as well. Jason Face's daughter was kidnapped last night, and I'm still in Knoxville. But I wanted to give you a call and get those records before this Lynch guy catches wind of it. From the way the bank's lawyers are screaming, he may already know. See what you can find out about it."

"Yeah, sure thing. I'll get on it first thing in the morning."

Chapter 36

Traffic on Hixson Pike was heavy as downtown workers escaped to the suburbs north of Chattanooga. I nosed my Saturn through the commuters, scanning my mirrors for tails. In bumper to bumper traffic, every car looked as though it was following me. I was sweating the last phone call, but while I honestly believed that Ron Close didn't suspect me *yet*, I realized that could change once he realized that Lynch and I were good friends.

From my suit coat draped on the passenger seat, I removed the burner phone that Cawood had set up under a bogus name. After my last freak-out encounter with Close, Weitzman had insisted we carry them, and I had not had time to return mine.

"Nothing makes us look guiltier than talking on pay phones," Weitzman had said. "And these are digital, so we should be okay."

I dialed Tom Lynch's phone, and after what felt like an eternity, I heard his voice: "Joe's Pool Hall. Joe speaking."

Oh, he was a funny man.

"Tell me this," I said trying hard to contain my anger. "Did you pay for our boots on your personal credit card?"

"What?"

"In Nashville, after we were at the state capitol, did you pay for our boots on your personal credit card?"

"Of course I did. I wasn't going to put a personal purchase on the group's card. That wouldn't be right."

"Damn it, Tom! Do you know what you've done? We don't have those cards to keep us from commingling funds. We have them to make us invisible when we stay at hotels."

"What are you so upset about?"

So I told him how a car pulled out of the muddy Mississippi River lead to bank accounts in Chattanooga.

"Shit!" was Lynch's first response. "Can he get my bank accounts?"

"Yes, he can. And he's asked me to help him do it."

"So I'm done for."

"Not necessarily. We need to generate an appropriate back story."

"Like what?"

"I don't know. Something like you bought the boots for a prostitute you spent a few hours with that afternoon."

"That'll never work."

"Why?"

"Because the clerks at the store may remember you."

"Good. Then maybe Close will think that guy was the prostitute."

"Oh, come on."

"No, it works perfectly. That gives you a reason for buying another pair of men's boots that aren't your size. You're a lonely widower with a high-profile job in Chattanooga, and for fun, you secretly drive to Nashville, and you purchased the boots for a young scamp of a cowboy who brought you much delight. You never met the young cowboy before, and you haven't seen him since. For all you know, he traded the boots for drugs."

"Where do I say I met him?"

"Line dancing."

There was a long pause as Tom tried to wrap his mind around that idea. "Why'd you leave the boots in the car, anyway?"

"In a million years, I never dreamed you'd pay for them with your own credit card. I thought they were clean."

"But Jack, I could never say I was with a prostitute."

"Would you rather tell him what you were doing on the Legislative Plaza with a .9 millimeter pistol?"

"No."

"Sounds to me like it's settled then."

"Do you think you can at least keep Close out of my bank records until we finalize a plan, maybe think of something better?"

"Maybe a day or two, but I can't even promise that. I'll do the best I can to stall it though."

"Thanks for the call, Jack," Lynch said. "After you bailed on us this weekend, I didn't know what to expect."

"Well, you fellows just stay low to the ground, all right? No more operations until this blows over."

"I'm sure Cawood and Weitzman will feel the same way."

Just my luck to go on a crime spree with a man too honest to bill two pairs of boots to the group. Lynch's Boy Scout sense of honor could sink us. Best case scenario, the prostitute story would appeal to Close's cynical cop nature, and he would move on to interviewing male prostitutes in Nashville. Worst case scenario, Close would take one look at Lynch's face and connect him to the police artist sketch in Nashville. Then, he'd would be sunk, and maybe the rest of us too.

PART V
The Horse Traitor

Chapter 37

I returned to my office after a busy morning in court to find Isaac Weitzman sitting in the lobby, staring at a worn copy of September's issue of the Tennessee Bar Association magazine.

I looked at him stonily, shaking my head as if to say *not here*. He took my cue and followed me without a word into the law library/conference room of the DA's Office. He waited until I shut all the doors, then said, "I'm sorry to bother you at work, Jack, but I needed to talk to you about Lynch."

"If you're talking about this thing with Ron Close, I'm afraid there's nothing else I can do."

"I know. That's why I'm here."

"I don't get it."

"The good news is that I think we found a way to get the TBI off his back. The bad news is that we'll need your help to make it work."

"No way. I'm not getting on that train again. I'd hate to see anything happen to Tom, but there's simply nothing I can do to help him at this point. Officially or unofficially."

Weitzman nodded. "Did you know that Barbara Briggs is speaking tonight at the Christmas dinner for the Women's Bar Association?"

"Here? In Chattanooga?"

"At the aquarium, actually. A last minute replacement for Justice Cox, whose gout is acting up."

"So what's your point?"

"My point is that this is the perfect opportunity to take advantage of Close's little conspiracy theory and get Tom the hell off his radar."

"I'm not following."

"It's simple really. All we have to do is to make the hit while Lynch sits in a public place in the company of a hundred honest people who can testify to seeing him. We owe it to him to generate a legitimate alibi."

I thought for moment and nodded hesitantly. "That could be the ticket to get the TBI off his case. But, you certainly don't need my help."

"Do you really think Cawood and I could pull this off alone? I've come up with a plan that I think is pretty foolproof plan, but we need one more person. I know you want out of this, and I do understand. But we need you to ride with us one more time, Jack, if only to get the heat off of all four of us."

I thought for a moment, desperate to talk myself out of it. "Does anyone get hurt?"

"Hurt? No. Scared shitless? Maybe."

I sat down in a chair at the head of the conference table and ran my hands through my hair. If it had been anyone but Barbara Briggs, I wouldn't even have asked the next question: "So what's your plan?"

Weitzman sat in the chair next to me and laid it out nice and simple. It all sounded pretty good except for one thing.

"You want my help? Fine. You can have it under one condition."

"What's that?"

"You cannot be the barrel man."

"Come on! Let's not forget that this woman freed my wife's killer."

"That's exactly why you can't be on point. You've got no objectivity. I don't want you making decisions on the street that are plugged into your emotions rather than your head. Among other things, I don't want you kicking another defenseless woman in the face. Or worse."

"But that only leaves Cawood," Weitzman said. "And there's plenty you don't know about him. I understand your point, but he may be a worse option than I am."

"What are you talking about?"

"Confidences that I promised not to reveal. Let's just say I'm a better choice for the job. Cawood's got too many issues right now."

"Isaac, we all have issues, or we wouldn't be going to group therapy together. Cawood may play a little rough at times. And I certainly don't want a repeat of what happened outside the Pyramid. But he's got less of an ax to grind with Briggs than you, and that means he's the better man for the job.

"Besides," I added, "I'll be right there if anything looks like it's getting out of hand."

"Come on, Jack. If anyone deserves a chance at her, it's me."

"It's too late in the game for any more mistakes, and I'm flat out not helping if you're directly involved with Briggs. And think about it. This should probably be your last job too."

"Last job?"

"Why not? Everything we've done is working, and after we create an alibi for Lynch, the best thing the three of you can do is to take a break for awhile. Let the TBI think they've seen a statistical ripple, a blip on the radar – something cooked up by politicians desperate to seem even more important."

"Fair enough," Weitzman said. "But leave Cawood to me, all right? I want to be the first one to talk to him about tonight."

Weitzman had a strange look on his face that I couldn't quite read.

"That's fine," I heard myself say.

And despite my curiosity about whatever issues Weitzman was talking about, it was fine. As far as I was concerned, the less I had to do with any of this, the better. But something about his tone bothered me.

"I just know him better, that's all," Weitzman said. "He needs to be prepped just right to understand the boundaries and rules of the game."

"No problem. I take it you're going to be the driver then?"

"I'll drive, if you don't mind being the bait."

"Bait, shill, setup man, whatever you want to call it."

Chapter 38

With my fork, I stirred cold wild rice around the chicken and feigned indifference as keynote speaker Justice Barbara Briggs was introduced. This was easy to do, given that the Women's Bar Association Christmas dinner had all the élan of a federal regulatory rule making hearing.

The banquet room of the Tennessee Aquarium was filled with red poinsettias. The audience was comprised mostly of lawyers and their coerced spouses, with attorneys from the big firms making the strongest showing. A Supreme Court Justice didn't come to town without the money lawyers standing in line to kiss her ass.

Applause rippled through the room as Briggs came to the podium at the head table. She was older than I expected, early to mid sixties, with high cheek bones, prominent chin, and sharp nose. Her hair was dyed brown and whipped up into poofy curls to hide its thinness. Her most striking feature were her eyes – big, shiny brown spheres that seemed to take in everything in the room. She was a former beauty who had faded to handsome underneath a liberal application of pancake makeup. No wonder she had gone so far in her career.

"I make the assertion, and I don't do it without some reservations," she said...

Typical lawyer. Can't say anything without qualifying it.

"...That the independence of the judiciary is at risk of being lost. I don't say that lightly or for shock value, but for the first time in years, I truly believe that in the criminal justice system the independence of judges is being challenged. Let's face it, criminal justice issues have become more of an opportunity to garner political points than to deal with deep-seated, significant social problems."

In my ear, I heard Weitzman's voice: *"We've located her car. She's parked close. A Cadillac Seville in the lot by TGI Fridays."*

Weitzman was driving a blue BMW 525i that I had stolen from a country club parking lot on the Georgia side of Lookout Mountain. Entry time: 24 seconds. Switched plates and bumper stickers gave the car some needed camouflage, and then we were in a go-mode with a fast exit vehicle.

"...causing an erosion of the judicial system. The rule of law is the cornerstone of justice in our country. The rule of law is the hallmark of every great democracy, and in fact, it's what guarantees a great democracy. And as a Supreme Court justice, I must be free to consider legal aspects of a case without being demeaned and castigated by popular political views and frustration with the problems of society. Yet, these attacks on the judiciary come with greater frequency. To attack an unpopular judge and unpopular rulings is easy. All it requires is the proclivity to be a bully."

"And her back left tire is flat. I'm getting ready to put the barrel man into play."

"As attorneys, you must strive to preserve the rule of law. Without it, we fall prey to special interest and the whim of public opinion. And this task falls exclusively to you. As you know, judicial ethics and traditions mandate that judges not respond to outside criticism and attacks."

"I'm in position." Cawood said in a tone of hushed excitement.

"Can you imagine how unseemly it would be for a Tennessee Supreme Court Justice to appear on the evening news and respond to criticism? Think how that could compromise the dignity of the court and pending litigation. Not to mention engendering an appearance that my decisions were not based *exclusively* on the facts and law as presented in court. And let's be honest, in a thirty-second sound bite, the public cannot even begin to understand all the things that go into courts' decisions. In fact, I don't think they can understand them in a newspaper article where the reporter's getting paid by the word."

She beamed at this last remark as if she was hitting the punch line on an uproarious inside joke.

But I wasn't laughing.

She reminded me of my smug law professors so caught up in the grandeur and theory of the law that they never saw how it affected real people.

Example: if a man robbed 10 banks and was on trial for the eleventh bank robbery, the jury would never know he had robbed a bank before. Why? Because by showing he robbed 10 banks, the jury learned he had the propensity for robbing banks – not that he actually robbed the eleventh bank. The theory was that the jury should make its decision on the facts – not on a person's propensity to commit crime.

That was the condescending intellectualism I couldn't stand about Briggs and those like her. They believed that a jury was not smart enough to handle the truth. That it was impossible for a jury to distinguish between propensity evidence and factual evidence and render a fair verdict.

And that was the type of hair-splitting that helped sap so much common sense out of the law. It was why juries hated lawyers. After all, what was the first thing the police did when solving a bank robbery? Check and see if the suspect had a record. Why was one group more entitled to the truth than another group?

To me, there are two basic ingredients that make our justice system work. First: the truth. Pure. Simple. Unadulterated. Second: the jury. Regular people with God-given common sense, smoothing out justice's rough edges with their collective life experiences and humanity.

And that was my beef with Barbara Briggs. She stood on that podium yammering that the public couldn't understand what she did, and that all of us lawyers were to rally to her defense every time she was criticized for making a boneheaded decision. She even had the gall to take a shot at special interest when she personally had spent half her waking hours since she put on a robe trying to dismantle the death penalty.

Well, tonight Barbara Briggs' true education would begin. She would learn that the first function of government was protection of its people, and I hoped she would be as skillful in pushing that agenda as all the others that had woven their way into her judicial decisions.

Our plan was simple. I was going to slow walk Barbara Briggs. With Rebecca Face, we had learned that nabbing our targets was easier if one of us slow walked them.

Note: *slow walking* is a technique of the more charming street thug. They put an arm around your shoulder, pretend to be your best friend and then slow walk you into the blade of a knife. Southern lawyers are fond of the term because that's such a common strategy among us. We smile at our opponents, extend extraordinary courtesy and then try to cut their throats in court.

When her speech ended, I headed up the stairs to the lobby. Last thing I needed was to get caught in a conversation with someone I knew, so with my cell phone glued to my ear, I pretended to be in a heated conversation.

As acquaintances passed by, I gave a curt nod or smile. I made out Harlan Griffin in the crush leaving the auditorium. If he saw me, he never showed it. He kept up an animated conversation with a senior partner from Milton & Martini as they made their way to the exit.

And then out came Barbara Briggs. A group of sycophants clumped around her genuflecting and tittering at her every comment.

"*Advise of status,*" Weitzman said.

With the cell phone to my ear, I could easily push the microphone button behind my ear and speak into my sleeve. "Speech finished. Target's doing a meet and greet in the lobby. How are things looking outside?"

Cawood answered: "*Better. The attendant in the parking lot has gone home, so there's no one in the booth.*"

Briggs had parked in a small lot in the corner of the Aquarium Plaza, and a Republic Parking booth was in the center. Attendants were always there during the day, but they usually left in the early evening after they had snagged parking money from the dinner crowd for TGI Fridays and Cheeburger Cheeburger.

"*A lot of suits headed to their cars,*" Cawood said. "*If she heads for her car, you'll have to try and stall her. There are way too many people out here.*"

Stall her? Obviously Bert Cawood had never tried to tell a judge anything before.

"*I agree,*" Weitzman said. "*Too many people at my location as well.*"

The lobby had thinned out quickly. Briggs waved goodbye to her admirers and walked towards the exit.

"Justice Briggs!" I called out loudly. Too loud. My nerves were showing. "Justice Briggs!"

She stopped by the door. "Yes?"

"How are you?" I said, taking her hand in mine and shaking it enthusiastically "My name's Jack Henley. I'm a lawyer here in town, and I just wanted to tell you what a big fan I am of your work. Big fan."

"Well, thank you, Mr. Henley, that's nice of you to say." She turned again as if to leave.

"Sorry, but I was hoping I could ask you one thing."

"Yes?" she said, turning back around.

"Umm, have you enjoyed your visit to Chattanooga?"

"Oh, yes, it's a beautiful city. I love what they've done with downtown."

"We've come a long way, haven't we?"

"Chattanooga has always been a unique place."

"I've always called it a city of extremes. Extreme geography. Extreme wealth. Extreme poverty. Extreme crime."

"Why the crime?"

"We're two hours from Knoxville, Nashville, Birmingham and Atlanta, and we're about as far as you can fly with an extra tank from a Latin American country. And don't forget, the climate's perfect to grow marijuana."

"So you're saying you're a hub—I hadn't realized that."

"Distribution's fairly entrenched, along with all the problems that go along with it."

"So I'm guessing you practice criminal law."

"I'm an assistant DA, actually."

"*Suits have thinned out,*" Cawood said in my ear. "*But you got one running back inside.*"

The lobby door flew open and a string-bean of a man wearing a gold and brown checked suit stumbled inside. Where his chin should have been was a token dimple, giving his head and neck a single eraser shape, and something about his big ears reminded me of two satellite dishes outside a mobile home. I recognized him as one of the sycophants from earlier.

"Justice Briggs," he said, "I was in the parking lot and noticed a blue car with judicial tags. Would that by any chance be yours?"

"Why, yes it is?"

"Bad news, I'm afraid. Looks like you've got a flat tire."

"Oh, no!" she said. "I need to get back to Nashville tonight. My daughter-in-law will be going into labor at any moment now."

String-bean beamed when he saw he had an opening. "I'd be happy to change the tire for you, ma'am."

I couldn't believe it. This guy was beating my time.

"Don't worry about it, fellow," I said. "I'm parked right next to her and have a portable hydraulic jack in my car. I'll get it."

Justice Briggs cocked her head to the side. "How do you know where I'm parked?"

Chapter 39

"How do I know where you're parked?" I said, with exaggerated slowness. "Just like this guy, I spotted your judicial tags on the way in."

"Of course," she said. "I forget that whenever I'm in that car I'm never anonymous."

"I would be more than happy to change your tire," String bean said again.

"Don't worry about it," I said. "I'm parked right there next to her, and if the spare's in bad shape we can use my cell phone to call a tow truck."

His eyes cut at me in irritation, and he focused back on Justice Briggs, waiting for a final ruling.

"Gentleman, you're both very kind. But this is precisely why I belong to Triple A."

"Fair enough," I said before the bean could jump back in. "At least allow me to walk you to your car and wait until they arrive. You've got to be careful this time of night downtown."

"Yes, that would be nice. Thank you."

"And I can stay, too." String bean said.

"Not necessary, but thank you for your offer." Her tone was crisp. She didn't want him to make any mistake about it – he was dismissed.

It didn't surprise me that this sent String-bean into a snit. I knew his type all to well. In law school, he was the guy who sat in the front row, his hand constantly in the air. "Gunners" we called them. They usually graduated to near obscurity as research grinders at big law firms.

I held the door open for Justice Briggs, and we walked out into the cold December air. Christmas lights bathed the Aquarium Plaza in a hazy yellow light, but the building itself still had its own quirky dark shadows, spawning from the unique architecture and design of the structure.

"He was rather intense," she said with a chuckle.

"Yes, he was."

"Funny how life is," she said. "I haven't had men argue over who changes my tire in a long time. You may find this hard to believe, but when I was younger, I used to turn a few heads."

"I don't find that hard to believe at all."

"You almost sound like you mean it."

"I do mean it."

"Well, that is certainly nice to hear. After I turned fifty-one – I think that was the same year I got half-glasses – it was like I became invisible. If my car got a flat, no one stopped to help me. If there was a long traffic line, men no longer let me cut in. And if I bent over to pick something up off the courtroom floor, lawyers kept talking. No one noticed me at all."

"They notice you now," I said.

"Yes, becoming a judge did restore some of the attention that came with youth. But frankly, it's not the same."

"Standby," Cawood said. *"I'm almost ready. See if you can steer her by the Visitors Center."*

"Don't you think you're being a little too hard on yourself?"

"That's what my son says, but let's face it, in the next twenty-four hours I am going to become a *grandmother*."

She shook her head ruefully and smiled. "I love the thought of it, but I could sure do without the title."

Briggs' insecurity surprised me, but I probably should have expected it. Life's most arrogant people are often overcompensating for Montana-sized insecurities.

We made our way over a small bridge and passed by the Visitors Center, which was a good choice on Cawood's part. No one could see us from Market Street, and the area was a blind spot for the Ranger's station. Another 25 yards and we would be around the corner of the building in the parking lot.

"So how long have you been in the DA's Office?"

"Seven years."

She smiled. "I read in the newspaper where one of your prosecutor's wife was murdered. How's that fellow doing?"

Without waiting for an answer, she said, "Someone told me that if he hadn't agreed to a lenient deal, the defendant would still be in jail and his wife would never have been murdered. Can you imagine plea bargaining out the man who kills your wife?"

"But that's not what happened!" I stopped and glared at her. Gone was any mask of civility. "I was the one who tried Jimmy Ray McElvy and who got him convicted. It was the Court that sentenced him to ten years. And you know as well as I do that that's an enhanced sentence in that range. It's not my fault if ten years equals sixteen months in the Department of Corrections."

"Oh my," she covered her mouth with her hand. "You're him."

"That's right."

"You're the one."

Weitzman's voice: *"Now! Now! Now!"*

Out of the corner of my eye, I caught a dark blur and turned in time to see Cawood whip a nine millimeter out of his trench coat pocket. His black ski mask was slightly askew from being pulled down too quickly, but his gun was pointed straight at Briggs.

"Give me your wallets and watches! Do it fast or I'll blow your fucking brains all over this parking lot!"

I took a step forward, shielding Barbara Briggs and trying to herd her behind me with my right arm. "We'll give you anything you want, mister. Just don't hurt us. *Please.*"

I feigned a slight tremor to my voice and acted as scared as I could. Cawood kept the gun on us. "Give it up. Now!"

I reached in my back pocket for my wallet. Behind me, I saw Briggs opening her purse.

"Hurry up, lady! Don't think I won't shoot an old woman."

With her left hand, Briggs shoved off me to the side and in her right hand she brought up a small revolver. "And don't think I won't shoot scum!"

Blam! Blam! Blam! She fired three shots right into the center of Cawood's chest. Cawood fell backward with flailing arms, his gun still clutched in his hand. The ground came fast, but he pointed the gun up and fired.

I kissed concrete, ducking a single gunshot high overhead.

Briggs, now with two hands on the gun and her legs spread wide, took aim at Cawood's head. She was obviously intending to finish what she started.

Cawood's eyes were wide with fear.

From my squatting position, I swung my leg around, roundhouse style, connected right behind her knees.

The gun went off twice as she fell backward. Glass rained down from a shattered street light above. *Thump!* Briggs' head smacked concrete. Hard. Too hard.

I scrambled over and yanked the gun out of her right hand. The barrel burned my fingers. Her eyes were open. Moans. Blood oozed out from the back of her head.

Cawood got to his feet. *Thank God for Kevlar.*

"That bitch!"

He straddled her before I knew what he was doing. His massive weight pinning her to the ground. A backhand. A hook. Then a series of trip hammer rights.

Briggs's limp body shook with each hit. Purple welts quickly appeared under her pancake makeup, which was splotched with blood from her nose and lips. Cawood's knuckles got smeared with her lipstick and blood. If he kept going, she'd be dead in no time.

I drove a shoulder into Cawood, knocking him off her and sending him rolling on the ground. He quickly scrambled to his feet. He tried to step around me, feint to the right and run to the left, but I grabbed his coat lapels and spun him away.

"Out of my way!"

"Leave her alone!"

Tire squeals made us both turn. A BMW popped up on the sidewalk. Weitzman stopped short almost clipping us with the fender and yelled through the window: "Get in! Get in!"

Then bullets started whizzing overhead, peppering the red brick wall of the Visitors Center. Chips of concrete and block rained on the ground.

"This is the police! Drop your weapons and put your hands up!"

In the circular driveway in front of the plaza, a paneled van unloaded a full tactical team: assault rifles, vests and night-vision goggles. Just in front of them was Ron Close crouched behind an unmarked car with a megaphone. They had been close, but not that close. We still had a few seconds until they were in position, but there was still no time to climb in the car.

My eyes found Weitzman's. "GO!"

"What?"

"GO! Don't wait for us!"

He understood and floored the car. The Beemer fish-tailed as he made a quick U-turn and headed straight for the TBI team. He was giving us time to escape.

"Come on!" I said to Cawood, turning to run.

"Fuck this! I ain't no track star."

Cawood lifted Barbara Briggs up by the collar. He wrapped an arm around her waist and carried her on his hip like a giant sack of feed.

"What are you doing? Let's get out of here!"

I glanced over my shoulder. The BMW popped off the curb and plowed right into the Crown Victoria Ron Close was crouching behind. Close ran for cover while the officers began firing. The BMW sped past the tactical van for the open road. White flames burst out of rifles. The back of the car punctured with a hundred bullet-shaped holes. You could have grated a hunk of cheese on the trunk. The engine roared, and Weitzman zoomed away at mach two.

The smell of gun powder hung heavy in the air, and as the officers scurried to train their guns on us. I ran after Cawood. He looked like a gorilla dragging a rag doll.

I caught up with him a few feet away from the aquarium entrance. "Let her go!"

"No!"

Again Close with the megaphone: "Last chance. Drop your weapons and put your hands up!"

Cawood answered with two shots above Close's head.

The police fired back. One bullet whizzed by my head, and I heard another ricochet off the concrete just next to my feet. I couldn't believe they were shooting at us. I hurried inside the aquarium door and dove behind an information counter.

I peeked around to see Cawood backing in the door. His gun was to Briggs' head, and he was using her as a shield.

"I'll kill her! Come one step closer, and I'll kill her!"

Close yelled to his men to hold their fire. "How do we know she's not already dead?"

"You don't. But if you don't back off, I'll put a bullet in her head, and then you won't have any doubt.

"Understand this! I got one Tennessee Supreme Court Justice, one Tennessee Aquarium and ten sticks of dynamite. If a cop puts so much as one toe in here, I'm blowing up the whole building! So back off!"

"What are your demands?"

"I'm demanding you back the fuck up and leave me alone. And if you don't think I'm serious, I'll feed this judge to the alligators!"

"Please! Don't hurt anyone!"

"Ten sticks of dynamite. Remember that!"

Then Cawood backed in shutting the door. I caught Justice Briggs as he dropped her to the floor.

"We need to find better cover and deal with the security monitors," he said.

"Security monitors? I don't think the guards will let us get to them. Did you think this building was empty? For Christ's sake, there's an entire catering company downstairs!"

"Then, we'll have to find a place we can make secure."

I pressed my fingers into Barbara Briggs neck and felt a slow but steady pulse. She was a mess. With a handkerchief, I tried to stop some of the bleeding on the back of her head.

"Good bluff on the dynamite," I said. "That might buy us time to get away."

"Who's bluffing?" Cawood ripped open his trench coat and pulled out two bundles of dynamite. He gave them each a kiss. "Daddy's little insurance policy."

Chapter 40

"Are you nuts?" I said, staring at the bundles of dynamite. "When did you start carrying dynamite?"

"I grabbed a few sticks from one of my construction sites after Isaac told me the TBI might be on to us. You never know when you may have to blast your way out of a situation. But listen...:" he paused and considered the space around us. "We need to find better cover. I'm nothing but sniper fodder down here."

Cawood bent down to pick up Briggs again.

"Don't touch her!"

"What?"

"I'll carry her up. You've done quite enough to this woman today. I don't want you anywhere near her."

"Fine. Just make sure you two stay between me and the window."

"I'll do it until you're in safely, but then we need to get this woman to a doctor."

I picked Briggs up in my arms and got onto the escalator. Cawood hunched down behind us as we rode up four stories to an empty black foyer outside the revolving door leading to the mountain cove.

The foyer was dark, with one large window overlooking the river. "They've closed the Market Street Bridge," Cawood said. "And it looks like they're shutting down Riverside Drive. They'll probably be cutting the power soon."

"Not here," I said. "Can't risk killing all the fish."

"At least something's going right," he said. "Let's go. It won't take long to get snipers on the Market Street Bridge, and that means a clean shot through this window. Come on."

The mist felt cold as we stepped into the mountain cove. Across the right triangle of the glass roof, a strip of neon light cast the forest in an odd glow. As I carried Barbara Briggs into the neon mist, I felt as though I was walking into a nightmare.

"I don't like this, Bert. I don't like this at all."

Cawood jogged ahead and climbed the steps to the deck above the otters' pool where Weitzman and I had sat only a few days ago. "Up here."

"Are you crazy? This woman needs a doctor."

"You don't get it, Henley. We're not running anymore. We're taking a stand, and I'm doing it on the highest ground this building has to offer."

"I'm begging you, Bert. Please let me get her to a hospital."

"Hold on, I need to take out the security cameras."

Cawood bounded down the stairs, then ran from camera to camera, taking each one out with a single shot from his pistol.

I hunched over Barbara Briggs, who had suddenly started gagging. Choking really. I rolled her to her side and patted her back. No good. I was afraid to try the Heimlich because I was pretty sure some of her ribs were broken.

Briggs' eyelids snapped open like broken widow shades. She grabbed at her neck. She started struggling to sit up, but I held her down, clamped my hand down on her chin, and stuck my fingers in her mouth. She might try to bite them off, but I had to get at whatever was obstructing her airway. At first my fingers only made her gag more, but then I felt something and brushed it away my index finger. I turned her head to the side.

"Now spit."

She complied and out came her two front teeth along with three or four others.

"Easy," I said wiping the blood off my finger on her dress. "Take some deep breaths."

Cawood came back up the stairs. "She okay?"

"Are you kidding? She almost choked to death on her own teeth. Let me get her help!"

"Damn it, Henley! Don't you get it? She's not leaving here. She's the whole point."

"Of what?"

"Of making it right."

"What?"

"Tonight we make a stand. I'm tired of pussyfooting around. Tonight, we even the score."

Cawood took a roll of duct tape out of his jacket pocket and began taping the sticks of dynamite to his bulletproof vest.

Briggs groaned. Her eyes fluttered and rolled back in her head. I eased her back to the floor, my rolled-up suit coat as a pillow. Her body was in so much pain it was shutting itself off from the conscious world.

"Bert, you're going to get us all killed."

Pulling off his ski mask, Cawood let loose with a fatalistic snort. "So what? It's not like it's the first time I got blood on my hands."

"What are you talking about? Your wife? Do you think you're responsible for Jeannie's death?"

Cawood didn't say anything. He tore another strip of duct tape with his teeth. "Oh, come on Bert. Kyle Burnette killed your wife. Not you. There was nothing you could do."

Still nothing. Cawood started twisting the fuses together on the dynamite. Then he stopped for a moment and his eyes, glassy and red, found mine. He had been drinking, and his words smelled of bourbon: "I was supposed to take Jeannie to an antique show in Atlanta. Going to those stupid shows was one of her favorite things to do, and she was desperate to find a new side-board for the kitchen. I promised her I'd be there, but when the time came to pick her up, I called and said that all hell had broken loose at the office, and that I'd be a few hours late."

"That's not your fault, Bert. We all have to work late sometimes."

He cut me off with sharp look. "But I was lying to her, Jack, so I could do what I had done every Friday afternoon for the past year, balling my twenty-year-old receptionist over at the Hampton Inn. Best I can figure from the time of death is that Kyle Burnette was cutting her throat about the time my receptionist was taking me hard up against the shower wall. If I had kept my promise, Jeannie wouldn't even have been at home."

"Bert, I'm so sorry."

"I know you've never farted sideways in your life, Henley, so you may have trouble understanding it. But the girl was just sex. Something I did, like playing golf. A reward for working hard. But I loved Jeannie. I loved her, and now she's dead because I decided to lay a little pipe with an office skirt."

I would have given anything to help assuage his guilt. But in the face of this astounding confession, I couldn't think of one thing to say that would be of any comfort.

"You know, it's funny," Cawood said. "I've been more faithful to her dead than alive. The night before the funeral, I climbed into the saddle one last time with my receptionist. I know, it was a real moment of despair, but I kept telling myself I needed comfort. And of course the girl was itching to seal a long-term deal. But in my head, each stroke into her became the slash of a knife across Jeannie's throat. And I went limper than a preacher's pecker – for the first time in my life mind you – and I ain't had sex since."

Cawood wrapped the fuses around the connectors of a small metal box with a large, round knob and taped the box onto the center of his chest between the bundles of dynamite.

"Jack, when you see me turn this switch. You've got exactly fifteen seconds to get the hell out of here."

"The woman who answers your phone at the office. Was that her?"

"No, that's someone new. Uglier than homemade sin. I paid my old receptionist fifty grand to leave and never, ever call me again."

"Weitzman know about this?"

"Some of it."

"But why this? Why now?"

"Today of all days, I've got to make amends... Today's the anniversary of her murder."

"I'm sorry, Bert. I didn't know."

"That's why I don't want to waste anymore time dicking around. Today of all days, I have got to do everything I can to make things right. And I promise you this, Jack, tonight I'm going to even the score. For Jeannie and Maisy and every other murder victim out there. Those bastards in Nashville let Kyle Burnette loose once, and I sure as hell don't want them setting anymore like him free. If this is what it takes to send that message, then so be it."

"But this isn't the way. No good can come from killing yourself."

"At least it'll stop the pain." His eyes filled with tears, and his lips twisted into a thin line of determination. He nodded his head, more to himself than me. "It'll stop the pain."

"I can stop the pain too, Bert, but first you've got to give me that dynamite."

"Not gonna happen. I'm sick and tired of these stupid games we've been playing. Everything we've ever wanted can come true after tonight, Jack. So high-tail it out of here and let me do this."

"I'm not leaving without Briggs."

"I'm serious, Jack. Now's the time to go if you don't want to leave in little pieces through the roof."

Maybe there was something in the wounded look in his eyes or that he was protesting too much or that I was such an arrogant lawyer I thought I could talk anybody out of anything, but at that moment, I was sure that if I had a good 15 minutes, I could talk Bert out of the room. But I didn't get that chance.

"You're so full of shit, killing yourself and this judge because you want to prevent more killings. It doesn't make any sense."

Plink! Plink! Plink!

Overhead panes of glass began breaking. I heard the whir of a helicopter overhead and watched in horror as a bullet caught Cawood in his right shoulder. Another round ripped into his left thigh. He sank to his knees and struggled to raise his pistol, but he couldn't make his right arm work.

I shielded Briggs with my body, glass falling on my back and head. I wanted to bolt for the emergency exit behind Cawood, but bullets chipped away at the floor in front of the door kicking concrete shards against the metal doors.

Cawood took a slug in the cheek. His glassy eyes filled with fear at the blood gushing down his face. Then three hundred pounds of All-American tackle keeled over. His eyes looked right at me but saw nothing. Then a spark. Trembling fingers found a large, round knob. A barrage of rifle fire cracked louder, but Cawood managed to somehow turn the switch before four shots from a sniper's rifle found their target. Brain tissue, blood and bone sprayed the air and across the floor.

My God, we only have 15 seconds!

I took to my feet, swinging Justice Briggs over my shoulder like a fireman. I bounded over a stone wall into shrubbery and made for the edge of the rock face above the otter pool. I swung Briggs down to her feet and held her like a marathon dance partner, all the while, eyeballing the water. If I jumped too far out, I'd be landing on some large stones at the edge of the water. Too far in and I'd hit on a rock ledge. I had to hit the pocket just right.

I jumped off the rock cliff straight into the mountain pool my arms tight around Justice Briggs. We sank deep below the surface, and I could make out the observation window, where tourists would press their faces against the window to see the otters playing under water.

I heard a deep, bassey rumble and felt the vibrations of the explosion.

In real life, explosions aren't the gigantic fireballs you see in the movies. Explosions are hot gases rapidly combusting and expanding, creating a high velocity shock wave that can destroy everything in its path.

And that's what we felt – the shock wave. But it came at us in a tidal wave of fresh water. Tons and tons of water propelling us forward and punching us right through the observation window. I can't begin to describe the pain of being fired through a four-inch thick window. Solid passing through solid. I don't think I could have survived if it hadn't happened so fast.

As the otter pool emptied into the observation room, I fought to hold onto Briggs. My fingers ached as they clutched a handful of dress, but she was sucked away before I could get hold of her. So I hooked my arm around a metal rail, and I held on for all I was worth.

My lungs screamed in protest, and I was beginning to think it would be easier to just let my lungs fill with water. But just as I was about to give in to the desperate impulse to inhale, I felt the flow being to slow.

Water still poured out of the tank, but I could inch my head above it. I looked at where the observation window had been and saw the moon shinning through a jagged hole of twisted steel girders. Gone was the trademark glass roof of the aquarium. The handcrafted trees had been blown to pieces. Everything was shredded. Everything.

Briggs. Where was Briggs?

I found her floating face down in a corner of the observation room. My legs sloshed through the water to her. A little mouth to mouth, and maybe she would be okay.

I flipped her over and screamed. Her left eye ball was hanging out of the socket, and the other eye was solid blood red except for a black pupil that stared straight at me. Fingers to her neck. No pulse. Her mouth hung open revealing her bloody gums.

I dropped Briggs back into the rippling water. She half sunk, and her left eye-ball, which was barely tethered to her face, floated an inch above her head.

My God, my God, what have I done?

Chapter 41

Several red pinpoints of light from laser gun sights danced around the otters' pool bed as snipers searched for a target from the chopper above. An entry team was already rappelling into what was left of the mountain cove.

It was time for me to go. I stepped into the ramps known as the canyon – a four story high black room lined by a series of inclined walkways that take visitors down through the display tanks. Water poured from an exhibit toward the top; brook trout and river chub sputtered and flapped as they fell over the balcony to a wading pool on the ground floor.

I worked my way down the walkways, jumping a rail to the next level and running like hell through a zigzag course. I vaulted the last rail into the wading pool and crawled on my hands and knees into the darkest corner under a ramp that led to the exit.

Shivering in the water, I lay flat with my head just above water. *Slow your breathing, Jack! Don't flip out now!* As the SWAT team worked its way up the canyon, I moved as quietly as I could through the water toward the exit. The ramp provided good cover, and when I got to the end, I climbed up over the rail and scurried out the canyon door to the lobby.

I had to take advantage of the confusion before it became a secured crime scene, but when I turned the corner by the gift shop, I found myself at the back of a line of waiters and waitresses who had been working the banquet. Police were herding us all toward the door, so in a lame attempt to look like a manager working in food services, I tucked my tie inside my shirt about midway down.

An officer holding the door open put a hand on my chest.

"You're all wet. And what's that blood on your face?"

I put a hand to my forehead and realized it was bleeding.

"A woman's hurt back there! Bad! She needs help now or she's going to die."

"Where?"

"Around the corner," I said pointing. "And up."

The officer nodded and ran in the direction of my wet footprints, talking into his radio. Another officer came up behind me and yelled, "Put your hands on top of your head!"

I spun around to find a stocky young officer in full SWAT gear pointing out the door and a line of waiters and waitresses leaving the building, all with their hands on top of their heads. They reminded me of the students who ran from Columbine High under police escort.

"Just do it until you're clear of the building," he said.

"Okay." I put my hands on my head and pulled my elbows forward, covering my face as I followed a large waiter wearing a red polyester waistcoat.

I ducked my head down as I ran and tried to get a feel for the situation outside the aquarium. Police were controlling the scene –but just barely. The CPD helicopter hovered above the smoking hole shining a bright spotlight down into the depths of the Mountain Cove. Three officers rappelled out of the helicopter into the building. Fire trucks, ambulances, police cruisers and television trucks were parked helter-skelter on the streets, and patrol men lined the area with yellow tape, holding back hundreds of onlookers and reporters.

We trotted a good block or more before police directed us into a make-shift corral they had set up in the tunnel by the movie theaters.

EMT's were already stationed in the area and gave each of us a once over as we walked by.

"Got a bleeder!" one said of them when she saw me.

They sat me on the bumper of an ambulance and draped a brown blanket over my shoulders. A short, stout blond haired EMT began cleaning the cuts on my face.

"So what happened to you in there?" she said. "You're may need a few stitches in your forehead."

"You wouldn't believe me if I told you."

"Try me."

"Explosion sent a stack of china into my face."

"Ouch." She did believe me.

"Do you have something for pain? I got a ringing in my ears like you wouldn't believe."

"Let me try some of this adhesive glue on your cuts. Once I tape it up, you may not need stitches at all. Then I'll get you something for pain."

My EMT seemed to be the only person on scene who actually knew what she was doing. Police officers were interviewing the other waiters and waitresses for information, but the process was far from methodical. *"Hey, did you see anything? Did you get a look at the guys? Did you see any bombs?" "No, no, no."*

I kept the blanket up around my face and let the EMT do her work. At the far end of the tunnel, next to the movie theaters, the police had set up a command center. A clump of Chattanooga police captains and lieutenants argued over a map on the trunk of an unmarked car. Harlan Griffin and Saul Jenkins stood nearby with other officers. Eventually, the police would roll in their mobile command center, a fully vetted RV with fancy communication equipment, decent coffee and all the Moon Pies you could eat.

And at this point, Close had to be on the outs. The Chattanooga Police weren't going to let an out-of-town TBI Agent run the show – especially when the jewel of Chattanooga's downtown renovation was at stake. The only thing he could expect from local law enforcement would be the blame.

"Let me get you something to help you feel better." The EMT stepped into the back of the ambulance and started going through the drawers looking at bottles.

Then I spotted Ron Close pushing his way through the crowd of waiters, waitresses and uniformed officers. He seemed to be looking for someone in particular. I had no idea if Ron had recognized me when I ran inside the aquarium with Cawood or not, but I wasn't about to stick around to find out.

After putting the blanket over my head like a shawl, I bolted for the yellow tape, ducked under, and pushed into the crowd.

"Hey!" The EMT yelled. "Come back here. I'm not done with you yet,"

I broke into a dead run and shuddered at the sound of a new voice from behind me. "Stop! Police!"

Ron Close.

No one had a stopwatch on me, but if this had been the Olympic time trials for sprinting, I'm sure I would have made the team.

I shot across Fourth Street by the Creative Discovery Museum, cutting into the driveway to the Clarion Hotel. Blue rollers zoomed by on Chestnut. I hit the stairs to the hotel's parking garage. First break of the night – a concrete block propped open the third floor door.

With both hands, I heaved the block through the driver's window of a brand new Toyota Camry. Car alarm blaring, I brought the brick down against the steering column knocking the turn arm loose. Sliding across safety glass, my fingers fumbled inside the jumble of wires in the column – prying, squeezing, twisting: and then the deafening roar of the air bag deploying.

The bag smacked my face into the headrest so hard I blacked out.

In the brief period of dreamy unconsciousness that followed, I saw myself giving a closing argument to a jury wearing only boxers with small yellow ducks: *"Ladies and gentleman of the jury, when the defendant ran from the convenience store he knew he was guilty. Under the law, flight shows consciousness of guilt. Why else does a grown man run into the night unless he knows he's guilty!"*

Judge Sacs – wearing a pink chiffon robe and rhinestone pearl-rimmed glasses – pounded the gavel again and again until it began to sound like...a blaring car alarm....

How long was I out? I'm not sure. But it took me a full two minutes to orient myself. Then the sound of tires squealing got me running again.

I jumped over the rail onto the steep bank behind the garage and scrambled up toward the YMCA on Sixth.

Keeping to the foliage, I watched traffic on Sixth and picked my time. Then, I dashed through the traffic.

Consciousness of guilt.

When I reached St. Paul's, Father Nick's car was still in back, and lights were on in his office. He taught a two-hour Disciples of Christ course every

Thursday, and by my watch it should have ended 10 minutes ago.

I locked the parish hall door behind me and tried calm by breathing. No other door of this downtown church would be unlocked. I was just starting to feel as though I wouldn't heave when Father Nick came around the corner.

"Hello? Is someone there?"

"Father Nick?"

"Yes, may I help you?"

My wet shirt was matted with patches of blood from Barbara Briggs and the brain spatter of Bert Cawood. My forehead was taped, but I could still feel a series of smaller cuts across my face. The airbag had given me a bloody nose, and a salty red film of blood clung to my upper lip and chin.

"Father Nick! It's me, Jack!"

"Jack? My Lord, what happened to you?"

Tears poured from my eyes, and my lower lip trembled. "I murdered a woman."

Father Nick's eyes took it all in, and when I saw the disappointment in them, I knew he believed me.

"I murdered a woman."

Chapter 42

With my back leaning against the wall, I slid to the floor and buried my head in my knees and cried. Father Nick sat next to me with an arm over my shoulder.

"Son, it will be all right."

"The fifth commandment, Father. Thou shalt not kill. I broke that one today."

"Calm down, son. It will be okay."

"No it won't. Nothing will ever be okay again."

"That's not true. It might seem that way at this moment, but God will make everything all right."

"Not this."

I leaned against the wall and wiped tears out of my eyes.

"Who was it?"

"Tennessee Supreme Court Justice Barbara Briggs."

If he was surprised, he didn't show it. "You've spoken of her," he said, "and if I recall, in less than flattering terms."

"It's a long story Father, but I promise you this, I never, ever meant for that lady to die."

"Of course you didn't."

"No one will believe that, but it's true."

Father Nick's eyes searched mine out. "I believe you."

"Things just got out of hand. One minute it's the perfect crime. The next it's total insanity. But I swear – I never meant for her to die."

"You will always have God's forgiveness."

"I don't know. Did God forgive Herod or Judas or Hitler?"

"Thinking an awful lot of our own sins, are we? You really believe that what you've done tonight puts you in a league with people like that?"

"So you're telling me there are shades of sin? Come on, your behavior is either right or wrong. At best, I was an accomplice in a felony murder, and at worst a co-conspirator in first degree murder. You can't tell me that I don't deserve to burn in hell alongside other killers."

"Jack, hell is filled with sinners forgiven for their sins."

"What?"

"Hell is filled with sinners forgiven for their sins."

"Then why are they there?"

"Because they couldn't forgive other people."

"Huh?"

"Welcome to Hell, Jack. Welcome to the Hell you created for yourself. Ask yourself how it feels and if you want to live in this place forever. Do you?"

"Please stop. I know I deserve it, but I can't take this right now."

"For Pete's sake, I'm not judging you, boy! I'm showing you a ladder to climb up. You want to be forgiven for killing someone? Well, you better start by forgiving Jimmy Ray McElvy."

"But my situation is different. I had better intentions than he ever did!"

"What's more human than Jimmy Ray McElvy trying to service the disease of addiction and provide for himself and his family? What makes what you did any better?"

I was about to tell him when the handle of the back door rattled. We both jumped at the noise.

Then a fist pounded from outside. "Open up! This is the police!" It was Ron Close's voice.

Father Nick gave me a what-do-we-do look. But before I could say anything, the telephone mounted on the wall by the doorway rang.

"Answer the phone," I said.

He picked up the receiver, and we both leaned over the ear piece. "Hello?"

"Father Humphreys..."

I recognized the voice immediately.

"...this is Harlan Griffin. Right now, I'm outside your back door with the police. We have reason to believe that Jack Henley is there. Have you seen him?"

"Yes, he's right here."

"Can you please unlock your back door and let us in?"

"I'm not so sure that's a good idea," Father Nick said.

I shook my head side to side. An emphatic no.

"Then let me put it this way, Father. The TBI and Chattanooga police are in pursuit of him for the crime of murder, and we are concerned for your safety. If you refuse to open the door, we'll have no choice but to break it down."

I stood and placed my hand over the receiver. "Tell him I've demanded sanctuary, and you've granted it."

"I don't think that exists anymore in the Episcopal Church."

"Please, just say it, tell him he'll have to get a warrant."

"Why not just cut out the shenanigans and turn yourself in? This isn't something you can run away from!"

"I need some time to sort through it. That's all I'm asking for. Please, Father, please. I don't want them to see me like this. All I want is sanctuary until they get a court order."

Father Nick reluctantly nodded.

"Father Humphreys, are you still there?"

"Listen, Harlan, here's the situation. I have Jack Henley right here. He's demanded sanctuary, and

I have temporarily granted it. So before you blow off the doors to the house of God, I'm going to need some kind of warrant or writ or something that says you can come in here and violate a man's sacred right to sanctuary."

He shrugged at me when he said the last part.

"Sanctuary! Oh come on Father, that's ridiculous. We're coming in."

"I think that would only make the situation worse. Give me some time. I'll walk Jack out the back door and hand him over to you."

"But I don't think there's such thing as sanctuary anymore."

"You better be right about that. You know United States District Court Judge Reese Anderson is on the vestry of this church. I'm going to call him as soon as I hang up with you."

Father Nick had dropped the name of one of the few men in Chattanooga more powerful than the District Attorney, so Harlan changed his tack: *"Father, you know I'm here to bring Jack in safely. As we speak, he's a danger to himself and other people, and every trigger-happy policeman in town knows it. If you can't get him to turn himself in, then I can't make any promises to you about Jack's safety."*

"I'll promise you this, Harlan. I'll do my best to walk him out that back door. Call me back in ten minutes."

Father Nick hung up. "Now what?"

"Oh, you were good, Father. When he calls back tell him again that I'm demanding sanctuary and insisting on a court order allowing him entry."

"You're not staying here, are you?"

I didn't answer him, but he could see the answer in my face.

"Please, Jack, stay here with me. Let me help you walk out of here. Let me..." His voice trailed off. He saw there was nothing he could say.

"Thank you for everything, Father."

He pulled me forward into a hug with a meaty hand behind my neck. "Go with God, my son."

"Hope to see you again sometime."

And then I was running.

Chapter 43

I rushed down the corridors behind the church sanctuary and into the building that housed a number of Sunday school classrooms. One room was filled with toddler-sized tables with a window that looked out into the driveway between St. Paul's and the St. Barnabas Nursing Home next door. If I could make it across the alley into the nursing home, there was at least a decent chance of getting away. And this was the only exit I could think of that provided a shot at cover.

I dragged a table next to the windowsill, and lying on my back, kicked the metal security screen bolted to the exterior brick. Three strong stomps and the bottom screws came out, so I scooted onto the ledge and dropped out underneath the screen onto the pavement.

My nose twitched in the December night to catch the smell of cops. My kicks had been loud, but how loud?

I was about to make a dash for the stairs that lead to St. Barnabas when I heard the unmistakable sound of a match striking. In the glow of the match's flare was the face of Saul Jenkins who was leaning against the wall of the nursing home.

"Do you think I'm stupid, Henley? Do you?"

"Damn it, Saul, you scared me to death!"

"Harlan might have bought that sanctuary crap, but not me. Like you're going to sit in there and lawyer your way out. No, I says to myself. You're going to slip out of there like a little rat – just like you did at the aquarium."

"Please, Saul," I said in a whisper, putting a finger to my lips. "Don't give me away. Just pretend you never saw me."

"I tried that once at McElvy's house, and it almost cost me my job. I'll be damned if I'll let you slip away again."

"But no one has to know you've seen me. Come on, Saul, after all these years, don't let our friendship end this way."

"Listen buddy, I ain't Rolfe. You ain't Liesl. And this ain't The Sound of fuckin' Music. You're under arrest."

The round fiery tip of the cigarette bobbed between his lips as he talked. His talk was tough, but he still leaned against the wall. He either figured that I wasn't going to put up a fight, or that kicking my candied-lawyer ass wouldn't be a problem. Knowing Saul, it was probably the latter.

"Saul, I promise that I'll turn myself in to you at noon tomorrow. You and only you."

"Yeah, right."

"I swear. I'm not going to set the precedent of having the TBI or the Chattanooga Police arrest a prosecutor. That privilege should be yours and yours alone."

"Taking a murderer off the streets is my privilege, Jack, and you're not a prosecutor anymore. So I don't care who arrests you."

"Saul, I've screwed up tonight as much as a human being can screw up. But I need some time to sort through this."

"Come on. Let's go. You'll have plenty of time to sort through whatever you want in jail."

"I'm not going anywhere. Hidden deep inside that church is six pounds of C-4 with a timer, and unless the right seven digit code is fed into the timer within one hour, that church will be nothing more than a pile of rubble."

Saul didn't say anything.

"I'll call you on your cell phone in thirty minutes with the code."

"Bullshit."

"That's what they thought at the aquarium. You already lost the best tourist attraction the city ever had. Do you want to be responsible for losing its oldest church as well?"

"You're so full of shit, Henley. Bomb, my ass."

The end of the cigarette burned bright as Saul sucked a final drag. And as I had seen a thousand times before, Saul cupped the cigarette in his hand between his thumb and index finger and tossed it to the asphalt by his left foot. Next would come the two-second toe grind, which Saul always watched.

Dipping his head down and watching the toe grind was as much a part of Saul Jenkins as the cigar wave was to Groucho Marx or the hand on the cheek deadpan was to Jack Benny.

Saul never saw it coming. An adrenaline-charged tackle, my shoulder driving into his side, pavement meeting us hard. A surprised Saul Jenkins: "*Hey!*" I still had the advantage and ripped his nine millimeter out of the holster and leapt backwards.

Saul rolled to his feet and kept coming at me, but I clicked the safety off.

He froze at the sound but tried to keep it casual. "Aww, knock it off, Jack. Give me my gun back, would you?"

"You've got to believe me when I tell you I didn't mean for any of this to happen. I never ever meant for Barbara Briggs to get killed."

"Yeah, whatever."

"I mean it! I never meant for her to get killed! You've got to believe me."

"I do. I do. Just put down the gun, and we can talk about it."

I started crying. "Everything I did, I did for Maisy."

My tears must have unnerved him. His voice shaky and dry, he said, "I know you did."

"Over by the church. Now!" I said. I remembered what Bert Cawood had told me about Muhammad

Ali and Sonny Liston. And I realized he was right. On a regular day, I was no more a threat to Jenkins than a moth to a windshield, but with Barbara Briggs being carried out of the aquarium in a body bag and me standing teary-eyed in front of him with a gun, he had to think I was nuts. Of course, he wouldn't be far off.

I used his handcuffs to secure his left wrist to the wire mesh cover on one of the windows of St. Paul's. I slipped his key and badge in my pocket.

"And don't think I forgot this." My fingers yanked up his pants leg and took out a slim .380 automatic from his leg holster.

"He's over here! He's over here!" Saul yelled.

"What are you doing?"

"I'm more scared of Harlan Griffin than guns."

"Thanks for nothing."

"You're holding the guns, Jack. Use them if you need to." Then, he leaned his head back and roared. *"Help! He's over here!"*

"Aww, hell!" I tossed his .380 down the driveway and beat it up the steps into St. Barnabas' lobby, locking the door behind me.

I must have been a sight. The woman at the information desk, maybe 75 years old with white hair and a cardigan hooked together with a chain on top, looked as if her teeth were about to drop out.

"Police." I said holding up Jenkins' badge in my hand.

"I heard shouting."

"That was next door, so we're asking you to lock all your doors. The shooter is disguised as a police officer. So whatever you do, don't let anyone in who's wearing a blue uniform. Now, I'm going to go check out your main parking area."

"Oh my goodness!"

"You've got to move quick, lady. This place is about to become Ft. Apache, St. Barnabas."

And then I was out the far lobby door into the parking lot. All the cars were at least ten years old, but I found a Pontiac Bonneville that looked roadworthy enough and shattered the window with the butt of the gun. The turn signal arm snapped like a twig, and before I fumbled for the slide, I leaned all the way over in case I triggered the air bag. Not a problem: car started on the first try, gas tank on full, entry time 11 seconds.

I jammed the pedal to the floor and sped up Sixth listening to the mournful wail of sirens.

Chapter 44

It's amazing how fast your mind works when you're fleeing from the police. As I sped through downtown Chattanooga, my mind could have crunched eight digit numbers, balanced the federal budget, or computed trajectories for intercontinental ballistic missiles.

Turbocharged thoughts burned up the synapses of my brain playing out scenario after scenario to their nth degree. Yet, I still couldn't figure out where to go.

Weitzman's? No way. He was probably shoring up an alibi at the hospital.

Lynch's? Not on my life. He was already targeted, and he didn't need me screwing up his perfect alibi.

Mexico? Belize? Brazil? Any of those might have worked with some planning, but I had no way to get any clothes, money or passport. Not that I'd use my real passport.

I wasn't even sure I could get to the airport, and if I did, the place was likely to be crawling with police.

Smokey Mountains? If the FBI couldn't find that abortion clinic bomber, I knew the TBI wouldn't find me. I could survive in a pup tent with canned beans for weeks. But my tent and camping equipment were at home, and I didn't have enough cash to get what I needed at Walmart.

Couldn't go home. Couldn't go to the office. Couldn't use my credit cards.

Georgia? Most criminals made a beeline for the state border, but I was an idiot if I didn't believe every sheriff's deputy in Catoosa, Walker and Dade counties would be waiting for me.

Think!

I circled around the West Side projects and turned onto South Broad. *Where to go? Where to go? Where to go?*

And then I knew in a blinding flash: Maisy! I wanted to be close to Maisy. But *where?*

Her grave was only ten minutes away on the other side of the river, so I pointed the car in that direction.

Big mistake. That was the first place Saul Jenkins would go. Might even say it was a *grave* mistake.

I slapped myself. I was getting punchy. Busted out in the open, no longer a covert operative for justice, I was cracking wise, trying to hold back the hysterical panic. Just get to Maisy. Just hold on.

When I was a new prosecutor, I always wanted defendants to think I was the Prince of Darkness, the baddest mother to wield the criminal code. How all those defendants would love it if they could have seen me now. Their howling animal-laughs echoed in my head: Assistant District Attorney General Jack "No Mercy" Henley on the lam and running scared.

And then I knew where I could be close to Maisy.

Ten minutes later, I parked the Bonneville outside the gate to the sculpture garden on the Bluff near Hunter Arts Museum.

A strong wind blew off the river. Peeking through a hole in the patchwork of winter clouds was a faint, curved sliver of moon.

Inside the garden, the sculptures looked like creepy black silhouettes, yet I still found solace there. I sat on the bench where Maisy and I had first kissed. Yes, she was in this place.

Think!

My palms pounded my temples to jumpstart the process. What had started as fear-based, adrenaline-enhanced lucidity had accelerated into a self-consuming forest fire.

I inhaled a deep breath and tried to exhale one smooth stream of air, but in the cold, all I could manage was spastic puffs of fog.

Even in death, Maisy would know what I had done. She would know.

And sitting on that bench in the garden of weird art, I knew what I had to do. All along, I think I knew what she wanted me to do. Maisy loved me for me, and she wanted me to keep being me.

I steeled myself in the garden, taking strength from her presence. Climbing out wasn't going to be easy.

Chapter 45

With a snap of my wrist, I ripped down the Budweiser beach towel that had been tacked above the window of the small bedroom. The sound of ripped terry cloth broke the silence, and I pointed my gun in the direction I had heard the breathing. A garish yellow light from a street pole streamed through the dirt-streaked glass.

Jimmy Ray McElvy lay face down sleeping in faded blue jeans and a wrestling T-shirt with Austin 3:16 emblazoned across the back. On his left leg was the black plastic box of the house arrest program.

His bed was a mattress on the floor with no sheets and sticky, half-congealed vomit clinging to the side. Judging from the smell, it was only a couple of hours old. On the floor next to the bed was a dog-eared copy of a naked biker chick magazine, a jar lid overflowing with cigarette butts, and five empty Robitussin bottles.

Looked like he was "Robo-ing." Robitussin contains Dextromethorphan which in regular doses acts as a cough suppressant, but in huge doses acts as a hallucinogen similar to mushrooms, PCP or LSD. A good choice to beat the house arrest program's drug screen.

I knocked some dirty clothes off a folding chair and took a seat to the side of McElvy's bed. My right hand stayed on Saul Jenkins' .9 millimeter as I nudged McElvy with my foot.

"Jimmy Ray, wake up."

He moaned, and a hand clutched his stomach.

"I said wake up!"

This time he bolted upright. His eyes scanned around the room trying to get a fix on the voice. Raw red lines ran across his face where I had beat him with the iron. The scars looked like fat worms grafted from his forehead to his chin. He screamed when he saw me holding the gun.

"Shhhh!" I held the gun barrel to my mouth as though it was my finger. "We don't want to wake Momma."

"Oh fuck! How did you get in here?"

"The back door."

"What time is it?"

"Two a.m."

I kept focused on his eyes. How messed up was he?

"Shit! I can't believe this! Why can't you leave me alone?"

McElvy grabbed his stomach and leaned over the mattress, retching up a black syrup-like bile. I leaned down and picked up one of the Robitussin bottles.

"I'm so sick." He wiped his chin with the back of his hand.

"That's because you used Robitussin DM instead

of Maximum Strength."

"Huh?"

"Robitussin DM has an expectorant in it."

"So?"

"You've overdosed on expectorant. That's what's turning your stomach inside out. Next time just get the Maximum Strength."

Sitting cross-legged, he sucked in air, and his eyes beaded in on me. "Are you for real?"

Throwing up had cleared his mind, and for the moment, he seemed lucid. But to what degree, I had no idea.

"Oh, I'm for real all right."

"If you're going to kill me, do it now because I feel like shit. I wish you had just done it in my sleep. I never woulda known how bad I felt."

"I'm not going to kill you. I came to apologize."

"Huh?"

"I came to apologize. I had no business attacking you the way I did. I can't imagine what it was like to have been in a coma or what it's like to have your face scarred for life. So I came to apologize and give you this."

"What is it?"

I held up a check made out to him in the amount of $50,000.

"What the-- ?" He rubbed the check between his fingers it a few times, as if to make sure it was real. "Are you serious?"

"As a heart attack. That should cover your medical bills, pain and suffering. Your attorney will tell you not to take it. He'll say that cashing this check will act as a settlement for our lawsuit. But this isn't a settlement for anything, it's just a gift. See?"

I leaned in and pointed to the memo line on the check. He flinched, probably thinking I would hit him again as I had in his house.

"See I wrote in 'Gift.' I don't want Wasserman to get one penny of this. Use it to pay off your Momma's house, go get yourself a decent defense lawyer or just go get some better Robitussin. I don't care. It doesn't matter. But I'm asking you for one thing."

"Here it comes."

"Dismiss your lawsuit against everyone else but me. Harlan Griffin had nothing to do with what happened. I'm the guy who clobbered you with the iron. Me and me alone. Sue me all you want. I won't be fighting you on it, but leave Harlan Griffin and everyone else alone."

"I didn't just fall off the turnip truck, mister. My injuries are worth a lot more than $50,000."

"Maybe. But that's all I'm paying you, and after tonight, it's all I'm going to have. Cash it, don't cash it. I don't care. It's a gift." I opened a pocket knife I found lying on the floor next to McElvy's wallet and stuck the check high on the wall with the knife. "It'll be here in the morning when you wake up."

"I don't get it. Why are you giving me money?"

"Because what I did was wrong."

"You're so fucked up, you know that?"

"Probably." I turned the chair around and sat on it backwards facing McElvy. "But that brings us to the most important reason for my visit. I wanted to tell you that I forgive you for killing my wife."

"Say what?"

"I forgive you for killing my wife."

McElvy stared at me, weighing my words. Then, he shook his head. "I don't think you do."

"You may be right, but right now it's important for me to act like I do."

"You're so full of shit! *Forgiving me?* Yeah, right! You know, I'd kill that bitch again if I had a chance. If it wasn't for her, no one would have gotten hurt, and I'd have gotten away clean. Your mistake was datin' a bleeder."

I jumped to my feet and kicked away the chair that stood between us, raising the gun with both hands. I wanted to cram it down his throat and squeeze the trigger. He might have figured me weak for giving him the check, but he had no idea how I would delight in seeing the back of his skull hit the far wall and slide down. No one could say the world wouldn't be a better place.

Then, the image of Barbara Briggs' eyeball hanging out of the socket flashed in my mind, and I lowered the pistol. McElvy was McElvy. Pathetic and sick and tortured. And what had scrambled his brains first was a real chicken and egg debate: chromosomes too closely related joining together to form a dark, bipolar version of Forest Gump or years of abusing airplane glue, marijuana and cough syrup. Pitiful really. His life for mine? Not worth the trade.

"Why are you looking at me like you jest ate a turd?" he staggered to his feet and balled up his fists. "What did you think I'd say? Did you think if you forgive me we'd hug and go to AA together. Fuck you! I'm gonna spend the rest of my life in prison because of that bitch! What did you expect, asshole?"

McElvy's face was contorted in fury. The scars on his face burned an angry red.

"I just thought that this would make me feel better," I said.

"You dumb shit. How dare you come into my home and look down on me. I ought to--"

And then he was vomiting again, holding himself up against the wall with one hand and aiming his head for the floor to keep the bile off him.

Pathetic. Sick. Tortured.

I left him there. That was a good way for me to remember him. Whether he would remember me in the morning was anyone's guess. He'd probably dismiss it as a Robitussin-induced hallucination until he saw the check on the wall. I didn't care if he remembered me or not; all that was important was that I remember.

On the way out, I pocketed his car keys off the kitchen table and slid out the back door. I was still a wanted man, and I only had a few hours left.

Chapter 46

After knocking for 10 minutes, I heard Chenester Jones unlock three dead-bolts on her front door. Her arthritis made her move slowly, and the creases from sleep showed in her face.

"It's three in the morning!" she said from behind the chain.

"I didn't have anywhere else to go."

Her eyes raked over me from head to toe. "Don't be bringing no trouble into my house."

"I promise. I'll be gone before the sun rises."

She shook her head and took the chain off the door. "You can use the shower at the top of the stairs."

After I dried off, I found clothes laid out on the counter. The white button-down shirt was loose in the shoulders, and the slacks baggy in the seat. But I was more grateful for those clothes than anything on sale at Brooks Brothers.

Back downstairs, Mrs. Jones cooked fried eggs turned over-easy, real grits, and homemade biscuits with honey. I didn't think I would have an appetite, but I ate everything she set in front of me.

"How bad is this trouble you're in?"

"As bad as it comes."

"I hope frying you these eggs don't make me an accessory to anything."

"No, ma'am, all of this is my fault and mine alone. No one will ever know I was here."

"Jesus will."

I didn't know what to say to that, so I took another swig of coffee. "Thank you for everything. The clothes, the food, but if I could impose for just one more thing I'd appreciate it."

Five minutes later, I was sitting in front of their brand new computer bought with the "donation money from the office."

An hour later, I covered a sleeping Mrs. Jones with an afghan and laid an envelope in her lap. Inside was my power of attorney, a letter signing over my townhouse to her, and a check for $500,000.

*

At dawn, the first rays of light did little to take the chill out of the downtown air. A heavy fog hung on the wet streets of Chattanooga – part of the wet gray that descends on the city in winter and stays until buds start appearing on the Bradford Pears. My body ached from fatigue and no sleep, and my muscles drew a soreness from the cold I never thought imaginable.

The courthouse appeared in the mist like an imperial castle from a science fiction movie. Unlike so many government steel and glass boxes, this building sat on the side of a hill with unbreachable walls designed with deep indentations, lines and modular squares.

A photograph of me stared out from a newspaper box just outside the Cherry Street entrance. A quick scan of the front page told me that Crimestoppers was paying $1,000 for any information leading to my arrest. I was to be considered armed and dangerous and reported to be emotionally unstable since Maisy's death.

No argument there.

At 6:30 a.m., I tugged the fedora, also borrowed from Mrs. Jones, over my eyes and slipped into the courthouse.

Behind a wraparound desk, an elderly security guard watched the morning news on a small television. He was too engrossed in the details of last night's explosion to even give me a once over. He must have thought I was part of an early morning cleaning crew.

Less than thirty seconds later, I set up camp in the cleanest stall of the second floor men's room.

By 8:45, a steady stream of voices filled the hallway with the morning rhythm of the courthouse: attorneys seeing if clients brought money, red-eyed police officers just off third shift grumbling about being in court, bondsman making sure defendants showed up, clerks toting armloads of warrants, prosecutors listening to victims complain, reporters trolling for anything to ease their boredom, and speeders looking to pay off tickets.

With two fingers, I pulled the hat low and stepped out into the gauntlet. A person's walk is as distinctive as his talk, and I had worked in the courthouse too long for someone not to recognize my gait. So I marched with a limp. Nothing big. Just a slight pull of the left leg to change my natural body motion. Nothing to call attention to myself.

With a billowing white handkerchief, I wiped what I hoped appeared as a chronic runny nose and strode past the doorways to Sessions Court and around the corner the Grand Jury room.

Walking inside the Grand Jury foyer was the equivalent to walking into a precinct roll call. Police officers sat in chairs along the wall waiting to testify, and at a desk in the foyer sat CPD Captain Jane Wayne Atkinson, the police liaison to the DA's office. She was the gatekeeper of who made it inside the grand jury room, and I doubted if she intended to let a wanted criminal, considered armed and dangerous, anywhere near the jurors.

Outside the door, I kneeled over and pretended to tie my shoe. I glanced up and saw a lawyer I didn't recognize heading for the door. Wild brown hair stuck out from the sides of his head, which was reminiscent of Larry from the Three Stooges. But this guy was no Stooge - round gold framed glasses, a conservative green tie and a hard finished brown suit with just a hint of pinstripe. Any hint of flash toned down to up-right respectability. This had to be my special prosecutor.

"Phil Ottoman?" I said, standing up and sticking out my hand.

"Why, yes?" he said shaking my hand.

"I'm Jack Henley."

Ottoman's mouth fell to China, and he blinked hard.

"Listen, I'm here because I am under subpoena, and all I'm asking is that you let me honor that subpoena. I know you're aware of the law that says out-of-state witnesses are free from service of process and arrest when they testify before the grand jury. I am asking you for that same protection until I'm finished testifying, and then I swear on the grave of my wife that I will turn myself in."

"You mean you want to testify?"

"I have to testify."

Ottoman's head darted from side to side to see if anyone else noticed who he was talking to. "But there's an outstanding warrant for your arrest."

"I know. But you don't let the police barge into a trial and snatch a material witness off the stand because there's an outstanding warrant. I'm asking you to protect the integrity of the grand jury process by allowing me to testify."

"Mr. Henley, you need to turn yourself in, and then I promise, next week some time, you can testify. From what I understand, this agg-assault is the least of your problems."

"You promised I could testify today."

"I did that out of professional courtesy, and if you think that extends to people with outstanding murder charges you're sorely mistaken."

"General Ottoman, that's what I'm here to testify about."

His eyes – which were the color of unpolished silver – scrutinized every nuance of my face. "You'll testify about the murder?"

"Especially that. You know you'll be appointed on it. There's no way the local office can prosecute me."

Ottoman recognized what I was offering him – a career case. The one they'd write about in his obituary. Every judge and lawyer in the state would know his name. Any prosecutor with a pulse would want a shot at trying the man involved in the death of a state Supreme Court justice.

"Come with me," he said grabbing my arm. "We're first up."

Ottoman pulled me into the Grand Jury foyer and shut the door behind us. Cpt. Jane Wayne Atkinson, a slender woman in her early fifties, leaned against her desk with the phone cradled between her shoulder and chin. She was the first to recognize me. The receiver slipped down and clattered on the metal desktop. Then the other officers recognized me and rose to their feet.

"Captain, I need this witness searched before he testifies," Ottoman said.

Jane Wayne Atkinson rocked back on her heels. "General, do you know who that is?"

"I know exactly who he is. That's why I want him searched."

I took off the trench coat and hat and threw them on the floor and assumed the position on the Captain's desk. "Come on, Jane Wayne. We don't have all day."

"This is crazy." She nodded to one of the patrolmen nearby. He ran his hands down my legs, up around my buttocks and under my arms.

Jane Wayne picked up my briefcase. "Is this going inside?"

"Yes, and you'll find an unloaded .9 millimeter inside with the magazine in the outside zipper pocket."

Ottoman and Cpt. Atkinson visibly tensed.

"Oh, please," I said. "The gun belongs to Saul Jenkins. I brought it in to give back to him."

She lifted the gun out by the trigger lock. The slide was already back in the locked position to show anyone who found it that the weapon was clear. "Somebody get me a plastic bag. Jack Henley, you're under arrest for–"

"Not so fast," said Ottoman. "He is under subpoena to this grand jury, and my witness until I release him."

"Jane, I'm sorry. If you could call Saul Jenkins and ask him to come down. I sort of promised him the honor."

Ottoman gave me a shove in the back. "Knock it off and get inside. Captain, I want an officer posted outside this door. No one is allowed inside until the grand jury is adjourned on this case. And I mean no one. I will prosecute anyone who violates the secrecy of grand jury proceedings by coming in this door."

Ottoman surveyed the room to see that each officer understood. They stood in frozen frustration as this out-of-town prosecutor hijacked their grand jury and the most wanted man in town.

"I'll watch the door," Atkins said, "because when he comes out, I'm going to be the first person to slap the cuffs on him."

Ottoman was getting a taste of what Atkins had been like on the street twenty years earlier – tough, unyielding and with a low tolerance for bullshit.

"Fair enough," he said.

As Ottoman closed the door behind us, I heard angry confusion break out among the officers, and above the verbal hubbub, Atkinson's voice shouting orders.

Chapter 47

"This is the State of Tennessee versus Jack Henley on the charge of aggravated assault," Phil Ottoman said, sitting at the grand jury's u-shaped table surrounded by 12 impartial civilians. "As you may recall, we heard testimony yesterday in this matter from attorney Ned Wasserman and his client Jimmy Ray McElvy. Today, we arranged for Mr. Henley to testify. State your name for the grand jury?"

"Jack Henley."

"And your occupation?"

"I'm a lawyer. Wait that's not true. I'm a recovering lawyer."

"Mr. Henley, do you have information you would like to share with the grand jury regarding the alleged aggravated assault on Jimmy Ray McElvy?"

"Yes, I do."

"Please tell them about that incident?"

"There's not much to tell that they don't already know except I did it. I snuck into Mr. McElvy's home and attacked him."

"But isn't it true he killed your wife?" Ottoman said.

"That's true, about five hours before this incident occurred. At the time of my attack, I was exasperated that the police were unable to get him into custody.

The whole stand-off seemed ridiculous. But, I was also enraged he killed my wife, and I went too far. I would also ask the grand jury to indict me for whatever they believe is appropriate –not just in this matter but also in the events surrounding the death of Barbra Briggs."

Silence. Not a peep. All of them stared at me rubber-necking the human car wreck of my life.

"You want us to charge you with murder?"

"I want you to charge me with what you believe is appropriate under the law. I know you were not prepared to hear that about these events today, so I went ahead and drew up an affidavit of the facts." From my briefcase, I produced a stack of papers. "I'm sure General Ottoman would like to review these. For later proceedings, I've also included a waiver of defense counsel and a waiver of jury trial.

"Please know this. I am guilty of the aggravated robbery of Barbra Briggs, and I realize that while you may believe that legally I'm guilty of her death based on the principles of felony murder, I promise you I never intended for that woman to get hurt. In fact, I was there to guarantee that she wouldn't be, but of course, I didn't know Bert Cawood would wig out."

"Tell us what happened," Ottoman said.

So I did. I told them how Cawood and I tried to rob Barbara Briggs, and how Cawood kept escalating events until Justice Briggs was dead and the top of the Aquarium was blown off. How I stole cars. How I assaulted Saul Jenkins. How I tried to kill Jimmy

Ray McElvy the night Maisy died. Words spilled out of me for almost an hour. And I told them everything.

Almost.

And Ottoman could sense it. "Did you and Bert Cawood rob any other judges?"

"Everything I've told you today encompasses all of the crimes I've committed in Hamilton County. Anything else is outside this grand jury's jurisdiction."

"If you refuse to be open about all of your conduct, how do we know everything you're telling us is true?"

From my briefcase, I pulled a trash bag and dropped it on the table. "This is the shirt I had on last night. The TBI should be able to find DNA belonging to me, Bert Cawood and Barbara Briggs. An EMT, Father Humphreys and Saul Jenkins can testify to seeing me in that shirt shortly after the explosion."

"Mr. Henley," said a middle-aged woman on my right. "Of all people, I never imagined you capable of being involved in something like this. Why? Why did you do it?"

"What reason could I give you that would be good enough to explain why someone was killed? What could I say that would make you say 'Oh, that explains it.' I've had cases where men were killed for fourteen dollars. And it's so senseless! Fourteen lousy dollars! But is it any better if he was were killed for fourteen thousand? Or fourteen million? There's nothing I could say that would be sufficient. Let's just say we had our reasons and leave it at that."

"Let's not," Ottoman said. "You come in here and pretend you're taking full responsibility, but you're not being fully candid. You won't tell us what other crimes you committed with Bert Cawood? And now you go mum on motive. And we're supposed to accept that?"

"General, I could give you a lot of explanations and rationalizations, but then what would I be? Just another lawyer suffering from moral ambiguity and the ability to rationalize any action. What I did is what I did. And everything I've said is everything this grand jury needs in order to consider the legal consequences of my actions. All the rest I'm leaving to God. I do suggest you talk to Ron Close of the TBI. By now, he's probably put it all together. For all I know, he may understand what I did better than I do."

"The newspaper said something about a blue BMW?" said Ottoman. "Were you and Bert Cawood being helped by another person?"

"Yes, that was our getaway driver."

"Who was driving that car?"

"It's one thing for me to take responsibility for my actions. But my recent behavior has hurt so many people. That's a choice for them to make. Not me."

"Them?" said Ottoman. "Were there more than one?"

I closed my eyes. Lawyers always make the worst witnesses. "Only three people were involved in the robbery of Justice Briggs. Me, Bert Cawood and the driver, and like I said before, I had no idea Bert Cawood was carrying dynamite. And I didn't know it was the anniversary of his wife's death. It was only after we were in the aquarium that I realized Cawood had a plan of his own. I didn't know he wanted to kill her. And, I promise you that driver had no idea that Bert Cawood was going to kill that woman..."

My voice trailed off. Could Weitzman have set the whole thing up? He knew about Cawood's affair with the secretary. He had warned me about Bert. Did he know it was the anniversary of Jeannie's death? Did he wind Bert Cawood up and point him towards Briggs?

"Mr. Henley, you seem a bit confused. Do you want to rephrase your last answer? Did the driver know Bert Cawood was planning to kill Justice Briggs?"

Cotton-mouthed: "I'm not sure."

Chapter 48

When they told me I had a visitor, I thought it was going to be that producer from Dateline again.

She showed up last week with a carton of Marlboro's and a tight-fitting shirt. Her name was something like Laurie or Lori, a late twenty-something go-getter who reminded me of myself when I was a brand new, hard-charging assistant DA.

"I'm guaranteeing you a personal interview by Stone Phillips," she said.

"Like I'm going to be part of some national television cry session. No way, sister. My story is going to be told the way I want it told, and the only way I know to do that is in a book."

"Don't be such a control freak. More people can experience your story through television. That could be the kind of pressure you need for early release."

"Haven't you heard? Tennessee doesn't have early release anymore. But thanks for the smokes."

"But it's *national television!*"

As they say here in the Barbara Briggs Correctional Facility – who gives a...well that's rude to say, and bless her heart, she was just doing her job.

And I should mention that authorities were beside themselves with the idea of me serving life without parole in a prison named after Barbara Briggs. It was one of the new concrete high-tech jobs built in Hohenwald, Tennessee, which is about two hours away from nowhere. In the last year, ground has been broken on five prisons in the legislature's new prison building program. Tennessee scrapped the Sentencing Reform Act and returned to its prior Class X Crime sentencing laws, and now the state is working overtime to meet the demand for prison space.

Today, when I shuffled into the visitors' room, I was surprised to see Isaac Weitzman sitting behind the glass holding the phone to his ear.

He waved as I sat down, and I picked up the telephone.

"Thanks for dropping by."

"Hope this isn't a bad time, Jack?"

"Not at all. Time's all I got."

Weitzman's eyes jerked up. "Sorry."

"Hey, congratulations. I heard Harlan got a guilty verdict in the Rawlins case."

"Yeah, he did. I was pleased. Mad as hell I had to go through that twice, but pleased. Harlan did a good job. Not as good as you did in the first trial, but we got what we wanted."

"Harlan's a good man. Looking back, I can't believe how much trust he put in me. I regret letting him down the way I did."

"How can you regret anything? We did more to change the criminal justice system in this state than the Union Army. Parole? Abolished! Work release? Cancelled. House Arrest? Gone! You saved more lives working with me than you ever did with Harlan."

"Maybe."

"What are you talking about? We kicked ass!"

Weitzman peered at me through the glass. My ambivalence frightened him. Given that we had been so close, he must have realized that he didn't understand me at all anymore. Maybe because all he had ever understood about me was my anger.

"So tell me," he said, "are you thinking about post convicting your pleas?"

"No, I chose to be here, and that was the right decision to make."

"What about the decision of *who else* should be in here?"

Sitting on the edge of his chair, Weitzman stared dead into my eyes, so I wouldn't miss his meaning.

"Did you know, Isaac?"

"Know what?"

"That night at the aquarium, did you know it was the anniversary of Jeannie Cawood's death?"

"Would it change things if I did?"

"So you did know."

He shrugged. "I knew."

"You used him."

"With Bert, it was a matter of time. That had nothing to do with me. Upset?"

"Upset that you manipulated all of us and took advantage of the most damaged among us to murder Barbra Briggs? Yeah, I was upset."

And I had been. My first month in prison I wore a hole in the gym's heavy bag on the place I imagined Weitzman's face to be. Some days I pictured Cawood –that lousy, sick-inside bastard who couldn't help himself. But, I got the most satisfaction imagining I was sucker punching Weitzman –that duplicitous son-of-a-bitch who somehow left me feeling conned. The odd thing was after months and months of punching that bag I was only angry at myself.

"I didn't take advantage of anyone," Weitzman said. "What Bert did was inevitable with us or without us. I just wanted him to do it in the most constructive place possible. Does this mean you'll implicate me?"

I leaned back in my chair and grinned. "Not in the way you think."

"What do you mean?"

"That day in the grand jury I made a mistake. I should have told the whole truth, but I was still too caught up in trying to manipulate and control things, and I was still acting like I had a monopoly on human pain. Hell, I even thought I was protecting you, but Isaac, I've had time to think. I mean really think."

"What are you saying?"

"I'm saying that I am writing a book that will tell everything."

"What the hell for?"

"Truth for its own sake," I said.

"Are you naming names?"

I nodded.

Weitzman started to say something then changed tracks. "So you're pissed at me. I understand that, but what about Lynch? Did you know that he's now in Washington, D.C. working as the head of a national victims' rights group? How can you do this to him?"

"I'm not doing anything to him that he hasn't already done to himself," I tilted my head towards the glass confidentially. "You know, prison's not that bad, and as I've come to find out, I'm no different than anyone in here."

"A book?" His head shook side to side in disbelief. "Why not just call Ron Close?"

"I've read too many police reports that get the facts right but fail to capture the truth."

"And this is going to go public?"

"Sometime next year."

"A *year*?" That surprised him, and he leaned back in his chair mulling it over. "A man can go a lot of places in a *year*. Listen, if anyone asks," he said punctuating his words with an unlit cigar, "tell them

I've moved to California to go beat the shit out of any O.J. lawyer I can find."

I knew he was joking, but I also knew Weitzman well enough to know it wasn't all a joke. Weitzman would never be able to let go of his fear and his hate.

"I'll pray for you, Isaac."

"You do that. You do that."

There was something odd in the tone of his voice, and if I wasn't mistaken, it sounded like *envy*. As if he understood that, through prayer, I had more of a sense of peace inside prison than he did out.

Crazy freakin' victim.

That was the last I saw of him. A few months later, I sent him a wallet I made in leather shop for Chanukah. I'm not even sure if he celebrates it or not, but I wanted him to know I was thinking of him. I worry about Weitzman alone in the world with nothing for companionship but fading memories of Fran and growing malice for a government he holds responsible for her death. He'll probably end up as some whacked-out militia leader with a cult following. I imagine he's ensconced on a ranch in Belize and involved in complicated arms deals to supply his own personal revolutionary movement.

Amazing what two people learn from the same events. Me? I learned of my horrible arrogance and facility for self-destruction. As one of the prison rehab counselors would say, I was on the worst kind of dry drunk. That's rehab counselor talk for self-centeredness. Weitzman? Well, he was emboldened through bitterness.

My wallet to Weitzman came back unopened with no forwarding address. I was glad, and if I was still carrying a grudge, I wouldn't have given him the gift of a head start.

As for me, I think God has given me time to finish the account of these events, so others can see the level of my stupidity. That's pretty presumptuous of me to say this or that is God's will, but what else could explain why I'm still alive?

I won't live much longer. The sheer fact that I'm a former prosecutor rankles other residents here. I know my end will be quick and brutal – just like the end was for everyone I've loved most.

I came into this world naked and wet, and I suppose that's how I'll go – a hand sharpened spoon gouged into my jugular vein in the showers. I always think I'll die in the showers because that's the room that all over-educated heterosexual people fear most in prison. I would feel more relaxed being strapped into the electric chair than I do picking up a small bar of soap and walking naked across wet tile into what I firmly believe is nothing less than Chapter 11 from the *Lord of the Flies*. As I step into the room, I can almost hear the natives chant: *Piggy, Piggy, Piggy!*

Anyway, I guess we all have to face Jerusalem. Christ didn't want to ride that donkey into town only to have himself nailed to two pieces of wood, but He knew it was something He had to go through. Me? I know I have to shower at least once a week.

My cellmate, Thor, laughs when I talk about facing Jerusalem. Thor says my spiritual awakening has made me worse than a reformed smoker flapping his hands at the first whiffs of smoke.

"Just a little bit of sin in the room, and you become Mr. Compassion. Well, kiss my ass. If you pull crap like that on Funeral Home Johnson in cell block D, you *will* get killed."

"By the way, why do they call him Funeral Home? Because he's so big?"

"Naw, because of his sexual *predilections*."

"Hey, good word."

"Yeah, it's on this week's GED vocabulary list."

"How's that going this time?"

"Better. Much better, thanks. But you know, I saw that word *predilection*, and I thought about the way Funeral Home loves to hump those corpses, and I thought – now there's a *predilection*."

God bless Thor. At six foot six and 325 pounds, he is one menacing black man. The Mean Joe Green of Cell Block B. But Thor protects me in the laundry and exercise yard. (I'm doing the legal work on his post-conviction for murdering his GED instructor in Memphis.) Yet Thor just doesn't understand that life being life - all roads lead to Jerusalem. My problem was I thought I had to face it alone.

But it was more than that too. Mine was the first sin. Like Adam, whose teeth tore into the bright red skin of the apple, I wanted to be like God and control everything.

But I could be wrong about all of that. I could also die in prison from old age. After all, what in the hell do I know? If I was half as smart as I always thought I was, I wouldn't be sitting in the Barbara Briggs Correctional Facility trying to figure out how to live while waiting to die.

"Every time you talk about the showers, you sound so fatalistic."

"Well, the showers scare the hell out of me, but what's fatalistic in knowing life ends in death? That doesn't mean I want to die."

And, I didn't. At first, I thought I did as if that was an express bus to an eternal life with Maisy. But once on the inside, I discovered a new purpose to my life. Maisy would like that; after all, from eternity's point of view, prison would be just a blip.

"So, Harlan Griffin and Ron Close get the book first?" Thor said.

"Yup. And maybe that chick from Dateline. It's gotta be worth some smokes."

"Is that all its worth? Cigarettes?"

"I don't know. I once knew this literary agent in Nashville. I'll see what she says, but I don't really care about that. I am more afraid of finishing. The book's kept me grounded, given me a purpose. I mean, what will I do next?"

"Write my story."

I looked up from my crude prison desk. "Are you serious?"

"May not be the life you wanted, but it's the life you got."

"No, no, this means a lot to me," I said. "You know, I already have an idea for the first chapter."

About the Author

This is the debut novel for John Bobo. A former Tennessee prosecutor, John has also worked at the American Prosecutors Research Institute in Alexandria, VA. His non-fiction book *The Best Story Wins: And other advice for new prosecutors* is an Amazon Kindle bestseller in Litigation. For more, please visit www.johnbobo.com.

Made in the USA
Columbia, SC
11 July 2023